All These Nearly Fights

By Richard Cunliffe

I take a deep breath and exhale slowly. What a week I'm having with all this fucking aggro – all these nearly fights. 'Charlotte Hibbs,' I say, 'that was miles out of character for you.'

'Maybe so,' she replies. 'But what an awful shithead he truly was.'

I sit quietly for a moment, and it dawns on me that the day may be coming when Charlie says something similar about me.

Disclaimer:

All These Nearly Fights is a work of fiction. Any resemblance between its characters and real people, or between its storyline and genuine events, is purely coincidental.

Dedication:

In memory of my fantastic mum, Jean, who sadly passed away recently, and for my dad, Ray, who's pretty fantastic too.

CONTENTS

1) Tuesday

1.1) Jimmy Harris, Just Doing his Job

It's no surprise when Ann and Rob ask for a few minutes alone to discuss the deal I've just put to them. It's normal for punters to want privacy at this stage, and I'm happy to give Ann and Rob the usual two options. Either they can remain at my desk while I make myself scarce, or the pair of them can decamp to the comfier chairs in our waiting area. But then Rob says they'd like to talk outside for a while, and I reply that they must be bonkers. It's starting to get dark out there, and the temperature will be dropping fast.

But they're pretty insistent, and so I let them go, telling them to come back whenever they're ready, but preferably before one of them gets hypothermia. Promising to be quick, they get up from my desk and make their way out to the car park. I keep track of them through one of the big showroom windows, and when Rob lights a cigarette I finally realise why they were so keen to head outdoors. Mentally, I take my hat off to the bloke. Back in the old days, when I used to smoke, I wouldn't have lasted this long without needing to spark up.

I go through my inbox while waiting for the two of them to return. After deleting a swathe of junk, I reply to a bloke who wants more info about the Impreza on our forecourt, and I acknowledge the complaint of a recent punter who reckons the car I sold him had a nail in the spare. I then forward the complaint to Graham, our sales manager here, asking him what he thinks we should do about it. ("Tell him to do one," will be Graham's likely response, although he'll probably soften his stance if I put in a word before going home.) Ann and Rob are still outside by the time I've finished emailing, and so I use up a few more minutes tidying my desk. After clearing away some paperwork, I take the wrapper from my sandwich through to the waste bin in the kitchen. Back there I find Cheryl from Accounts, filing her nails and humming a tune while waiting for the kettle to boil. Cheryl's normally good for a laugh, and I get her giggling by repeating the joke that Graham told at this morning's meeting.

I take my time returning to the showroom, heading the long way round via the connecting corridor to the workshop. Although I'm hoping that Ann and Rob will have come back indoors, I reckon it's more likely that they're still outside – still thinking, still talking, still making up their minds. And of course there's always the chance they won't be here at all, because they may have run away home the minute they realised I was no longer watching them. That kind of thing happens pretty regularly, actually – guys 'n' gals doing a runner. People will come for a browse, asking questions about the cars we're selling, and wanting a price for their old one. They say they're "just looking", and well they may be, but the flipside is we're never "just showing". We come here to get deals done, which means we'll try selling a car to anyone who rolls up on our forecourt. And punters will go along with that, up to a point at least. The "just looking" brigade will sleepwalk their way to the verge of a deal, before suddenly realising they've gotten in deep. That's when they'll quietly shit themselves, requesting a moment to step outside and consider the numbers in private. Next minute, they're tearing out of here as though we'd set a pack of dogs on them.

People like that make me laugh, or sometimes they make me angry, depending on my mood and whether or not I've done enough deals for the month. But although I've been wrong about punters in the past, I'm not too worried about Ann and Rob pulling a getaway stunt of that sort on me. They've been here over an hour, we've all got on well, and they were happy with our car on test drive. Also, they seem pretty realistic about the age, condition and likely exchange value of their current motor. I reckon they're straightforward people; I reckon they'd simply front up and tell me if they didn't want to do business.

Back on the sales floor, hanging round the coffee machine, I get chatting with Rudi. He's clutching his usual frothy latte, no doubt with his usual two sugars. I don't get how a short, slightly-built man can drink gallons of sweet, milky coffee without putting on weight. But that's Rudi for you – he's a fucker like that. He asks me, 'How are you getting on? Are your people buying it, do you think?'

'I reckon so. They're taking a few minutes to talk it over.'

Rudi glances to one side and lowers his voice. 'I think you've got more chance than Carl.'

Carl has the desk nearest the coffee machine, and he too has a punter on the go. But Carl's punter is different to the ones we normally get. Tall and rangy, the bloke has an easy authority about him, together with an air of confidence which sets him apart from our usual customers, most of whom are so defensive when they walk in here that they may as well be wearing body armour.

I take a good look at the man at Carl's desk. His clothes stand out as immaculate. In addition to a silk shirt and tie, he has on a rich woollen suit which I don't reckon he bought off the peg. 'The bloke looks loaded,' I whisper to Rudi. 'Whatever car he's on, I'll bet he can easily afford it.'

'That's as maybe, Jimmy. But I still wouldn't back Carl to deal him up. Right now I wouldn't back Carl to deal anyone.'

I tell Rudi he's made a fair point. Carl has lost the sales knack nowadays. The bloke used to do okay, but lately he couldn't sell a presidential pardon to a death-row inmate.

Back at my own desk, it turns out I was right about Ann and Rob. They haven't run off, and they are still outside. There's just enough daylight left for me to watch them hovering near the car they test drove – a high-end Vauxhall Astra, smart and sleek in gunmetal grey. Rob's a short, beefy barrel of a bloke who does everything slowly, and right now he's plodding about at the Astra's rear end while lighting another cigarette. Ann's much lighter on her feet, even though she's six months pregnant, and her body language is livelier than her husband's. She's darting round the car, pointing stuff out, seemingly doing most of the talking.

The two of them show no sign of coming indoors, and so I sit back down and try to keep busy. I take out my order file and begin making a list of things I need to do for some of my other punters. There's a tow-bar to sort out for the Robinsons' Mazda, drive-away insurance to process for old Harry Bell, and then there's a settlement letter required for Yasmin Mellor's finance agreement.

But actually, this is completely fucking hopeless. I can't concentrate on admin right now, because all I'm thinking about is the state of play with Ann and Rob. Truth is, even though I no longer need the money, I'm still a sucker for the buzz that comes from selling someone a car. And I love moments like these, moments when I've got punters hovering on the edge of a deal – they're easily the best part of the job.

By now it's almost too dark to see anything beyond the showroom windows. But I can just about spot Rob doing the thing that blokes do when they're looking at motors, namely bouncing the car on its springs and then kicking the tyres. Rob moves from the rear of the Astra to the front, repeating the same trick at each corner, and as I watch I think: *Give me fucking strength.* Seriously, I've got loads of time for Ann and Rob – literally loads of time, because it's nearly Christmas and trade is quiet – but bouncing the car like that is no bloody use to them, and serves only to tell me that they've had long enough out there, dicking around in the dark. And so I get up from my desk – it's time I went out, had a word, and got them back indoors.

But for all my urgency, I'm curious about the smart-suited punter at Carl's desk, and so I slow down for a closer look as I walk past. I reckon Rudi's prediction was accurate, because the man doesn't appear to be buying a car. He looks bored and pissed-off, and is leaning back from Carl's desk with his arms folded and a frown on his face. Meanwhile, Carl's doing all the talking, and that's never a good sign in this game.

In spite of everything that's on my mind these days, I add to the load with a mental note to find out more about the tall man in the smart suit. I'd like to know not only who he is, but why he's even walked into our used-car supermarket. The building has a linoleum floor, glary strip lighting and low-budget furniture, whereas this bloke wouldn't look out of place in a showroom selling Bentleys or Astons.

But right now I need to concentrate on my own punters. I step outside and call out to Ann and Rob. 'Hey, you two! Do I need to send a search party?'

'Jimmy, don't be a smartarse,' Ann fires back. She takes Rob's hand pulls him towards the showroom. 'We're coming now. We've had a good chat.'

'That's not what I'd call it,' grumbles Rob. 'Ann talked. I listened.'

I hold the door for them. Ann lets go of Rob's hand and slaps him playfully across the arm. 'Oh yeah?' she says, heading inside. 'He's a right one, Jimmy. He's had lots to say, believe you me.'

'Sure I have,' says Rob, shaking his head.

We sit at my desk, and I give them a minute to settle down and finish their bickering. Then I swivel my computer screen round so they can see it, and reopen the document we were looking at before they went outside – the document showing the deal that's on offer for them to buy our car. Displayed on the screen is the price of our Astra alongside Graham's valuation of their old car in part-exchange. Also shown are some optional extras, a total balance, and a monthly repayment plan.

We study the offer in silence, and then I make my second attempt at closing the sale. 'Okay,' I say, 'here are the figures we were looking at before you ventured into the frozen wastes. What are your thoughts as of now? Would you like to buy the car?'

They both look at me. Their cheeks are rosy red because they've been a good while out in the cold. Rob says, 'Well, it's like this...' But he clams up after that, appealing with his eyes for help from Ann.

She looks from him to me and says, 'Actually, Jimmy, Rob was right. I did do most of the talking while we were standing outside.'

'You always do,' he replies.

She slaps him playfully again, but this time the look she gives him is harder. It says: *Just shut up a minute while I handle this.* It's a look I recognise well – I see it often from this side of the desk, often from the bloke but sometimes from the missus.

'So yes,' continues Ann, 'I did have the most to say. But what Rob said was really important. It's made up our minds for us.'

Suddenly, I don't have a good feeling about this. I ask Ann, 'So what was it Rob said?'

'He said that our baby isn't due until March.' Ann sits back slightly in her chair, and doesn't quite meet my eye. Then she comes out with the killer line: 'And so we're in no hurry to get a bigger car.'

I too sit back, trying to act cool, not wanting to appear frazzled. Composing myself and working hard to keep a smile on my face, I say, 'But you do like the car, don't you?'

'I love it.' She looks at her husband. 'We both do. It's a great car. But we don't need it just yet. And you've been brilliant with us today, Jimmy, but this is the first garage we've come to, and we don't need to make any snap decisions.'

I glance from Ann to Rob and from Rob to Ann. With their cheeks already flushed from the cold, it's hard to tell whether either of them feels guilty about backing out now. Briefly, I think about reminding them of what they said immediately after their test drive – that they loved the car and were ready to buy it if I got them the right deal. But it would be hard to bring that up without embarrassing them, and I've found that I rarely sell cars by embarrassing people.

In the end I say, 'That's fine. I recognise this is a significant decision, and that you need to consider all of your options. Also, I respect your right to look at other cars on other forecourts.'

'Thanks,' says Rob, looking and sounding surprised. He puts a protective hand on Ann's knee, and they both do something I've seen dozens of times before: they visibly relax, all their pent-up tension leaving them because they think they're off the hook. It's as though they're a pair of fairground puppets, one minute held erect by wires and strings, then suddenly released when the puppeteer goes for his tea break.

'Jimmy, you do talk posh,' says Ann, stretching in her chair. 'For a car salesman, anyway.'

'How do you mean?' I ask her.

'Well, you say it's a "significant decision", rather than a "big deal". And you talk about us considering all our options – that sounds posh as well.'

'Fair point,' I reply. 'When I need to say something important, I slow down and choose my words carefully. Sometimes, without really meaning to, I end up sounding posh. It's my girlfriend's influence. She teaches English, and I reckon it's rubbing off on me.'

Ann smiles back. 'She's lucky to have you, Jimmy. What's her name?'

'Charlotte. Although I often call her Charlie.'

'Charlotte's a lovely name. Have you been with her long?'

'A while. Two years.'

'And do the two of you live together?'

'Bit nosey, aren't we?' says Rob to Ann.

'It's okay,' I reply before she can slap him again. 'We do live together, or at least we do when we both have the same day off. We've shared a house for about a year-and-a-half.'

Ann pats her belly. She has a baby bump starting to emerge. She asks, 'Any little ones on the way?'

'Not just yet.'

'One day, Jimmy? You'd like children?'

'Who knows? We'll see, Ann. We'll see.'

She looks disappointed by the answer. I ask them, 'What about you guys? There'll be three of you soon. Are you planning to be four after that? Five, one day, maybe?'

Their faces light up, but all Ann says is, 'Like you said, Jimmy, we'll see.'

Rob says, 'It's a big responsibility, you know. Having a kid.'

'I'm sure you're right,' I reply.

'You need to be ready for it,' he adds.

'Which is why you're out and about, looking at cars.'

'Exactly,' says Ann. 'So we'll know what we want once our baby's born.'

'And that's going to be in March, you say?'

'Early March,' says Rob, as Ann sits and nods.

'Well, good for you.' I reach into my drawer and take out the A4 sheet headed *Customer Requirements* – the one on which I made some notes about the features Ann and Rob told me they wanted in their next car. I can actually remember perfectly well what they said to me, but Graham likes us to use the sheets because he reckons they make us look professional.

'Just confirm a few things, would you?' I ask them. 'That way I can help you out when the time does come to buy.'

'No problem,' says Rob.

'Thanks.' I make a brief show of rereading the sheet, before taking out my pen and randomly underlining a couple of words. 'So, first of all, you want a nearly new car. Say, six months old. Something that's old enough to save some money compared to brand new, but new enough to expect good reliability. I do understand that reliability is a must, and that's because you, Rob,' – and here I point my pen at him for emphasis – 'particularly don't want Ann breaking down when she's out and about with your baby in the car.'

'That's right.'

'And you want a bigger car than your old Punto because you've got to fit in everything that goes with a baby – pushchairs and the rest. Agreed?'

'Agreed,' says Rob.

'I like the way you say "the rest,"' says Ann, having a giggle to herself. 'Have you got the first idea what "the rest" actually is?'

'Course I have,' I reply. 'It's stuff. Baby stuff. All that stuff you cart around with babies.'

Now they're both giggling at me, but I need them to be focused, and so, just for a few seconds, I let them joke among themselves while I glance around the showroom. I notice that Carl's smart-suited punter is standing in the doorway with one hand on the door. Carl's trying to persuade him to sit back down, but the bloke is shaking his head and is clearly impatient to leave.

Then I look back at Ann and Rob. I put on my serious voice. 'The other major consideration is safety, isn't it?'

'Definitely,' says Ann.

'That's the biggest thing,' says Rob.

'Of course it is,' I agree. 'And that car out there – the Astra we drove – we talked about how safe it is. We talked about *Isofix* fittings for your baby's seat. We talked about crumple zones and side impact protection. We talked about ABS and EBD and VSC. And we talked about front airbags, side airbags, curtain airbags.'

'We did,' confirms Ann.

'And it's all good stuff,' says Rob.

'So in other words,' – and now I pause for effect, looking down at the list, then up at the ceiling, and finally back at them – 'what you'd like to buy, once your baby comes along, is a car just like that Astra outside.'

'Yes,' says Ann.

'Pretty much,' says Rob.

'And you both drove the car, didn't you? You were happy with how it performed on the road.'

Ann nods, and Rob says, 'Yes, Jimmy, we were.'

I allow another brief pause. Then I say, 'In which case, I've got something to say to you both.'

I pick that moment to lean forward – only a little, but enough to cause a subtle change in their postures. Both of them sit more upright. The puppet master is back. I have their attention.

'You've found a car you like,' I remind them. 'You're telling me you don't need one until March, and I respect that position. I can't force you to buy now, and I'm not going to try. But I'd like you to think again about that Astra out there, with all the safety systems we discussed. It would protect you in the event of a collision, much more so than your current car would. So my question is this: Does your baby need to be born before you want to protect him from an accident?'

Ann draws a breath, but says nothing. I've shocked her, I can tell. Rob just looks at me stony-faced.

I press on: 'I think you both know the answer to that question. And so I'd like to point out that you could benefit from that car's advanced protection systems in forty-eight hours from now. Because that's how quickly you could drive it away.'

Neither Ann nor Rob replies. I sit back again. Quietly, I add, 'I don't mean to come across as pushy, and if you think I'm guilty of emotional blackmail then I won't disagree. But that doesn't mean my point about safety isn't valid. Besides which, you do like the car, and anyway – let's be honest – you know I'm here to try and sell it you.'

But there's still no reply, just the same serious stares. I reckon I've seriously fucked this up, and I realise that I'm the one doing all the talking now, just like Carl with his bloody punter. I can't help myself, though, and I find myself blathering on. 'I didn't mean to offend you,' I tell them. 'And if you choose to walk away, that's fine. But look, you've found a car that you really like. If you are up for buying it, I'll go and talk to Graham, my boss, about the figures I quoted. It's nearly Christmas, and maybe he could offer you some kind of seasonal incentive to do a deal.'

They look at me a moment longer, and then Ann says, 'You said, "protect him."'

'Sorry?'

'When you said the car could protect our baby, you said him, not her. Do you think you know something we don't, Jimmy?'

'No, of course not. "Him" is just what came into my head. Maybe I'm boy centric or something.'

'Boy centric? More posh words, then.'

'I suppose.' I shrug at her. 'Sorry, Ann. I didn't mean to annoy you.'

She clams up again, and Rob doesn't say a word. Everything feels strained and awkward now. I've overplayed my hand here, and a deal looks miles away. Not even my hinting at discount has provoked a response. Instead, all we're left with is an argument about fucking vocab.

But I don't like to part on bad terms, even when I haven't sold people a car. And so, holding up my hands, I say, 'Look, I can see neither of you appreciate what I just said about accidents and safety systems. Please accept my apologies – it's clear you're not ready to buy a car, and I should have understood that. Also, I didn't mean to suggest you were definitely having a boy. What are you hoping for, by the way?'

I keep getting the silent treatment from Ann. She looks at me coolly, saying nothing. Surprisingly, it's Rob who gets the whole thing back on track. Turns out he's just a slow burner.

'I'll tell you what I'm hoping for,' he says, leaning forward and setting his big forearms down on the desk. 'I'm hoping that this Graham of yours is feeling generous. Because if you're looking for a deal, Jimmy, we'll do one with you. But you'll really need to play Santa if you want to sell us that Astra.'

I'm surprised he's taken charge like that, and from the look on her face so is Ann. But I've seen plenty of weird goings-on from this side of the desk – enough by now that I'm never lost for words. And so I put my business face back on and look Rob in the eye. 'We're ready to be generous,' I tell him. 'Tell me what kind of deal would persuade you to buy our car.'

1.2) The Big Boss in his Cave

Rob begins by asking for too much discount. I have to point out that we already run a tight ship and can't grant discounts running to thousands of pounds when our profit margins are measured in the hundreds.

It's an uphill negotiation after that. For a few minutes I fear I've lost them again. But rather than give up, I cajole and prompt and haggle. I stay positive and I hang tough. I remind them both how much they like the car, and I launch a charm offensive at Ann in an effort to get her back on my side. Finally we get there. We arrive at a number which works for them and which I think will be okay with Graham.

Before I go to Graham's office, I get Ann and Rob some hot drinks from the machine. And while I'm about it, I talk briefly with Carl's punter in the super-smart suit. Carl has also been hanging tough, managing to talk his punter out of leaving, and now the man's waiting alone at Carl's desk, presumably while Carl does for him what I'm about to do for Ann and Rob, namely ask Graham to approve a better offer.

I offer the bloke a coffee while he waits for Carl. He tells me no thanks, but asks if I could please let Carl know that time is short. He's polite enough with me – and more softly spoken than I'd imagined – but his body language remains negative. His arms are firmly crossed, and the way he's tapping his foot confirms he's running out of patience.

I tell the man I'll pass the message on to Carl. He thanks me for that, and then I return to my desk with Ann and Rob's coffees. Once I've set down the drinks, I reconfirm with them the price at which they'll buy the Astra, subject to Graham giving me the okay. But although Rob's still happy to go ahead, Ann now wants a tank of fuel thrown in. She smiles when she asks, though, which I think means we're friends again, and I tell her I'll do what I can about the petrol.

Rudi has the desk closest to Graham's office. Although this is prime position when Graham sticks his head out the door with a sales lead up for grabs, it's harder for Rudi when he's got punters on the go and they can hear Graham bollocking someone on the other side of the wall. But over the years Rudi has maximised the upside of sitting where he does, while learning how to minimise the downside – he's gotten good at making light of the shouting matches which can randomly kick off while he's trying to do a deal.

Right now he doesn't have punters with him anyway, and so he needn't give a fuck that we can hear Graham and Carl yelling at each other in the office. Rudi has got someone at his desk, though – namely our younger colleague, Kevin – and I can make a good guess as to why. Physically speaking, Kev's a younger version of Rudi – short and slim and not that much to look at – but that's about all they have in common. Rudi's our top salesman, and has been for years, whereas Kev, who joined us fourteen months back, is consistently one of the worst. In comparison to Carl, who's forgotten how to sell cars, Kev seems never to have known, and the reason he'll be sitting at Rudi's desk is that he tries to compensate for his lack of sales by helping out in other ways. When I see that he's studying a list of names and vehicles registrations, I can easily figure out that Kev will have agreed to do some of Rudi's legwork: most likely he'll have volunteered to progress Rudi's customers' cars through the workshop or valet bay.

Kev gets up from the desk, clutching the customer list. After nodding timidly at me, he heads off to do Rudi's bidding. Once he's out of earshot, Rudi says to me, 'Don't start. And don't give me that look.'

I watch Kev scuttling away through the door to the workshop corridor. 'You're not helping him,' I tell Rudi. 'He'll never learn to sell if you keep using him like a dogsbody.'

Rudi looks at me cold-eyed. 'He'll never learn, anyway,' he says. 'It's been over a year with Kev, and if he was going to be any good he'd have shown it by now. Just face it, Jimmy – he is a fucking dogsbody. Harsh, I know, but true. I say let's make the most of him while we can, because Graham's bound to fuck him off before very much longer.'

When I don't reply, Rudi changes subject: 'Anyway, your people – are they dealing?'

'I need Graham to sweeten the deal for me. But that's a big fucking argument he sounds to be having in there. I hope Carl isn't pissing him off so much that he refuses to help me on price.'

'You'll be fine,' says Rudi. 'It's an everyday thing with Carl at the moment.'

It's true that Carl isn't Graham's flavour of the month, and inside the office I find the two of them facing off across the desk. Carl is giving Graham the big stare – which I don't reckon is a smart move – whereas Graham is letting Carl have the benefit of his considered opinion. He's doing so with both barrels.

'Carl, this is fucking hopeless,' says Graham. 'I don't know what you want from me nowadays. For the life of me, I don't.'

'I want you to stack a proper deal,' replies Carl, seemingly happy to give as good as he gets. 'It shouldn't be fucking difficult. I want you to give me some discount for my punter out there.'

Each is clearly pissed off with the other, and when Graham is pissed off he looks vicious. He still sports the crew cut from his days in the parachute regiment, and although he's in his mid-forties now, and beginning to get paunchy, he still seems in pretty decent shape. Carl, like me, is a decade younger than Graham, and although Graham's a big bloke, Carl is bigger still. But Carl is in far from decent shape – I don't reckon he's been to the gym in twelve months, and all I see him eating is chips and chocolate. A lot of his muscle has turned to flab, and I reckon he'd get battered if he picked a fight with Graham.

Not that Carl is backing down. Throwing his customer notes onto the desk, he says, 'You remember when you used to help me sell cars, Graham? When I used to come to you, and you'd stack a fucking deal for me? Back when you –'

But Graham has heard enough. He slaps the desk with the palm of his hand. He slaps it hard. Hard enough to make pens and pads and the keyboard jump. Hard enough to make me fucking well jump, even from three yards away. Hard enough to stop Carl in his tracks.

I think Graham's about to really erupt, but when he speaks his tone is low and menacing, like the head of family in a clichéd mafia flick. 'Enough, Carl,' he says. 'You're going to listen to me for once.'

There were times when I'd have left the office by now, or possibly not have come in at all. I used to feel embarrassed about being here when there was an argument going on, or when Graham was bollocking the fuck out of somebody. But I came to learn that I'd only lose my place if I stepped away from the queue, and then I'd end up waiting even longer. Eventually I got into the habit of ignoring the fireworks and settling in for the wait. And so settling in for the wait is what I do right now, perching myself on the corner of the big table we use for our morning sales meetings.

Graham says to Carl, 'I help you sell cars when you fucking help yourself. But you only help yourself when you do the job properly. And today, and too many times lately, you ain't doing it properly.'

'And what's that supposed to mean?'

'You know what it means, Carl. It means you've come in here asking for a deal when you've got no commitment from your punter. He ain't had a test drive, and you're telling me he's buying it for someone else anyway – someone who might not even like the bloody car. In short, your bloke's giving you nothing – no buying signals at all – and yet here you are, asking me to work him out a fucking deal.'

'Yes, but –'

'Yes, but bollocks,' interrupts Graham, jabbing a finger in emphasis. 'What is the point?' he asks. 'You tell me, Carl. What is the fucking point?'

Carl has gone red in the face. He squares his shoulders and thrusts out his jaw. He says to Graham, 'The point is we might just sell the man a car.'

'And pigs might fly to the moon given the level of commitment you've got. Or rather not got.' Graham half turns and points at the big whiteboard behind his desk, the one that lists each salesperson's deals for the month. 'Based on current performance, Carl, and on last month's performance, and on performance the month before that, I'd say pigs will build Moon Base Fucking Porky long before this man buys a car from you.'

Carl's face is even redder now – he looks like a fucking beetroot. He winds himself up to reply, but it's clearly time I intervened, given that this is going nowhere and I've got punters waiting.

'Carl,' I say quickly, 'you need to go and talk to your bloke. He hasn't got a lot of time.'

Graham glances at me, then looks back at Carl and throws his arms in the air. 'That's brilliant,' he says, his tone thick with sarcasm. 'Brill – Eee – Ant. There you have it, Carl. Your man hasn't the time to buy a fucking car anyway.'

Carl turns to me, pricklier than a cactus on steroids. 'How come you know that then, Cooter?'

'Come on mate,' I reply. 'How do you think? It's that mind reading programme I've got hard wired into my chair.' Immediately, I feel bad. I didn't need to be sarcastic with him when he was having a shitty moment. But then again, he didn't need to call me by my least favourite nickname, the one only he uses nowadays.

Graham certainly doesn't mind hurting anyone's feelings. 'Look Carl!' he shouts, pointing outside, at the darkness beyond the window. 'There go the pig astronauts!'

Carl turns back to Graham. 'I'm just saying –'

'You ain't saying nothing, not now.' Graham makes a zipping motion across his lips and launches a proper tirade. 'Over half an hour the bloke's here. And in all that fucking time there's no rapport, no test drive, no commitment, no nothing. Just you wanting a deal for a bloke who's ready to leave and ain't got the time to buy a fucking car anyway. You tell me, Carl – why are you even in here bothering me? How the fuck is this selling us any cars?'

Maybe Carl has finally given in. The blood is draining from his face, and his shoulders have drooped. Graham comes round from behind the desk, grips him hard by the arm, and walks him to the door.

'Get out,' he hisses in Carl's ear. 'Get out and reappoint the bloke for some future point when he can find time to test-drive the fucking car. Then I'll talk a deal, Carl. Not fucking before.'

Carl skulks away, into the showroom. Graham returns to his desk and his old executive chair – the one he flatly refuses to throw out and replace. Worn and creaky, it moans in protest when he drops his big arse into it.

'Next,' he says, waving me to the harder chair on the other side of the desk.

I walk over from the big table and sit down slowly. I shouldn't keep Ann and Rob waiting any longer than I have to, but the first thing I say is, 'You were hard on Carl.'

Graham's eyes flicker furiously, but when he answers his tone is more sorrowful than angry. 'I was hard on him?' he asks. 'Someone needs to be hard on him. If he doesn't sort himself out, he'll be out the fucking door. Even if it is nearly Christmas.'

'You'd really sack the bloke?'

'Just look where he's at for the month.' Graham leans back, causing the old chair to creak some more, and taps his knuckles on the big whiteboard behind him. 'Just look at the state of play.'

I already know the state of play – I always know the state of play – but I make a point of studying the whiteboard anyway. Rudi has the most sales this month, with eleven so far. I'm only two behind with nine, and Emma is close to me with eight. Next, there's a gap to Marlon, Kate and Wes, each with five apiece. Kev trails them with four.

And then there's Carl. Carl is in last place on two deals. December is always a quiet time, but two deals by mid month is piss-poor, especially for someone of Carl's experience.

'Five years,' says Graham, his tone still regretful. 'That's how long he's worked for me. Longer than any of you, except for Rudi and maybe Kate.'

Rudi, Kate and Carl. Graham's three old stagers. Salespeople come and go – the odd one sticking it a year or two, others lasting only months – but the three of them have hung around a good long while. Me too, I suppose. My four years mean I'm nearly an old stager. But I won't complete a fifth year. I'll be gone before Easter, one way or another.

'Come on, boss,' I say. 'I know Carl can be a dickhead, but he can also sell cars when his head's in the right place.'

'What do you mean – can be a fucking dickhead?' Graham offers up a nasty little smile, and casts a glance at the ceiling. 'He's been a dickhead from day one – a proper pain in the arse. God's gift to the car trade, or so he thinks. But I've never had anyone generate so many complaints, from customers and from fucking staff.'

'He and I have never been best mates,' I reply. 'But we've learnt to get along.'

'Rude, arrogant, sexist, short-tempered,' Graham continues, as if he hadn't even heard me. 'That's what people say about Carl. And people are fucking right.'

'But like I said, he can sell cars.'

'Can sell cars, sure. But can sell and does sell ain't the same thing. And Carl's been shit at the job since the summer. I shouldn't have carried him this long.'

I try to read Graham's face, not convinced that he's really ready to kick Carl out. Normally, when he sacks people, he doesn't tell me first – he just bloody does it. But on the other hand, he looks and sounds very serious right now. It's possible that he's not fooling around.

'You do remember,' I remind Graham, 'what happened to Carl in the summer.'

'His wife left him, sure. But she was back after six weeks.'

'But boss, that doesn't mean everything is hunky-dory with them. She might have had nowhere else to go. Or they might still be together just for the kid. Seriously, when did you last see Carl looking just a little bit happy? Never mind having a proper laugh about something.'

'But he's always been a miserable twat, even when he was selling cars.' Graham sighs and leans further back, lacing his hands behind his head and resting the sole of his shoe against the edge of the desk. He listens to the old chair creak, almost as if it's talking to him, and then he adds, 'Besides Jimmy, I've always told you that this ain't marriage guidance, or a club for fuckers with problems. We come here to graft and sell and earn good money, not to get dragged down by whatever shit's going on at home.'

'I know. But –'

'This is a selling operation. Selling, selling, selling. You've been here long enough to know that.' Abruptly he sits up straight again. 'I mean, you remember when your missus left you?'

'My missus? You mean Isabel?'

'Yeah, Isabel.' He nods appreciatively. 'Fit bird, but a gold digger as it turned out.'

'Alright, well so she was. Anyway, funnily enough, I do remember her leaving me, since you ask.'

'Sorry – you know what I mean. My point is you were fucking rubbish for a couple of months afterwards. It all happened just after I'd finally taught you to be a salesman – you were performing for me at last, hitting the numbers – and then that bird walks out on you and you're rubbish again. You're no longer Jimmy Harris, you're suddenly Jimmy Shit.'

'I remember it well,' I reply, thinking back three years and remembering it very fucking well. Isabel leaving me was like a thousand kicks in the bollocks.

'But you were only rubbish for a couple of months. Then you got it sorted. Jimmy Shit was gone. Jimmy Harris was back. But that twat out there...'

Graham gets up and crosses the room. He looks into the showroom through the thin strip of window running down one side of the door.

'He's doing it now! He's got his punter gone, and he's back to doing what he does all fucking day. Pissing about on his fucking phone.'

'Yeah,' I admit. 'He does that a lot lately.'

'Then, when a new punter comes in, looking to buy a car, he goes and fucks it up. It's all rush rush rush with him. No proper qualification, no demonstration, no test drive, no fucking nothing.'

Graham falls silent. Still looking into the showroom, he tenses up and says, 'That couple at your desk – the ones from earlier. I forgot you were with them. How are you getting on?'

'Ann and Rob Jones? I need you to take a look at the deal.'

'Fuck's sake.' He comes away from the door and moves back behind the desk. 'Why didn't you say so sooner?'

'It won't hurt, me being in here a while. They'll think I had to work hard to persuade you.'

'How much money do you need?' Graham asks. He's staring at his monitor, fingers poised over the keyboard.

'I need you to get the payment under two-fifty, without increasing the term. Same deposit, and keep the extended warranty in.'

The boss taps rapidly at the keys, stares for a moment at the screen, and then, because he doesn't trust the computer, he double checks the figures on a calculator from his drawer. 'That's okay,' he finally says. 'Two-forty-nine and twenty eight pence. I've had to discount the car by three-fifty, and tweak the rate a bit, but we still make over six hundred GP. Good enough for me, especially as we've sold fuck all today. If you can get this done, and Emma can close the people she's with, we'll finish up with two deals. That'll be alright.'

'Thanks boss,' I reply, before suddenly remembering that Ann also asked for fuel. 'Oh yeah, sorry, but I need a tank of petrol too.'

'Fuck's sake, Jimmy – that's another fifty quid. But whatever. Just get it done. I'll send the new offer to your screen.'

'Alright, I'll go and sign them up.'

I'm almost at the door when Graham says, 'There's still time for you to catch Rudi.'

I turn back. Graham is standing at the whiteboard, already adding the name Jones to my list of deals. I'm only one behind Rudi now.

'Remember the bonus,' says Graham. 'It's worth a thousand quid.'

He doesn't need to remind me, because I know all about our December incentive. Graham will pay a thousand pounds, on top of our normal commissions, to whoever sells the most cars this month.

A thousand pounds happens to be less than one tenth of one percent of the money I currently have on deposit at my bank. But Graham doesn't know that, just as he doesn't know a lot of other things. He'll have no idea that I'm likely to resign pretty soon, nor that I've been thinking a lot about Isabel, the "fit bird" he remembers leaving me a few years back.

Not knowing I've gotten unexpectedly rich, Graham expects a thousand quid to motivate me. And I am motivated, although more by the kudos of beating Rudi to top spot than by claiming the bonus money. Rudi's my mate and I respect him loads, but I'm fed up with him being the main man around here. It's time for a new name at the top of the leaderboard.

'I'm having a beer with Rudi after work,' I tell Graham. 'I'll let him know I'm hunting him down.'

'That's what I want to hear,' says Graham, sitting back down. 'Make sure you smash the fucker this month. Even though we love him, I'm fed up paying Rudi so much money. He's earning more than me, and I'm relying on you to take him down a peg.'

'I'm on it,' I reply, heading for the door.

1.3) Drinking with the Kids

Rudi and I had planned a simple after-work beer at one of the downbeat little pubs neighbouring the showroom. But then Emma and Wes decided to come along, and they persuaded us to head somewhere livelier.

When I say they persuaded us, I really mean Emma persuaded Rudi. Emma's a pretty girl, with a cute smile and great legs. She has a wardrobe full of short skirts and a knack for getting blokes to do exactly as she wants. Although she's young and raw, and only three months into the job, she's already posting some impressive sales numbers, and Graham's whiteboard shows she's third in December's league table. People will call me sexist for claiming that her good figures owe plenty to her good figure, but blondes do sell more cars in my opinion, and I think Emma herself would agree. Anyway, she certainly did a job on Rudi tonight. Getting a venue change past him is no easy matter for your average Jack or Jill, but it's clearly a piece of cake for the sassy, brassy new girl. And that's why we're here in a noisy, bustling boozer on the edge of town, one with live music, cheap beer and a crowd of punters too young to shave. And when I say a crowd, a crowd is what I mean – it's packed in here, with Rudi and I are queuing three deep for a round while Emma and Wes go looking for a table.

I take a good look around as we scramble our way to the bar. I might actually be the second-oldest punter in the entire pub, with the eldest being Rudi. We're the two old-timers wearing our trousers conventionally – namely round our waists – not slung so low on our hips that everyone gets to admire our pants. But for all that, I'm glad we rocked up here. I like the vibe and the change of scene. I like the bright lights and the loud music, even though the band look like refugees from a kindergarten and their name means nothing to me. I also like the way the barmaid smiles at me when I finally reach the front of the queue. She's a welcome upgrade on Derek, the sour and moody landlord at the Lamb and Musket.

In the past, despite the crowd and the noise and the mayhem, I'd have hung around the bar after getting served, so that I could flirt with the barmaid and maybe swap phone numbers. But not anymore – my freewheeling days are done, dusted and consigned to history. So instead, after a moment's suggestive eye contact, the barmaid and I go our separate ways – she to serve the next clamouring face in a sea of punters, me to help Rudi carry the drinks.

Meanwhile, Emma has done really well. Towards a back corner of the pub, she's actually found the one table that's going begging, although whether it's really going begging looks to be up for debate. I can see her arguing the toss with two blokes – both of whom look closer to my age than many of the kids in here – and as Rudi and I draw near I hear one of them complaining that they spotted it first.

Emma has claimed one of the chairs for herself, while throwing her bag onto another and her coat over a third. She says to them, 'So what if you saw it first? I got here before you guys, and that's what counts.'

I nudge Rudi and we move in, backing up Emma's claim to the table by setting down our drinks. I smile neutrally at the two blokes, but get only grim stares back. One of the guys looks a proper piece of work. Bare-armed in a sleeveless denim jacket, he's got some macabre tattoos of skulls and the grim reaper, while his greasy hair is tied back in a filthy pony tail. He smells ripe too, like he might not have showered lately, and after we've put down our drinks he demands, 'Fuck do you think you're doing?'

I look him in the eye. 'Like my friend said, I think she got here just before you.'

'No, we was here first.' He points at Emma. 'She just jumped in.'

'That's life, mate' I reply. 'It's a crowded pub. It's not like there's a queuing system.'

'Well, we want the fucking table.' He steps closer, into scrapping range, and raises his voice. 'We saw it before her.'

His friend puts a hand on his arm and says, 'C'mon, Josh. Just leave it.'

'Good advice,' says Rudi from beside me. 'Possession is nine tenths, isn't it, fellah?'

'Fuck that,' says the bloke to his mate, shaking his arm free. He smells especially rancid now that he's stepped so close. 'This lot aren't having it. We are.'

'I don't reckon so' I tell him. 'We've already got it.'

'Yeah, we have,' pipes up Emma, smiling at him sweetly. 'So back off, Josh. Like, back off, go home, have yourself a frickin wash.'

I think: *Fuck's sake.*

That's the other thing about Emma. When she isn't charming people she's pissing them right off, and sure enough Mr Rancid looks fucking livid. He moves round the table towards her, his eyes wide and full of anger. I need to get between the two of them, but the table's in my way and I know I'm not moving fast enough. Meanwhile, Emma has finally realised that the bloke is full of menace, and she's hurrying to stand up and back away. Trouble is, she isn't moving fast enough either. This is really fucking bad. And it's only going to get worse. But then...

... from somewhere over my shoulder a loud voice says, 'Hold it, fuck-face!' and everyone – our foul-smelling mate included – seems to freeze. That's when a calloused black hand clamps briefly on my shoulder and moves me firmly aside.

Wes is here, and not a second too soon. I'm bloody glad he's on the scene.

He steps forward and says to the bloke, 'Touch her and I'll kill you.' He doesn't speak loudly, but then again he doesn't need to because it's fallen quiet all around us.

Of course, people often go around casually threatening to kill each other, mostly without any serious intent. But I believe Wes literally when he threatens to kill our stinky new friend. I believe him because I've noticed how much he thinks of Emma. It would have been hard for me not to have noticed, given the way he looks at her when he thinks no one's watching.

For a moment there's a stand off, Rancid Josh looking angrily from Emma to Wes and back again, his eyes still livid and a little vein in his temple pulsing like a warning beacon. He's clearly a nasty fucker, but nor does Wes look like someone you'd mess with. My workmate isn't huge, but he's all muscle, and it's obvious how strong he is from the way he's carrying an extra chair with just one hand, almost as if it were made of balsa. As if that weren't enough, and even though he's a really nice lad, Wes has a psychopath's stare – everyone backs down when he puts it on them.

Everyone, that is, except this bloke, who stands his ground and stares right back. I don't like it that he's so cocky. I know that Wes is one of the main men at a local boxing club, and he certainly carries himself with confidence, but the scumbag facing him looks unfazed. That worries me. I'm asking myself whether this bloke knows a few tricks of his own, or whether he might be carrying a blade. He looks the sort who would.

Fortunately, we don't get to find out. The other guy, now with greater urgency, again says, 'Josh, leave it.' And this time, lowering his voice, he adds, 'We're on camera, you know.'

We all look around. Most of the people surrounding our table have sensibly backed off from the aggro. But they're all still watching, and at least four blokes are filming us with their phones. Thankfully, that seems to do it for our new buddy, Josh. He finally turns to walk away, but not before he's returned Wes's death stare, and made noises about our not having heard the last of this.

We watch them go, and then we all sit down. I realise that my heart's racing. Rudi and Emma look pale. Only Wes appears unshaken.

'Well done, mate,' I say to him.

'It was nothing,' he replies. 'I'm sure you'd have dealt with the bloke just as well.'

'My hero,' says Emma to Wes. She applauds briefly, and switches on her smile, but it's a few watts short of full power. It's clear that she's shaken, and I feel like tearing into her for provoking the bloke like that. But then again, I wasn't blameless myself, and what's more I don't want to give the moviemakers round here any new material. So this time I hold my tongue, and it's actually Rudi who speaks next when he deadpans, 'Anyway, it's always great to come somewhere new.'

We all start laughing; Rudi makes a show of clenching his fists. 'Fucking good job you were here,' he says to Wes. 'I'd have killed those wankers by now.'

We all laugh some more, and Wes says, 'Listen to Rudi – he's great. You've just got to love the old guy.'

'Hey, less of the old,' says Rudi. 'I won't even be forty for another couple of years.'

Emma and Wes exchange a look, and Emma says to Rudi, 'You're still, like, nearly twice our age.'

Rudi looks a bit crushed, and I decide to make things worse for him, just like good mates do. I put down my beer, point at his hair and say, 'Another thing – your hair's not so dark today. Forgotten to shampoo with your magic bottle?'

Emma and Wes laugh again. Rudi's hair does look darker on some days than others. He take a quick sip of beer and replies, 'What about you, you fucker?' He points to where my hair is greying at the temples and says, 'You're not many years behind me.'

'Six.'

'Like I said, not many. You'll need a special shampoo soon, and that's not all. Started trimming back the hair in your ear holes yet?'

'That's so gross,' says Emma. 'My dad has got big tufts in his ears. It's like he's got armpits on the side of his head.'

I think back to when Emma's old man rocked up at the showroom, not very long after she began working with us. He said he was interested in getting a car, but he never bought one, and I reckon he was just fathoming out the kind of place where his little girl had begun work. He had a none-too-subtle line in questioning, and I remember telling him that I had a long-term girlfriend (true) and that I hadn't thought of making a move on his daughter (lie). But thinking about doing something and actually doing it are different things – I hadn't tried it on with Emma when he asked, and nor have I since. Surprisingly, as far as I know, nor has anyone else – not even any of the younger mechanics, for all their big talk and their testosterone to spare. Maybe, like me, they've scented Wes's interest, and maybe they're scared enough of him not to get in his way. But it's got to be said, he's taking a fucking long time about making his move.

Rudi takes another mouthful of beer, pats his pockets and produces cigarettes. He waves the packet at Emma. 'Coming for one?' he asks her.

'Not just yet. I want to get warm before I get cold again.'

'No worries. I'm going to brave it, though.' He looks at the heaving mass of punters. 'Which way do I go?'

Drawing an arc in the air with my finger, I tell Rudi, 'Make your way past the bar, head towards the toilets, and keep going until you find yourself outside. There used to be a patio heater, but I don't know whether it's there these days.'

'Thanks.' He gets to his feet, once again eyeing the masses separating him from his fix. For a minute I think he's going to change his mind, hesitating like a reluctant swimmer on the edge of a pool when he knows the water is freezing. But then, next second, he's away into the crowd, following the path I described. I watch him mouth "excuse me" here and there, pushing people gently when asking alone doesn't work.

Wes is looking at me. 'How did you know where to send him?' he asks.

'I used to smoke.'

'But you used to come in here?'

'Wes, I haven't always been an old bloke. And in my head at least, I'm still a young one.'

'And in mine,' says Emma. She nudges Wes with her elbow and says, 'Jimmy's still down with the kids.'

Wes smiles his biggest smile, a boyish grin that's the total opposite from the evil stare he conjured up for the rancid bloke's benefit. 'Hey, Jimmy,' he says, 'no offence meant. It was just with Rudi complaining about coming here, you know?'

'Sure, mate.' I reply. 'No offence taken.'

Giggling, Emma elbows him again, and says, 'You're lucky Jimmy doesn't kick your ass.'

He pushes her playfully back. 'You're lucky I don't kick yours.'

I watch them play-fight and mickey-take, and I wonder quietly about the two of them. I ask myself whether Wes might be waiting for some kind of encouragement before making his move, and whether Emma, in turn, is waiting for him to make that move before offering the encouragement he requires. Chicken and egg, so to speak.

Then, suddenly, as if someone had flicked a switch, they both stop laughing. Wes's smile fades and a sour expression comes over Emma's face, as if she'd bitten into rotten fruit. I look in the direction they're looking, off to my right, and I'm surprised to see Carl standing nearby, wearing the same thick overcoat he puts on for work. I'm surprised he's here, because he rarely gets asked to the pub and it's a long time since he bothered to invite himself. He certainly doesn't look comfortable now he's arrived: if Rudi's the oldest punter in here, Carl has got to be the lardiest. His forehead's glistening with sweat, and he looks pretty breathless from pushing through the crowd.

Carl comes closer. He dislikes Wes, and he especially dislikes Emma. He dislikes them in the resentful way that experienced salespeople dislike novices who are already outselling them. But dislike them though Carl does, he isn't above pretending to be their best mate when he happens to want something.

'Right then, kids,' he says, putting on a big false smile. 'Where's Rudi? Outside having a crafty fag, is he?'

'There's nothing crafty about it,' replies Emma. 'He's, like, a grown man, out for a drink. He's allowed to smoke.' She raises her glass in a mock toast to Carl. 'So are us kids, in case you were wondering.'

Carl's smile turns down a fraction. 'Whatever you say,' he replies, unknowingly mirroring Rudi by patting his pockets, but without actually producing any cigarettes. 'Lend me one, would you,' he says to Emma, 'while I go looking for the skinny fellah.'

'He's slim, not skinny,' says Wes coolly, almost too quietly to be heard above the din that's picked back up. 'And you're a fine one, anyway, to be talking about other people's appearances.'

'Besides,' adds Emma, 'where are your own fags?'

Carl pats his pockets some more. He stretches his matey smile back to full beam. 'Must have left them in the car.'

After that, he and Emma just look at each other. He makes no move to go for his ciggies, and she doesn't offer him one of hers.

Carl then looks to Wes – who doesn't smoke, and only stares pityingly back – before finally turning his attention to me.

I try to be the peacekeeper, the man who's everyone's friend. 'You know I stopped smoking long back,' I tell Carl, 'otherwise I'd let you have one. But if you want one off Emma, you could try saying please. Otherwise, yeah, Rudi is smoking out back. I'm sure he'd crash you a fag.'

'Sure,' replies Carl. 'Maybe I'll ask him. Being as Princess Perfect here isn't playing nice.'

'You're pathetic,' says Emma, taking a cigarette from the packet, and throwing it down on the table. 'Here, take one you lard arse. Take one and fuck off.'

Carl picks up the cigarette. 'And I was trying to be friendly,' he says.

'You weren't trying to be friendly,' says Emma. 'You were trying to act friendly.'

'There's a difference,' adds Wes.

'And you'd know, would you?' replies Carl, his smile suddenly superseded by a nasty little sneer. Any pretence of friendship on his part has disappeared, and I get the idea, just for one second, that he's going to make to Wes's face one of the racist comments I've heard him make behind Wes's back. I don't know what Wes will do if Carl calls him "black lad" or "Samuel L", but it won't end happily – I'm sure of that much.

But thankfully, Carl holds back. He just looks at Wes a second or two longer, before once more turning to me. 'You've made some fucking freako friends,' he mutters. And then, to Emma, while sidling away: 'You don't impress me, sweetheart – far fucking from it.'

Emma looks wound up and ready to snipe back. But she's too late – Carl's already out of earshot. We watch him merge into the crowd, bulldozing his way towards the smoking area. Wes studies him with narrowed eyes. 'How did he know we were coming here?' he asks.

'Maybe Rudi told him,' I reply. 'Or maybe he just overheard.'

'I can't stand the bloke,' says Emma.

'That make two of us,' says Wes.

'Carl's a prick,' I tell them both. 'But you shouldn't let him get to you.'

Emma takes a drink, and I notice her hand holding the glass isn't quite steady, which is hardly surprising given all the aggro that's gone on in here. She puts down her glass and says, 'Carl can wind anyone up. I've even seen him get to you, Jimmy – he winds you up when he calls you that name.'

I nod, and tell her she's made a fair point.

'What is that name again?' she asks. 'Gooter?'

'Cooter.'

'I don't get it,' she says. 'I mean, I get why Marlon gets called Brando. But I don't get Cooter.'

'Yeah, Jimmy,' says Wes. 'Why does he call you that? Unless it's none of our business.'

I take a sip from my pint. 'I'll tell you about my nickname if you promise not to use it.'

Wes says it's a deal, but Emma just smiles and winks, knowing I'll tell them anyway.

'Alright,' I begin, 'you'll find this hard to believe, but there was a time when I wasn't good at selling cars.'

Emma feigns a little gasp. Wes laughs and says, 'You, Jimmy? Never.'

'It's true,' I reply. 'Took me a long while to get the hang of it – for the first three or four months I was totally crap, and Graham came close to binning me off. Part of the problem was that I worked as a mechanic before I got a job in sales.'

Emma asks, 'So, why was that a problem?'

'I knew so much about cars that I spent too much time talking about them. I was desperately trying to impress the punters with all my knowledge, but actually I was just boring the poor fuckers to death.'

'I get it,' says Wes. 'But why the nickname?'

'Cooter was the mechanic in *Dukes of Hazard*. Graham reckons it he liked it on TV when he was a kid. So when I was talking more like a mechanic than a salesman, he'd start calling me Cooter. It was my cue to snap out of it and get my shit sorted.'

'Coooo-ter.' Emma rolls the name around her mouth, as if trying it for size. I give her a look, and she says, 'Only joking, Jimmy. But why does it upset you so much?'

'I'm not sure, Em'. But back then, Rudi, Kate and Carl all picked up on the name, and they'd use it when they wanted to tell me I was fucking up. Then, later on, when I got to grips with the job, the nickname died a death. Everyone stopped using it. Everyone except for Carl, that is. He still calls me Cooter when he wants to piss me off.'

'But Jimmy,' says Wes, 'like you just told us, you're smart enough not to let him get to you.'

'You're right, mate. But sometimes theory is easier than practice.'

While I've been explaining the Cooter story, Emma has begun toying with her cigarette packet – opening and closing it, turning it round and round in her fingers. Now she says, 'I really want one of these. But I'm not going for one while he's out there.'

'I'll come with you,' says Wes.

'But I don't want any trouble. What if he starts?'

I tell her that the three of us will go, and that we'll all make a pact not to get wound up by Carl. Wes is happy with the idea, and between us we persuade Emma that everything will be fine. I glance back once after we've moved away from our table, to see that it's been pounced on by other punters, like seagulls will zone in on a fistful of crumbs. Emma and Wes, meanwhile, manage to manoeuvre their way through the crowd faster than me, not because I'm heavier on my feet, but because I'm carrying Rudi's pint as well as my own. He's only sipped at it so far, and I'm trying not to spill too much of his beer.

Once outside, the smoking area is as I remember it – a long, narrow patio, the high walls putting me in mind of a prison yard. In the centre of the patio stands a ramshackle old heater, one I remember from years back. Its dancing orange flames generate more light than heat, but it's a freezing night out here and most of the punters are drawn to it anyway. Rudi and Carl are exceptions to that – they're lurking in the far corner, Rudi with his back to the wall and Carl towering over him. From the way they're standing so still, in spite of the bitter cold, I reckon the discussion they're having is a serious one. It isn't blokey banter about women or football.

I catch up with Emma and Wes. He's holding her drink while she lights a cigarette. Emma blows smoke in the air and asks, 'Is Rudi alright, do you reckon? Carl is twice his size.'

'Twice his size,' I agree, 'but only half has smart. Rudi can handle Carl, alright – he's been handling him for years. But I'll take his pint over and make doubly sure.'

'Want me to come?' asks Wes.

'Only if I get knocked out.'

I make my way to where Carl and Rudi are standing. It isn't only a serious talk that they're having, but a quiet one as well. I have to get pretty close before I can hear them, and even then I can't properly make out the words, only Carl's injured tone. He sounds aggrieved and put upon, as if Rudi's pissed on his chips or done him some other disservice. Rudi spots me and whispers urgently to Carl.

Carl shuts up and glances over his shoulder. I walk right up to them, close enough to join in the discussion they're no longer having. I say, 'Well, fellahs, this is cosy. Rudi, I brought your pint.'

'Cheers mate.' He takes it from me, downs a good third, and says, 'That hits the spot. Carl, how about I get you a beer?'

'I don't want a drink,' Carl replies moodily.

I look closely at Carl. He's stopped sweating out here in the cold, but his face is red, just like earlier when he got angry in Graham's office. Also, despite the poor light in these shadows, it's easy to spot the wounded look on his face. Another thing, too: although there's no sign of the cigarette he scrounged from Emma, I can smell its odour clinging to him, which means he smoked it in a frenzy.

'Funny you not needing a drink,' I say to him. 'Funny that you've come here, I mean, what with this being a pub. Namely a place that serves drinks.'

'I wanted to talk to Rudi,' he replies. He gives me a mean little look, but I'm not bothered by his hard man act. He can eyeball me all he wants – I don't give a fuck.

'I was the same,' I tell Carl blithely. 'I wanted to talk to Rudi, too. That's why we came out for a drink.'

Carl looks at me for a long moment. Then he turns his attention to Rudi, who draws himself up to his full height and says, 'Carl, I've told you the score.'

Carl turns his tough stare back on me. He says, 'I was going anyway.' Then, to Rudi: 'Give me a fag for the road.'

Rudi produces his cigarettes. 'Take the pack,' he says. 'There's only half-a-dozen.'

Carl's eyes flash angrily. 'I don't need the pack.'

I'd tell Carl to get lost, but Rudi shrugs and opens the packet. Carl takes a cigarette and slides it into the pocket of his coat. He begins walking away, but then turns back and says, 'Rudi, have a good think about what I've said.' Then he finally does leave. Shoulders back, strutting like a gunslinger – in as much as fat blokes can strut like gunslingers – and without even a glance at Emma or Wes, Carl goes back inside, from where I guess he'll head out the front door and go home.

I wait to see if Rudi wants to explain. When he doesn't, I say, 'Tell me to keep my nose out, mate, but what the fuck was all that about?'

Rudi steps away from the wall, puts his glass on the floor, and lights a cigarette. His hands, like Emma's earlier, aren't totally steady. 'I'm not exactly sure,' he replies. Then he stands and smokes while I make a show of checking my phone for messages, each of us waiting for the other to speak next.

Rudi cracks before me. 'What I mean,' he finally says, 'is that I'm not sure I should tell you anything. No offence, Jimmy, but I'm not sure Carl would want me broadcasting the stuff we were talking about.'

'That's fine by me.' I shrug to say it doesn't really matter. 'But you look bothered, mate. If you want to share what's going on then I promise it goes no further.'

I step aside and look away, giving Rudi chance to work out how much he wants to tell me. I watch Emma nattering with Wes, and I notice a couple of lads eyeing Emma up from the huddle round the patio heater.

Finally, Rudi says, 'Carl's got problems.'

'Oh, yeah? What sort? Fallen out his missus again?'

'No. Well, actually, yeah. But that's just an ongoing thing with him.'

'So, he's got other problems as well?'

Rudi just nods and draws on his cigarette.

I say, 'In which case, it's got to be money.'

'How did you figure that?' he asks. 'Was it the phone thing?'

'What phone thing?'

'Obviously not, then. I'm talking about how he uses his phone. You know how he's always on it in the showroom?'

My mind casts back to this afternoon. I remember Graham complaining that Carl always has his phone out in the showroom, and sure enough, when I picture Carl at work I see him with his head down and a thumb dancing manically across the screen of his phone. On the back of that image, another one of Carl comes to mind – one of him spending heavily on lottery tickets one evening last summer, the time I bumped into him in the off licence on the way home from work.

'It's gambling, isn't it?' I say to Rudi. 'He's been gambling, mostly online, and losing, by the sounds of it.'

'That just about sums it up. Roulette, football, horses... you name it and he's thrown money its way. I mean, he knows I like a bet myself, and if you go back to the summer he was spending every spare minute showing me different sites on his phone, telling me what he'd won here and what he'd won there. Won this. Won that. Won blah-blah, bloody-blah. Well that was then and this is now, and he's stopped telling me what he's won because he's won absolutely fuck all for months and months.'

Rudi gives his head a shake and takes another deep drag on his cigarette. 'Anyway,' he says, 'how did you guess Carl had money troubles if you didn't know about the phone gambling?'

'He hasn't been selling cars,' I reply. 'Not enough to pay his way. And when a bloke comes to the pub, doesn't have a drink, and he's cadging smokes – well, he must be skint, mustn't he?'

'I suppose so.'

'But mate, why was he here, looking for you?' Have you been lending him money?'

Rudi crushes his cigarette underfoot. 'I lent him three hundred quid. I've told him that's the end of it and he's getting no more – I've got my own fucking family to feed, after all – but he just keeps on asking.'

'So, was he threatening you just then?'

Rudi lets out a little sigh. 'No, not really,' he replies, but he doesn't sound convincing, and I'm getting pissed off now. Carl will have me to answer to if he's been leaning on my mate.

Only I was forgetting that Rudi reads minds sometimes – that's how the fucker sells so many cars – and now he says, 'Jimmy, do me a favour. Don't get involved in this.'

'Why not?'

'Because I'm asking you not to.'

I look at him hard. 'Are you sure about that?' I ask.

'Yes I am, for now at least. But I'll talk to you if it becomes an issue. Anyway,' he adds, rolling his shoulders, as if to shake off the problem, 'you fancy another pint?'

I study what's left of my beer. Truth is, I don't want another one. Setting aside that two pints is borderline illegal for driving, I'm worn out by all the fucking grief in here.

'Mate,' I tell him, 'I'm going to pass. Long day and all that.'

He makes a bad joke about how I'm definitely getting past it, but a joke is all it is – there's no malice on his part and no problem either. When I tell Emma and Wes that I'm going home, they're okay with it too. We all go back inside, and I leave the three of them queuing once more at the bar.

On my way out, in the small entranceway separating pub from street, I once more cross paths with the barmaid. She's put on a Santa hat, and is selling tickets for some event they're having on Christmas Eve. I tell her I don't want tickets, and she says that's a shame. She also says she's disappointed I'm leaving so soon, and that she hopes to see me here again. I'm as bad as anyone at imaging nuances when I've had a drink, but there's a spark in her eyes that tells me she means what she says.

I wish her goodnight, and then I step out into the cold and dark with a smile on my face. I may have had a bellyful of aggro, but I leave the pub feeling pleased with myself. Not only am I seriously rich, but I can still pull a bird without trying too hard.

1.4) No Rest for the Wicked

Charlotte's car is already on the drive by the time I get home, and there are lights on behind the curtains of our front room. Bearing in mind that I stayed out for only one pint, I'm surprised to find Charlotte made it home before me. She goes to the gym on Tuesdays after work, and normally sticks around afterwards for a glass of wine and a natter with her mates.

As usual, she's parked her old Clio at the front of our drive, leaving me the room to tuck my company Golf in behind. Trouble is, I no longer have the company Golf. Graham took it off me this morning as its mileage had gotten too high. Telling me to get the Golf cleaned and priced up for sale, he handed me the keys to a Ford Mondeo in replacement. I like my new car, but it's a bloody big beast, and I'd only fit it on the drive if Charlotte were to park halfway into our porch. So I leave the Mondeo on the road outside our house, folding in the roadside door mirror as a precaution against it getting smashed. We may live in a quiet cul-de-sac, but it only takes one bloke driving like a dickhead to get too close and cause a piece of damage.

I was driving like a dickhead the night I reversed Charlotte's car into a concrete bollard at the cinema. It's not that I was reversing too fast; I just wasn't paying enough attention. Then, next second, a big crunch for the car and a red face for me. It was completely my fault, because I simply hadn't noticed the bollard. I've certainly had time enough since to notice the dent – which is fist-sized and ugly – because Charlotte won't let me get it fixed. "It's only a car," is what she says, "and it's old nowadays, so I don't see any point in spending the money. A little dent won't stop me driving it, or am I wrong about that?"

She isn't wrong about that. The bumper is not hanging off, and the little Clio still drives okay. Even so, walking up our drive, I stop and do what I've regularly done ever since I caused the dent – I put my hand on the bumper and try giving it a shake. It's a routine I've gotten into to make sure that the thing hasn't worked loose, and tonight I find, just as I've found on all the other nights, that the bumper is still fixed firmly in place. But not everything is okay with the Clio: one of the rear light clusters has condensation on the inside, and there's rust forming where the wiper joins the tailgate. Also, while I'm here, pissing about in the dark and cold, I make a quick check of the tyre treads. They're safe and legal for now, but I reckon this car will need new rubber soon.

Finally, I let myself into the house. It's warm in the hallway, and I can hear the quiet gurgle of scalding water perking in the radiator near the stairs. I don't bother with the light switch as the door to the front room is ajar, allowing enough light through for me to move around without crashing into the coat stand or stumbling over Charlotte's gym bag. I can hear violin music playing softly on our stereo – it's the kind of thing Charlotte puts on as background when she's got schoolwork on the go, and on that basis I reckon she'll be busy marking. After taking off my coat, I head into the front room to see if I'm right.

Charlotte is sitting cross-legged at one end of the sofa, which is where she always sits when she has marking to do. With a green pen in one hand, she has a schoolbook open on her lap, and another twenty or more piled up beside her. Close by, on a little coffee table, is a good-sized glass of white wine, recently poured and still cold, judging from the spread of condensation round the outside of the glass.

I say hello. Charlotte pushes down the reading glasses she's recently begun wearing, and looks at me over the top of the frames. 'Hi, sweetheart,' she replies, smiling. Charlotte has a sexy smile, with or without the glasses.

She puts the marking aside, and begins to get up. I go to her, and we briefly kiss while she's halfway to her feet. Everything about Charlotte is fresh and zingy. Her jeans and jumper smell newly clean, and her long, tawny hair, still damp and shiny from the health club's shower, has the lemony tang of citrus shampoo.

'Good day?' I ask.

'Pretty much,' she replies, sitting back down. 'And you?'

'Same here.' I nod at her glass and ask, 'Not drinking with the girls?'

'I was too tired after my work-out. Plus, I have to get this lot marked. We're awarding prizes on Friday for the best Christmas essays.'

'That's three days away. You've got loads of time.'

Again, Charlotte peers at me over the frames of her glasses. 'I've got tonight,' she says. 'I need to be finished by tomorrow, because that's when we're due to discuss who's won.'

'Fair enough. So how long do you need?'

'About an hour,' comes her answer. And I must look sceptical about that, because she quickly adds, 'Alright, maybe two.'

'Which means I'm cooking dinner, right?'

'Sweetheart, that would be great. And don't delay it on my account. We can eat whenever it's ready, and I'll get back to marking afterwards.'

'No worries. I'll go and crack on.'

I get as far as the door before Charlotte asks, 'Did you sell any cars today?'

'I did. Just the one, but one's not bad for a weekday in December.'

'I'm sure it isn't. Who did you sell it to?'

'A nice couple, Ann and Rob. They're about our age; maybe a bit younger. She reminded me of you.'

Charlotte casts me an amused look. 'Really?' she asks. 'In what way?'

'In the way that she's the boss, and runs Rob ragged making him do what she wants.'

Charlie takes a sip of wine and studies me carefully. She says, 'You don't look run very ragged from where I'm sitting.'

'Remind me who's cooking dinner, would you?'

She giggles a little. 'Fair point. Best get on with it before I have you whipped.'

'There you go, overpromising again.'

She giggles some more, miming a whipping action with her pen, before picking the schoolbook back up and returning to her marking. I'm probably supposed to get my ass into the kitchen at this point, but instead I hang back in the doorway.

When Charlotte looks up again, I say, 'Anyway, this couple – Ann and Rob – because she reminded me of you, I got to thinking about something.'

'And what was that?'

'Well, they're getting a new car, and I wondered whether you'd like one.'

'Me?'

'Yeah, you. How do you fancy changing your car?'

'My, my.' Once more, she puts the book aside, uncurling from the chair to sit up straight. 'What's brought this on?'

'Well, your car's seven years old and will need money spending soon, so it makes sense to change it now. I'm Graham's blue-eyed boy at the minute, or one of them at any rate. That means he'll let me have a terrific deal on pretty much anything we've got in stock.'

While Charlie digests the idea, I sidle from the doorway back to the centre of the room. 'It's the right time to do it,' I tell her. 'We've got some great cars available at the minute.'

She laughs at that last part. 'You sound just like a car salesman. Sweetheart, it's a lovely idea, but even this terrific deal from Graham will cost loads of money, won't it? How much would this set me back?'

'Not you. Me. Or us, if you like. I can take some from the business fund.'

'No way!' she says, her eyes widening. 'Not the business fund – definitely not.'

'How come?'

She takes off the reading glasses and looks at me directly. 'It's your money, that's how come. The money you've saved to quit your job, start a business, get rich – all of those things. What's happened to that idea? Are you giving up on it?'

'Of course not.'

'So why raid the fund now?'

I take a second to gather my thoughts, and I perch myself on the arm of a nearby chair. Then I tell Charlie my latest half-truth. 'Look at this way: work has been going well, as you know. I've been putting good money into the fund, and I reckon we can get the business up and running soon – I'm having a drink with Ash tomorrow so that we can start firming up our plans.'

'I know,' she replies, 'and that's great. So coming back to my previous question, why raid the fund now? The staff-room gossips have only just stopped banging the drum about Little Louis.' She points at the Louis Vuitton handbag sitting on the arm of the other chair. Sleek and dark, it looks magnificent, even to a bloke. It looks fucking expensive too, which it bloody well should, being as it cost more than a normal month's pay. 'First, you buy me one of the world's most expensive handbags,' continues Charlotte, 'Now you're talking a car. People will think we've won the lottery.'

'Let them think what they want.' I feel my face colouring, and so I get up and move away, picking up the remote for the TV and fiddling with the piece of tape which holds the broken battery cover in place. 'Just let me get you a car, Charlie. It is Christmas after all.'

'Nearly Christmas.'

'Okay, so it's nearly Christmas. What do you say?'

For a moment she says nothing. Just leans forward, elbows on knees, staring hard at Little Louis.

'I think you're spoiling me,' she finally says, a bemused smile playing across her lips. 'And I can't think why.'

'Does there have to be a why?'

'I suppose not.'

'So come on, Charlie. Let me do this.'

Charlotte looks at the handbag some more, and then takes another sip of wine.

'Sweetheart, I'm starving,' she says, putting down her glass. 'Why don't you go and get the dinner started? Make us something really nice, and let's talk properly after we've eaten.'

1.5) Sitting Alone, Staring out at the Dark

Later in the evening, I head up two flights of stairs to my den on the top floor. My den isn't a big room, and it was tight for space even before I crammed in all the big and bulky stuff that didn't much belong anywhere else. My running machine takes up the most square feet, my desk not many less. They both get regular use, but I ought to free up some space by ditching the big old beanbag in the corner. I used to sprawl there when I played my Xbox, but I haven't done any gaming in more than two years.

With my usual manoeuvring and contorting, I manage to wriggle in behind the desk. I turn on my laptop, and while I'm waiting for it to boot up I sit and stare at the darkness beyond the window. I can remember the estate agent describing the properties in this block as "townhouses", for the simple reason that they each have third floors. Meanwhile, the surrounding houses are only two-storey, and so all I see is the dark when I sit here and look out at night, not the lights of other people's homes. The blackness out there creates a sense of isolation, especially when Charlotte is two floors below and I can't hear anything of what she's up to. It makes me feel as though I'm alone at the top of the world. Sometimes that's a good feeling; other times it isn't.

My laptop is ready to do its thing, and so I open up the spreadsheet showing the cash-flow forecast I drafted as part of my business plan. I wrote the forecast nearly a year ago, and putting it together didn't come naturally to me. I read some accounting-for-beginners books, and then swatted up about spreadsheets, all in the name of doing things professionally. Looking at it now, I still feel proud of my work, but I've reached the stage where I know the numbers off-by-heart, and in truth I've opened the document only in case I need a decoy: if Charlotte comes in I can point at the screen and tell her I'm working on my flow-of-funds projections. Flow-of-funds projections – fuck me, that makes me sound like some big-shot corporate bean counter.

Next thing, I get round to my real purpose in coming up here. I unlock my desk drawer and take out the manila folder containing all the gubbins relating to my lottery win. I extract the bank statement advising that I've got three-and-three-quarter million pounds on account, and idle away a few minutes simply staring at the thing. I look at my name – Mr James Michael Harris – and at my address. I look for a longer time at the big number – the one with nine digits including the pence. Mentally, I compare the big number with the smaller ones in the cash flow forecast on my computer screen, and think: *what's the fucking point?* It's all well and good having ambition and making plans to start a business, but when the best part of four million quid lands in your lap you begin asking yourself whether to bother.

Three or four months ago, everything seemed clear cut. I was saving as much money as possible, so that I could go into business with my best mate, Ash. The business would be about me buying and selling cars, and Ash fixing them up. Our plan – or my plan, really – had been to work hard, work smart, and get rich. But then I found out that I could get rich anyway, and do so overnight, if I'd only bother to claim the winnings that had actually been mine since the summer. Suddenly, my ideas about the future weren't so straightforward, and I was left asking myself whether to bother starting the business or, alternatively, simply sit back and enjoy an easy life of indulgence. The decision might seem an easy one when it's only hypothetical, but I've found it far harder having won the lottery for real. An "easy life of indulgence" may sound attractive, but "floating rudderless in a morass of luxury" – an alternative description I picked up from the web – feels frankly dangerous. But even then, this particular conundrum – to strive or to retire – is only the second biggest dilemma I find myself needing to resolve at the moment.

I slide the bank statement away and take out a different folder from my drawer. I call this folder my Pitfalls Folder – I use it to store the lists and articles I've printed off concerning the stuff that goes wrong in the lives of lottery winners.

Some of the pitfalls just seem bonkers. They make me think: *Only in America*. There are stories, for example, of people throwing themselves in front of lottery winners' cars so that they can then sue them for huge amounts of dough. And there are other accounts of winners' relatives hiring hit men to bump them off, so as to claim all the millions for themselves.

I'm not too worried about off-the-wall stuff like that – although who know what may happen when I finally tell my family that I've won? – but there are other pitfalls I take much more seriously. Becoming delusional is one of them, and losing friends is another; I can see how both those things could easily happen if I'm not careful. And then there's one risk I'm really conscious of at the minute: it's what I call the Pressure for Perfection. The gist of it is this: I'm rich, and so my life should be perfect – I have no excuses for it to be anything less. People who aren't rich obsess about what they'd do if they did have money, and how great their lives would be if only their bank balance was bigger. Well here I am, with bundles of cash, but living a life that doesn't feel great at all. Not by a long bloody way.

There's more than one reason why I've failed to build a perfect lifestyle in the months since I got rich. But by far the biggest reason is the worry I'm feeling about Charlotte and how things are between the two of us. My relationship with her is front and centre of the biggest dilemma I've ever had to face.

My brooding is interrupted when our landline phone starts ringing. Hardly anyone dials it these days, only cold-callers and Charlotte's mum. If I were to lean over and stretch out, I could answer the upstairs extension, the one that's on the floor round the side of the desk, all tangled up with power cables and printer leads. But it's very late for cold-callers, and so I leave Charlie to answer because I reckon it's got to be her mum who's phoning.

I get back to thinking about the biggest dilemma I'm currently facing. It's simply this: I don't know whether to leave Charlotte or stay with her. I love the woman, but I feel bored and straitjacketed by our relationship, and I've no idea what to do for the best. My having a big pile of cash doesn't help – I reckon it's clouding the situation rather than helping with matters. Quite frankly, I don't know whether I'm restless because of the money, or whether I'm restless in spite of it. And so I don't know whether it can cure my fatigued relationship with Charlie, or only make things worse.

Surprisingly, that phone is still ringing. I lean across and stretch out my arm, reaching down for the extension, but it falls silent just before I can grab hold. For a second I simply hang there, one hand hovering over the phone, wondering whether Charlotte's picked up downstairs and is now nattering with her mum. If she is, then maybe she'll tell her about the talk we had after dinner, the one when I had another go at persuading Charlotte to let me buy her a car.

'Why, Jimmy?' she replied when I raised the subject for a second time. 'And why now, especially?'

'Because I can.'

'No, sweetheart. I mean, really, why now?' She pushed her plate aside and looked at me interrogatively. I may as well have been one of the kids in her class, caught doing something he shouldn't and required to explain himself.

'Well your bumper's dented, for one thing,' I replied.

'My bumper's been dented for flamin' months, as well you know. Which brings me back to my question: why now? Why do you suddenly want to splash out when you've been saving money for almost as long as I've known you? You used to be proud of how much you were salting away, and you were forever telling me about your plans for the business.'

'Hang on, Charlie – '

'But you've stopped talking to me about any of that. And now you want to buy me a car. Are you sure you haven't given up on going it alone?'

'Given up? No, of course not.'

But she had a point of course – a bloody good point come to that. It's been eighteen months since she moved in with me, and I've been banging the drum about starting a business for most of that time. It's only in the past few weeks that I've gone quiet about the idea.

'Something has changed,' said Charlotte, getting up from the table and clearing away the plates. 'Whatever happened to all that energy and vigour? You were ferociously ambitious, sweetheart, but where's that ferocity gone?'

I think those last questions were rhetorical. I certainly hope they were, because I didn't have any decent answers at hand. Instead, I made a crappy little speech, telling her I was still ambitious about the business and I then promised to get back in the habit of sharing my plans. Finally, I finished off by assuring her that my business fund remained in good shape, and asked once more whether I could please just buy her a bloody car.

Charlotte said she'd think about my offer, and then she apologised for appearing ungrateful, claiming she didn't want me to spend big and then regret it later. When I asked why she thought I might regret the idea, it was her turn to struggle for answers. She took the conversation off on a tangent, and we somehow ended up discussing her Pilates class at the gym. After that, it wasn't long before she went back to marking books, and I came up here to stare at these poxy sheets of paper and have another go at figuring out which way my life is heading.

What with my having left the laptop alone, it's gone into sleep mode – the screen is black and empty, just like the night-time view from my window. I jiggle the mouse to bring back the desktop display, and then spend a minute restoring my spreadsheet. I glance at the numbers displayed – at my projections of income and expenditure – and try to remember the time when the size of them scared me a bit.

What I find scary nowadays are the decisions I need to make concerning me and Charlotte. I'm scared of leaving her, and I'm also scared of staying. I haven't told her about the money because I reckon her knowing will cloud my judgment all the more, and yet I need to move on from this twilight world of secret-keeping where I look for contrived ways of spending money on her just to ease my guilty conscience.

And my decision regarding Charlotte is tied up and intertwined with my feelings for Isabel, my former long-term girlfriend, recalled by Graham as a "gold digger" when we were talking at the showroom earlier. Isabel left me three years ago, after more than eight together, to hook up with a bloke who, then at least, had more money in his wallet than I had in the bank. I was down and busted-up for a long time afterwards, and it was Charlotte who picked me up and pieced me back together when all the king's horses and all the king's men would have given it up as a fucking bad job. That means I owe Charlotte, big time. But although I can pay her in cold hard cash, I'm not sure I can offer anything more.

I reach further back in the desk drawer and take out the piece of old tin I recently found in the loft. It's Isabel's piece of old tin, and although it isn't much to look at it gives me the excuse I need, after three years without contact, to pick up the phone to her. I'll be nervous when I make the call, more so than when we first met. Life was simpler back then, a decade ago in a crowded nightclub, when I walked up to a stunning blonde girl and asked her to dance with me. She said no to that, and then knocked me back again when I quickly followed up with the offer of a drink.

I put on a brave face, told Isabel it was her loss, and began to walk away. My pride was bruised but not broken. Sure, Isabel was the best looking girl in the club – and didn't we both know it? – but I wasn't a bad pull myself, and although the clock was ticking I'd have other chances with other girls long before the humiliating fallback of a taxi home with the reek of failure for company.

I'd walked almost out of earshot before Isabel spoke to me again. I was looking around for my mates, so that we could regroup and get a round of drinks in. Then, only just audibly: 'You're a mechanic, aren't you?'

I turned back. Brilliant blue eyes, sizing me up. 'Don't you work at Kinning's garage?' Isabel asked.

I tried to think of something to say – something cool or funny or a little bit savage. What I ended up saying was, 'Yeah, that's right.'

'Thought so,' she replied. 'Well, my car needs fixing.'

This time, a reply came to mind. I looked at my watch and grinned. 'I'm afraid we're closed until Monday morning.'

She didn't so much smile as twitch her lips, but that was all the encouragement I needed. I winked at her cheesily. 'Besides,' I added, 'I haven't got the booking diary on me.'

'Dickhead,' she said, but without any malice. 'Do you want to look at my car sometime? I mean, you must do work, cash-in-hand?'

Truth was, I did not do work for cash-in-hand. I wasn't interested in that. I was twenty-two, or thereabouts, still living with my mum and working long hours, for which I was well paid. Plus, there was overtime available whenever I wanted it. All of which meant I could enjoy my time off, not spend it crawling around someone's poxy old motor in return for a bit of pocket money.

'Yeah,' I replied. 'I do work, cash-in-hand. When do you want me to take a look?'

This time I got the bare bones of a real smile. 'Do you want to phone me?' she asked.

My phone was new. It was also at home. The previous weekend, in the very same club, my old one had slipped from my pocket and gotten trampled to bits in a mosh pit. I'd replaced it with my first ever smartphone, something so expensive I hadn't wanted to risk bringing it out. All of which meant I had to scrounge a cloakroom ticket and a pen to write down Isabel's number. She huffed at me, called me a dickhead again, and told me that the thing about mobile phones was they were supposed to be mobile. But I didn't mind her mini-tantrum, because I knew by then that she fancied me – maybe only a little bit, but that little bit was something I could work on. Later on, I was happy enough to share a taxi home with Ash and CJ, the two of them swapping war stories about women they'd chased without success. I didn't reckon I'd failed – I'd got the number of the best looking bird in the club.

I'm brought back to the here-and-now by the sound of footsteps, first on the stairs, then on the landing. By the time Charlotte knocks on the door and pushes it open, everything she shouldn't see is back in the drawer, and I'm staring fixedly at my spreadsheet.

'Hi,' she says softly from the doorway.

'Hi, yourself.' I glance at her tired face. 'How's the marking going?'

'Finished for tonight,' she says. And although I had hoped she was here to offer me coffee, Charlie then adds, 'And so to bed.'

I look at my watch. It's even later than I thought. I feel angry with myself because I know I spend too long up here, staring at bits of paper, waiting for my head to magic some easy answers to these difficult questions.

I must look angry too, because Charlotte asks me if I'm alright. I let her know that I'm fine thanks, just tired. I tell her I've lost track of time and that I'll be just a couple of minutes behind her. She squeezes into the den and kisses the top of my head. She murmurs, 'Don't be long with your numbers, business boy.'

Then she goes, closing the door gently behind her, leaving me staring into space and thinking about my dilemmas. Should I stay with Charlie? Should I pick up the phone to Isabel? Should I still start a business with Ash? It would be great to know what I actually want. I wish I had all the answers to all my questions. Fuck me, I wish I had even some of them.

I haven't found time tonight for my third biggest dilemma – that's the one concerning how much money to give away, and who to give it to. Of course, I'll look after Charlotte whether we stay together or not. I'll take care of my mum as well, plus my dopey brother and his dopier wife – they are family after all. But regarding who gets what after that, I just don't fucking know. I'm not sure whether to give twenty-five grand to each of ten people, or ten grand to each of twenty-five.

Or both.

Or neither.

Or whatever.

And that's to say nothing of charity, of putting right some of what's wrong with the world. There are a zillion good causes out there, and I don't know which ones to choose or how much to give them.

But I don't have time for anymore of this tonight.

I power down the laptop, and while I'm waiting for it to switch off I take that piece of old tin back out of the drawer. I unearthed it a week or so since, while scouring the loft for some documents I needed so that my solicitor could draft what he called an "emergency will" - a simple, no-thrills document which would serve a purpose until he had chance to construct something more intricate. He told me that to have millions in the bank, without a final will and testament, was to invite trouble for those you leave behind, and I'm bloody sure he was right.

I turn the piece of tin over in my hands, marvelling at it less for what it is than for the opportunity it offers. Given that Christmas is coming, and therefore New Year too, I ought to make some resolutions and get my life moving in one direction or another. And so I decide, here and now, that there'll be no more pissing about – I'll phone Isabel tomorrow. With that decision put to bed, I realise it's time I put myself there too. I stash Isabel's piece of tin back in the drawer and get up from my desk.

By the time I make it to the bedroom, Charlotte's already asleep. I undress in the dark, before slipping into bed and snuggling-spoon-like against her back. She mutters something dreamy, which I can't make out, and when I whisper, 'What's that, Charlie?' she doesn't reply. Instead, her breathing resumes its restful beat – deep and slow, deep and slow – with a little low whistle at the end of every breath.

I just lie in bed, tired but unable to fall immediately asleep. I think about Isabel for a while, and then about Charlotte. But for some reason, before I drift away, my mind fills up with thoughts about Carl and his money problems. At best he's a pain in the arse, and at worse a horrible piece of shit, but part of me thinks I ought to help the bloke out of his troubles. After all, I wouldn't have won the lottery in the first place if it weren't for the fucker sticking his oar in. I finally fall asleep thinking about how Carl got inside my head that evening, and wondering again whether there might be such a thing as fate.

1.6) Booze 'n' Fags 'n' Filthy Lucre

Until recently, I'd always thought that fate didn't exist. At least not in the sense that our futures are mapped out rigidly and each of us is powerless to change them. I just don't subscribe to stuff like that. The idea that our tomorrows are written in the stars? And that a big, supernatural hand is guiding us towards them?

What a load of bollocks – that's what I used to think about it.

And actually, that's what I still think about it. Or at least it's what I think for ninety-nine percent of the time.

But the other one percent is different. That's when I get around to wondering about the freaky stuff – things so freaky that they seem beyond coincidence. These are the times when events seem to conspire, when outcomes are forced, and people seem powerless to change destiny because destiny really has been decided by a higher authority.

Sometimes, when I look back on the summer evening when I won the lottery, I reckon it was a one-percent episode. No, I don't believe in fate, and yet it seems that fate had a hand in everything that happened at the time.

Saturdays are usually our busiest day at the showroom, and it tends to be late before we leave for home. But that particular Saturday had been the first really hot one of the summer, ensuring trade was down and footfall low, which was why we were all out the door and locking up not long after five. I remember I'd sold only one car, and not even Rudi had done any better, but we were all in high spirits because the weather was so fantastic.

Graham seemed happy enough. The month overall was looking good, enabling him to write one poor day off for what it was. Besides, he had a date planned for that evening with a woman he'd met on the internet, and to impress her he decided to take the sporty red Audi convertible. After finally getting the roof lowered – not without some help from me – he sped off sharply, wearing his Ray-Bans and a big grin, with two fingers raised to those of us still locking up the building.

It was only because I stopped to help Graham with the Audi's roof that I ended up at the off licence. If I'd left earlier I'd have been nearer home by the time Charlotte phoned, and I'd have gone to the supermarket instead. But as things turned out, I'd driven less than a mile from the showroom, and was stopped at the Appleby Road lights when Charlotte's call came through. She said her sister Michelle was coming round in a couple of hours, and we were out of Malibu – could I please stop and pick up a bottle? The lights changed green as I hung up, and in the same instant, about a hundred yards ahead, an aged Vectra pulled out of a space immediately in front of old Raymond Cooper's off licence. I hadn't been inside Raymond's shop in years – I'd been just a kid the last time, and he'd refused me cigarettes. But it seemed now as though the shop were beckoning me back through the door.

Once I'd parked up and walked in, not much looked to have changed. It was one of those small, old-fashioned shops, where the aisles were narrow and the goods piled high. Of course, Raymond was still there, still standing proud behind the counter in his pale brown shopkeeper's smock and a knitted woollen tie. His hair was whiter and thinner than before, but otherwise he looked the same, his reading glasses still worn on a cord around his neck. Stupidly, irrationally, I felt a little bit frightened of him, as if he might round on me again for trying to buy those cigarettes while under-age.

There were four people queuing. And bloody Carl was one of them. He was third in line, and we nodded briefly at each other as I squeezed past on my way to the spirits shelf. He'd made it up to second by the time I joined the queue in fourth. Turning towards me, he spoke across the middle-aged woman standing between us. 'Shitty day, huh?'

'Yeah,' I agreed. I knew he'd done no business at all, but for conversation's sake I asked, 'You sell anything in the end?'

'Fuck all,' he replied.

The woman in the queue was laden with shopping. She looked fatigued by the heat, and I don't reckon she had the energy to be offended by Carl's swearing. But I felt embarrassed for her, and so I didn't reply because I didn't want to give Carl any further excuse to open his mouth.

But my colleague was persistent, wanting to mitigate the big fat zero he'd racked up for the day. 'I've got a young couple coming back tomorrow,' he said. 'On the dark grey Megane. They seem keen enough.'

'That's good. Let's hope you deal 'em.'

I didn't really give a rat's arse whether he dealt them or not, and Carl said nothing further because by then it was his turn to be served. He dobbed a six-pack of lager down on the counter, and then asked Raymond for cigarettes. I thought he'd be leaving once he'd paid up and received his change, but I was wrong about that. Instead, he produced a fistful of hand-filled lottery tickets and slid them across the counter to be processed. With them he pushed back his change and a fresh twenty from his wallet.

'Six lucky dips as well,' he said. He turned away from Raymond, wanting to check his phone – maybe for messages, maybe, as things have turned out, for the racing results. Raymond didn't trouble to reply, but put on his reading glasses and began *processing the lottery tickets. He glanced up once while doing this, flashing a sly look of contempt to which Carl remained oblivious.*

Finally, as Raymond pushed tickets and change across the counter, Carl slid his phone away and looked at me. 'Here's hoping,' he said. 'If I win tonight, Jimmy-Boy, I won't be dealing anyone tomorrow. I won't even be turning up.'

'Well, good luck Carl, but the odds aren't good.'

'Some fucker's going to win. I can feel it in my bones.' He slipped the lottery tickets in his pocket, and stepped away from the counter with his beer and smokes. 'The jackpot's rolled over from Wednesday, as well.'

'Like I said, good luck.'

'Aren't you playing?'

I help up the bottle of Malibu. 'I'm buying booze. I don't play the lottery.'

'Next please,' said Raymond. He'd served the heat-weary woman, and she was on her way out the door. Now he was giving me the hurry-up because the queue had grown behind me.

'Suit yourself,' said Carl, as I stepped towards the counter. 'If I'm not in tomorrow you'll know why. You can have my fucking customer if you want.'

I put the bottle and my money on the counter. 'Just the Malibu, please,' I said to Raymond, before turning to look as Carl did his gunslinger's strut through the door – he was less overweight than he is now, and could just about get away with it. I'd heard Carl's wife had walked out on him the previous week, but if he was missing her then he was hiding it well. I kept track of him through the window, heading for his car, looking for all the world like he owned the street. Here was a salesman who'd come to work that morning and sold nothing all day, but was going home high on the hope – the expectation, even – that he was going to win the fucking lottery.

I picked up my Malibu and my change. I said my thanks to Raymond and turned to go.

I don't know what it was that made me turn back. I can only reckon it was a crazy fear that Carl might actually win the big one, and that having done so he'd come in tomorrow just to large it up. He'd be unbearably smug; he'd be full of, "What did I tell you, Jimmy?" Or, more likely, "What did I tell you, Cooter?"

Anyway, for whatever reason, having stepped away from the counter, turn back I did. The man behind me in the queue had moved in to be served, but I sidled back in front of him, sheepishly muttering my apologies. Raymond gave me a stern look like the one he gave me when I was fourteen and trying to buy John Player Special. 'Look, I'm sorry,' I said, 'but could I please have one of those lucky dips.'

Just briefly, I thought Raymond was going to refuse me again. But then, after a moment's pause, he wordlessly took my money and pressed a button on his machine. That was the deed done. I was in the draw. And not that he knew it, but Carl had finally persuaded somebody to buy something that day.

2) Wednesday

2.1) Kate Makes an Entrance, Eventually

At the next morning's sales meeting, it's a case of new day, same old faces. Everyone from the pub last night, Carl included, is gathered round the big table in Graham's office, all waiting for the boss to finish his phone call and get the meeting underway. Marlon, Kev and Kate weren't at the pub, and nor are they at the meeting. It's fine that Marlon and Kev aren't here because Wednesday is their regular day off, but Kate should have rolled up by now. I know she's arrived at work because I can see her car parked outside the window, but I'm guessing she'll only come into the office at the last possible minute. That's the way she plays things these days, avoiding Emma so far as she can, and Graham to some extent as well.

Emma and Rudi are nattering at one end of the table. They're nattering quietly, what with Graham being on the phone, but their body language is upbeat. Emma is bouncy and fidgety, playing with her hair and fiddling with the bangles on her wrist; Rudi is less animated, but his expression is alert and eager. The two of them might be showing it in different ways, but each has their game face on.

Wes is a different story. He looks on bleakly, a little slump in his broad shoulders indicating that he's not the happiest man in the room. Wes isn't a morning person at the best of times, but he gets tetchy when he sees Emma hitting it off with another bloke, even when bloke is Rudi, who's not only happily married, but is also old enough to be Emma's dad, and, for good measure, happens to look like the "before" photo in an advert for a bodybuilding course.

Carl, meanwhile, looks even worse than Wes. He has the harried look of a convict on the run, and he can't sit still, not even for a second. I watch him check first his phone, then his big blingy watch. He takes a few seconds to chew his thumbnail, before checking phone and watch again. He glances across to where Graham is reclining at his desk, and mutters under his breath when the boss's call drags on and on.

There's no point trying to talk to Carl or Wes, so I stay silent and watch Graham on the phone. Eventually, he rocks himself upright in his chair. 'No sweat,' he says into the mouthpiece, 'we'll sort it before New Year.' Then there's a pause while he does some listening. He shakes his head a little and rolls his eyes at me. 'Yeah, yeah,' he says, 'it's a sure thing.' He listens some more and adds,

'Whatever, Pete, whatever. Gotta go now – we're having a sales meeting.' A final pause, this one shorter, impatience showing all over his face. 'Yeah, like I said, gotta go. Speak soon. Bye.'

Graham puts down the phone and eases out from behind his desk to join us at the big table. 'Head office,' he says, sitting down. 'Always keen to tell us our jobs, but there's no fucker there who could sell a car, even it were a new Ferrari for fifty quid.' We all laugh, except for Carl, who just sits there with his face downcast. After milking the laughter, Graham says, 'Right then everyone, it's December the thirteenth and…'

But he quickly tails off, looking first at the faces round the table and then at the rota on the wall. 'Hang on,' he asks, 'Bloody Kate, again – where is she?'

We all look at each other, and Emma manages a disdainful little sniff.

'I've seen Kate's car,' I tell Graham. 'She's definitely on site. Maybe getting coffee?'

'Or in the bogs,' says Carl, with another glance at his watch. 'Trowelling on her make up, probably.'

Carl's comment meets with tight-lipped silence. None of the rest of us, not even Emma, would bitch about Kate like that in front of Graham, not given how close the two of them are. Graham's always had a soft spot for Kate, and probably always will, even though word is the affair they were having has run its course.

Sure enough, Graham bites back, 'You're a fine one, Carl. When God was handing out faces you ended up with a second arse.'

That gets the boss another laugh. Then, once the room quiets down, there's a brief lull while Graham stares at the door, as if expecting Kate to walk in. When that doesn't happen he looks at each of us in turn, as if deciding who he'll pick to go and track her down. But in the end he doesn't bother. He simply sighs and says, 'Right, I daresay she'll be here in a minute, and on current form she won't be listening anyway. Besides, what I've got to say won't take long.'

Carl checks his watch for maybe the tenth time, and that doesn't go unnoticed either. Graham asks whether he has a train to catch or something, and when Carl grudgingly admits that he hasn't, Graham tells him to start paying better attention, before then picking up where he previously left off. 'As I was saying, it's December the thirteenth.'

'Only twelve sleeps to Santa,' pipes up Emma.

Carl's tetchiness simmers over. 'For Christ's sake,' he moans. 'This isn't a nursery school.'

'But it's okay for you to act like a big kid?' Emma snaps back. 'Bad-mouthing Kate about her make-up.'

'Don't talk such bollocks. No one slags her more than you'

'You think so? Well –'

But then Graham slaps the table hard, just as he slapped the desk yesterday, and with a similar result. Everyone shuts up and looks at him.

'You two, zip it,' he says. 'Take your bitch fight outside once I've finished talking.'

Emma blushes a little, and hurriedly says sorry to Graham. But her tone is sulky, and if looks could kill then the one she gives Carl would hospitalise the fucker at least. In turn, he gives her a mean stare back, one which won't serve him well if he needs to scrounge any smokes today.

'Apology accepted,' says Graham. 'Thank you, Emma. Yours too, Carl.'

'Sorry,' mutters Carl.

'Good – so glad that's sorted and everyone is friends again with everyone else.' Graham looks quizzically at Emma and Carl, and then continues, 'Right then, as I was saying – and don't make me repeat this again, or someone will die – today is December the thirteenth.' He pauses, ever so briefly, as if daring anyone else to interrupt or wisecrack, and then he continues. 'As Emma reminds us, there's only twelve days left before a fat man in a red suit drops down our chimneys and leaves presents for all the good boys and girls who haven't been thieving, fighting or generally acting like bastards.' He glances round the table and says, 'I reckon you lot have no chance.' Again, we all laugh apart from Carl, who shuffles in his seat while grumbling quietly to himself. Risking Graham's disapproval, he snatches another glance at his watch – it's clear that something urgent is going down with him.

'For two of you,' Graham continues, pointing first at Emma and then at Wes, 'this is your first December in the motor trade. And what this pack of wizened old scrotes will tell you is that the second half of December is very quiet, and for pretty obvious reasons.'

'But be ready for January,' says Rudi. 'January goes mad.'

'Yeah, Rudi's right,' says Graham. 'January will be busy. But from now until Christmas it will be quiet round here. Which means we have to make the most of every enquiry we get. When you think about it, the punters who do come in will be serious about getting a car. Nobody interrupts their Christmas preparations to come in here, kick tyres and just piss about – and you need to remember that when you're talking to them. These are serious people, and it's your job to sell them a fucking motor. So we deal them, not burn them. Understood?' He looks briefly around the table. 'Good. Glad we've got that sorted.'

Graham takes a moment to fiddle with his cufflinks, and then he adds 'Now, another thing. You all know there's a thousand quid for finishing top this month?'

Rudi sticks his oar in again. 'Why don't you pay me now?' he asks. 'Why not just have it done with?'

Graham casts him a wary look, like a prize-fighter weighing up his next opponent. Rudi stares straight back, his eyes full of frank self confidence. Rudi believes he's going to win. He always believes he's going to win, and his record suggests he's justified in that belief.

'You know I'll pay you if you actually finish top,' says Graham. 'But you won't have it as easy as you think. You've got Jimmy breathing down your neck, for one thing.' He looks hard at me, and then his eyes move away, searching the faces of the others round the table, looking to see who else is up for the fight. I reckon he likes what he sees in Emma, and he tells her, 'You're not far behind, Em'. You could overtake these two fuckers easily enough.' He casts around some more. 'Wes, you could still get there with a big push. You've yet to show me you can be a top performer, but this would be a great time to start. Carl, what can I say? You've fallen off a fucking cliff just lately, but you used to sell me cars, and I know you still can if you put your mind to it.'

Graham leans forward. He asks, 'Everybody got the message?' When we all respond with the right noises, he asks if we have any questions for him. But before anybody can actually ask one, he says, 'Right. Meeting over, then. You all know what happens next. Let's get the pitch sorted.'

Carl says, 'Graham, can I talk to you after the meeting?'

Graham points at the rows of cars outside his window and says, 'You can talk to me once the pitch is in good shape.'

I look out the window and make some mental calculations. Sorting the pitch means getting our outside display looking polished and professional. It means straightening the rows of cars, and it means picking up litter. It also means bringing the newly valeted cars on display, while moving the sold ones off. And on a morning like this, it means scraping ice off all the windscreens so that punters can see the price boards and point-of-sale material.

There are six of us working today. There are maybe a hundred-and-fifty cars out there. That's twenty-five windscreens each.

And it seems that Carl hasn't got time to clear his twenty-five screens. 'Graham,' he pleads, 'I could really do with talking to you now.'

Graham sits back, arms folded and eyes cold. 'If I agreed to that,' he asks 'would I be helping you sell a car.'

'Not in the sense of –'

'And I mean now, Carl. Have you got a deal on the go that you need to discuss? By stopping behind and talking to me, rather than helping your colleagues sort out the pitch, can you sell me a car in the next twenty minutes?'

'No.'

'I see. In that case, is there an urgent problem with a car you're due to hand over today?' Graham looks at the sales board before sarcastically adding, 'Oh no, my mistake. You've only sold two for the fucking month, and they've both gone out already.'

'But I must talk to you now.'

'Pitch,' says Graham, standing up and pointing outside. 'All of you, Carl included. Get out there and get the pitch looking right. I'll grant interviews afterwards.'

It's once we're on our feet, heading for the door, with only Carl still trying to hang back, that Kate finally shows up, coffee in one hand, notepad in the other. Although she's late she doesn't appear hurried – her hair, clothes and make-up are all immaculate, as per usual.

'Sorry I'm late,' she says. 'I was just –'

'The meeting's over,' interrupts Graham. 'It's time to sort the pitch.'

Kate presses on anyway. 'I was just getting coffee,' she says, 'when I saw was this old man bringing his car back for repair. He was struggling to park, so I took a minute to help him.'

'Whatever,' says Graham. He shakes his head and moves back behind his desk. 'I'm going to work on some price changes. You lot get my pitch sorted. You might just find a customer while you're out there.'

I reckon Kate's got something else she wants to say. She looks at Graham, but he doesn't look back. Instead, he pulls his keyboard towards him, and suddenly he has eyes only for whatever's on the screen. Kate shrugs her shoulders, and files out the door with the rest of us. I'm close enough to hear when Emma puts on a mocking tone and says to her, 'Ever feel no one's listening, poppet?'

'Talk to me once you've grown up,' replies Kate, without even looking at Emma. 'But only once after you've found a brain to put in your stupid big head.'

Outside Graham's office, we peel away to get our coats. It may well be December the thirteenth, but the season of goodwill is yet to descend around here. It could be we're in for a long couple of weeks until Christmas.

2.2) We'll Never Get Finished at this Rate

There are plenty of people who envy me my job, thinking it's a cushy number. The lads I used to work with, back when I was a mechanic, certainly reckon I have it easy nowadays. And many of my customers think the same way, choosing to believe that selling cars is about sitting around, drinking coffee and chatting with the public. Well okay, it is, up to a point. But what people usually fail to appreciate is that I need to do the "chatting" part really well – so well that punters open up their wallets and hand me money. A salesman's in trouble when there's too much chatting going on and too little money flowing in – just ask Carl about that. Each of us is only as good as our last month, and if our last month wasn't good then we're living on thin ice.

The constant pressure to hit targets is something that people who aren't in sales simply don't comprehend. They don't see the long hours in the showroom, nor the late evenings spent cold-calling old prospects on the phone. They've no idea how many rejections we get (even the best salespeople, myself included, typically close only one in three leads), and they never know the shame of finishing the month placed last in the league table displayed prominently on Graham's office wall.

I think that's why many people try their hand at this game without sticking it for long – selling cars for a living looks far easier than it really is. And apart from the remorseless pressure, there are other sides to the job which no one in their right mind enjoys. People don't get into sales because they want to go outside and move cars around when it's dark and cold and pissing down with rain. And nobody ever signed up to work at a car dealership because they like doing what we're doing now, namely scraping ice off windscreens – roughly twenty-five cars apiece.

None of us are happy defrosting screens, and I reckon I know why that is. It's not that the work is all that tough physically – no, there are far harder jobs out there in the big wide world. The real problem is that it's a *lonely* thing to do: I've got my row of cars to work on, and the others each have theirs. That means we're working in isolation, and that's a big, big deal for people like us, because to succeed in this job we need to be the kind of people who like the company of others. We have to be so good at building rapport with complete strangers that they agree to spend thousands of pounds just an hour or so after we've met. We salespeople are socially minded boys and girls, and this can cause problems when we're given lonely jobs to do, because being socially minded isn't something we can easily turn on and off.

It's because of our social mindedness that we'll be seen to cluster together when business is quiet, congregating round each other's desks for a coffee and a natter. It's also why we're so rubbish at scraping ice off windscreens – give us each a row of cars to defrost and some mystical force will pull us together again. In short, we'll slope off to each others' rows and have a good old chat.

Rudi breaks cover before I've got five screens cleared. It looks from here as though he's barely done three, but still he downs tools – scraper and aerosol – and heads my way, moving cautiously as the pitch is slippery underfoot. I think I know what's on his mind – the same thing that's been on mine for the past five minutes.

'You're not setting a great example,' I tell him, as he takes up position at the bonnet end of the BMW I'm de-icing. 'Bunking off for a natter with only three screens scraped – Graham would expect more from his second-in-command.'

'The best example I set is selling a fuck-load of cars. Bollocks to everything else.'

Rudi's red-faced and slightly breathless, which ought to trouble him when all he's done is scrape a bit of ice and then saunter across the pitch. But he mustn't be worried about it, because next thing he sparks up a cigarette. He says, 'I know I shouldn't smoke on the pitch. But bollocks to that as well.'

I take a glance around the place. 'Well, there are no customers to see you.'

'No Graham, either.' He exhales a big lungful of smoke. 'He'll have his hands full with Carl.'

I look across at the row of cars abandoned by Carl after he'd scraped only one screen. More than five minutes have passed since Carl jacked it in and went back inside. I fully expected Graham to throw him out again – physically, if needs be – but so far Carl hasn't returned.

'What do you suppose they're talking about?' I ask, lifting the BMW's wipers so that I can scrape the screen low down. 'Money, do you reckon? Same shit as last night?'

'I guess so,' Rudi replies. 'But I don't know how Carl supposes Graham will help him.'

'Has Carl asked you for money, today?' I ask.

'No, he hasn't.' Rudi draws on his cigarette and stands silently for a few seconds. Shoulders hunched against the cold, he watches cars go by on the road outside. 'If I'm really honest, I've been avoiding Carl all morning. I normally have a smoke round the back, but I didn't want to bump into him there.'

I repeat the question I asked last night: 'Mate, is he threatening you?'

'I wouldn't call it that, and I'm not frightened of the fucker. But he must have real problems, because when he asks me for money he's so fucking intense about it. So demanding, so full on. I don't need it, Jimmy. I really don't.'

I put down my scraper and my aerosol. 'How much do you reckon he owes?'

'Thousands,' replies Rudi.

'Sure, but how many of them?'

'I don't know. Too many for us to think of bailing him out.'

Just briefly, I think of explaining that I could afford to be more helpful to Carl than Rudi might imagine. But this isn't the time or place to reveal to anyone here that I'm minted. Instead I say, 'I'm sure you're right. And I don't reckon I'd want to fucking help him, not when he carries on the way did in the meeting.'

Rudi nods to say he agrees. Then he stamps out his cigarette and kicks it towards a drain. 'Anyway,' he says, walking away, 'it's time I got back to work.' Not that he's talking about clearing windscreens. There's a punter on the pitch – a youngish bloke in a quilted jacket, peering at a frosted-over Mini – and Rudi, as he so often does, has seen him first.

It's one thing to spot a punter first, but getting to him ahead of your colleagues is another story. I could race Rudi across the pitch if I wanted to, and probably beat him easily enough. What's more, from the concerned way he glances back at me, I reckon he's had exactly the same thought. But I decide to let him go. On another day I might have gone for it, but when the pitch is so icy I could end up in Accident and Emergency having my face stitched up.

Instead I get back to scraping screens. And I manage to clear only two more before it's Emma's turn to come over and talk.

'Was Rudi smoking here?' she asks, her face hopeful. She has a cigarette in one gloved hand and her lighter in the other.

'He was.'

'That's good.' She pops the cigarette into her mouth, but then takes it out again and looks at me, maybe sensing disapproval on my part. 'So… ' she asks, 'I can smoke here as well, can I?'

'You know the rules, Em'. No smoking on the pitch. Rudi chose to break the rules. You can do the same.'

'Err… right. Okay...' She looks puzzled and uncertain, her hand holding the cigarette hovering halfway to her mouth.

I say, 'If you're going to light it, light it. I won't grass you up. I'm just saying, this isn't some magic little corner of the pitch where smoking's suddenly allowed.'

'But you don't, like, mind?'

'I don't, like, mind.'

Emma looks warily around before sparking the wheel of her lighter. A little pop of flame, and then she's smoking avidly, greedy for the nicotine. But still she glances nervously about the pitch, holding her cigarette close so that it's less noticeable to anyone looking our way.

I concentrate on clearing ice off windows. I'm now on with a wide Volvo saloon, and I have to stretch to reach the middle part of the screen. After a minute or two of my leaning and scraping, Emma says, 'Wes has asked me out.'

'Oh, yeah' I reply, without looking round or stopping work. 'He certainly took his time.'

After a few more seconds, Emma asks, 'Jimmy, have I pissed you off or something?'

I put down the scraper on the Volvo's bonnet, and rub my frozen hands together in a hopeless effort at warming them up. Then I run a rueful eye over my row of cars, contrasting the few windscreens I've cleared with the larger number still remaining. It's a shame that it's Kev's day off and he isn't here to help us – we'd get it done quicker if he were around. For my part, I'd like this shitty job done and dusted so that I can get on with other stuff, principally that phone call to Isabel I've resolved to make. Fat chance of that when the likes of Rudi and Emma want to bend my ear.

I say, 'You haven't pissed me off, Em', but I wish you'd try harder to get on with Kate.'

Immediately she snaps back. 'I didn't start it. She did.'

'Yeah. And she'd say the same about you. But does it really matter who said the wrong thing first? It's been dragging on for way too long.'

Emma doesn't answer. She just smokes and pouts and glowers, and then turns away to look across the pitch. I follow her line of vision to where Rudi has got the Mini opened up for his newfound punter.

A wordless half minute passes into oblivion before I say, 'Okay, so Wes has asked you out. What are you going to do?'

'I don't know.'

Emma keeps her back to me and smokes some more, no longer trying to hide the cigarette from prying eyes.

I've returned to scraping the big Volvo's windscreen when she turns back around and says, 'I'm like… I don't know. I mean, I love Wes to bits – as a mate – but this is…'

'This is different,' I acknowledge. 'This is a date.'

'That's just it. This is a date we're talking about.'

'And you don't know whether to say yes or no.'

'Exactly.'

'Okay, then.' Once more I put down the scraper and give her my full attention. 'Answer me this: what was your gut reaction when he asked you out? What's the first thing you thought?'

Emma seems to think about the question. 'I don't know,' she replies, shaking her head.

'So, the two of you are good mates. He fancies you. Do you feel anything for him? Any attraction, I mean?'

'I don't know.'

'You don't know much, do you, Em'? Could it be that you don't want to say yes, but don't know how to say no?'

She tosses away what's left of her cigarette without bothering to stamp it out. Then she shrugs and says, 'Jimmy, I just don't know.'

I pick the scraper back up. 'Emma, did you tell me about Wes asking you out because you wanted my opinion? Or did you just want to tell someone?'

She laughs, a little bitterly, and says, 'Guess what?'

'You don't bloody know.'

'You're right – I don't.' Emma stuffs her hands in the pockets of her coat and starts to walk away. 'We need to get these screens cleared,' she says, as if I was the one needing a reminder of that. 'Bet we end up doing Carl's share. What an arsehole that bloke is.'

I watch her go. Her shoulders are tense and there's a pissed-off look on her face. Whatever it was she wanted from me, I don't think she got it.

But once she's gone, I clear my head and put in a shift. For twenty minutes, maybe half-an-hour, possibly even longer, I just attack those windscreens. And by the time I step back and take a breather I've cleared nearly twenty, with only six left to do. But I reckon Emma was right when she said we'll end up clearing Carl's screens as well, and I'm not happy about that idea because my fingers are already raw and numb. I ought to dig out those fucking gloves I had last winter.

Looking around, I've cleared more cars than everyone except Wes. He's gone hard and fast at the job, and is scraping his last-but-one windscreen. In comparison, Emma and Rudi are just sloping off together – most likely for another smoke – whereas I noticed Kate heading indoors five minutes since. Like Carl, she's yet to return.

I'm undecided whether to finish my row of cars or sneak off and make the call to Isabel. While I'm mulling it over, Kate comes back from the showroom and stops by to chat. I've already frittered away enough time nattering, but I can't give short shrift to Kate when she's been such a good mate of mine, supporting me when I was struggling to learn the job, and again when Isabel upped and left me. And as if that weren't reason enough for me to be nice, Kate has brought us both a coffee. It isn't coffee from the machine, either. We're talking big hot mugs, brewed up in the kitchen.

Kate passes me one of the mugs. It's got a chipped rim and some cool graphics of Spiderman swinging across the New York skyline. 'Wrap your fingers round it,' she says. 'It may warm you up a bit.'

I do as she says, and I offer her my thanks. My fingers start to go tingly when I curl them round the mug. Unlike me, Kate has found her gloves and put them on. They're white, and they match the Russian Ushanka hat she's wearing with the ear flaps pulled down. For working outside on the ice, Kate's also swapped her usual heels for a pair of green wellington boots. She shouldn't look good in those, but somehow she does.

'You're getting on with it,' she says brightly, glancing along my row of cars.

'I just want to get the job done.'

'You always do. Although it looks as though Wes will finish first.'

'He should,' I tell her. 'He's younger than me, and a bit fitter too.'

'That's some admission on your part,' she says, stepping slightly to one side for a better view of Wes clearing ice from the last of his screens. Then she casts me a cheeky grin, something I'm glad to see because she's been so moody in recent weeks. 'You're right, though,' she adds. 'No offence, James, but he certainly is fitter than you.'

'Ah, but I'm the better kisser.'

'Oh yeah?' she replies. 'What makes you so sure?'

'All the girls say so.'

'Probably because you paid them to.'

I tell her to fuck off and we both have a laugh. This is the first time I've felt properly comfortable around Kate in over a month – the first time I've felt we could talk without her biting my head off. Briefly, I just stand and watch her while she watches Wes. Eventually I say, 'Thanks again for the coffee. It was thoughtful of you.'

'You're welcome.' She turns her attention from Wes and chinks her mug against mine. 'I haven't made you one in ages.'

We sip our drinks for a short while. Then I ask, 'How much fitter would you say, exactly?'

Kate sniggers, mischief playing round her eyes. 'Don't go there, James,' she says. 'You're not in bad nick, but if I had to choose between you and Wes, well...'

'I see.'

'Don't be hard on yourself,' she adds. 'Like you said, you're not as young as he is. Mind you, nor am I, and at least the two of us are in better shape than Carl.' She nods pointedly back towards the showroom, from where Carl is yet to return. 'What's wrong with the pratt this time?' she asks. 'He was in with Graham when I went for these coffees. Do you know what's up with him? He's stopped talking to me these days.'

In truth, we've all stopped talking to Kate, for the reason that she's made herself largely unapproachable. But if she's finally returning from the dark side of what Rudi calls Planet Woman, then I'm happy to have her back. I take a big gulp of coffee before saying to her, 'Rudi knows more than I do, but it looks like Carl has himself some problems.'

'I'm guessing it's gambling,' she replies. 'Or he's addicted to pornography all of a sudden. When a man with no mates spends so much time on his phone, it's got to be one or the other.'

'That's a bit brutal of you, Missus, but you're spot on about the gambling. You're asking me what's wrong with Carl when you already have it figured out.'

'Yeah, I thought I had. I was just looking for confirmation. And anyway, James, it's your turn next.'

'How do you mean?'

Kate toys absentmindedly with one of the flaps on her hat. She says, 'I want to figure out what's going on in you head. You haven't been yourself for a month or two.'

I could say the same about her. And I'm on the verge of doing so when I spot movement from the showroom. It's not Carl, but Graham, who walks outside. He stands with his arms folded while he looks around the pitch. Then he points at the two of us and beckons us indoors.

2.3) Rallying Round a Mate?

Graham ushers Kate and I into his office, where there's now no sign of Carl. Telling us he'll be back in a minute, Graham goes off to find Rudi, and when they both come back Rudi smells of fags. Graham has the three of us sit down at the table, and then he goes back outside, where he talks to Emma and Wes while we watch through the window. From the way Emma folds her arms and tosses her hair, it's obvious she isn't happy. Graham will have told the two of them to clear the ice from Carl's row of screens – a request Emma won't have thanked him for. Sitting next to me, Kate's more or less purring at Emma's irritation. She nudges me and says, 'It's time the little cow did some work for a change.'

When Graham comes back in, he closes the door and joins us at the table. His first question is to Rudi: 'What happened to your man?'

'Bloke on the Mini? The car's for his wife. He says he'll talk to her, and they'll most likely come back for a test drive on Thursday.'

'Most likely?' Graham's tone is deeply sarcastic. 'He sounds really sold on it, I have to say. Maybe he'd have been keener if it wasn't still caked with ice.' The boss gives himself a moment, fiddling agitatedly with a pen he's taken from his jacket, and then says, 'Alright, I want to talk to you about Carl. He's been a fucking idiot.'

None of us replies. Graham looks at each of us in turn and puts two and two together from reading our faces. He says, 'Alright – it looks like you already know about his problems.'

His stare lingers longest and most accusingly on Kate. She shrugs at him and says, 'Hey, I only found out this morning.'

'How much do you all know?'

'Not a lot,' I tell him. 'Only what Rudi and I were figuring out last night.'

'And all we can say for certain,' adds Rudi, 'is that he's been gambling heavily for weeks – perhaps months – and now he's asking to borrow money.'

'You lend the fucker any?' asks Graham.

'No, not me.' Rudi flashes a fleeting, conspiratorial look my way. I suppose he's lying because he doesn't want to look like a soft touch in front of Graham and Kate.

Graham doesn't miss much, and I'd be surprised if Rudi's sideways glance went unnoticed, but for now at least it does go unmentioned. 'Okay,' Graham says, leaning a long way back, staring at the ceiling and apparently gathering his thoughts. The tubular metal frame of his chair creaks and groans in tortured protest, and I want to tell him to sit up straight. The chairs around the big table aren't designed to recline like the one at his desk, and if he snaps the frame he'll go down hard and heavy.

But Graham seems oblivious. 'What about those two outside?' he asks. 'Anyone said anything to them? Or to Brando and Kevin?'

'Not me,' I reply. 'I haven't said anything to anyone outside this room.'

'And like I said,' says Kate, 'I've only just found out.'

'Besides which,' says Rudi to Kate, 'you don't talk to Emma, anyway.'

Kate pokes out her tongue at him, but doesn't bother to reply.

'Alright,' says Graham. He rocks himself upright and leans on the table. 'I'll tell you what's gone on this morning. Firstly, you'll have noticed that Carl didn't scrape many windscreens earlier before he came back indoors.'

'I counted one,' I say.

'Like I said, not many. I wasn't impressed with him, and I told him to get his arse back outside. That's when he pleaded to talk to me, and when I asked him what it was about he asked if I could lend him a few quid.'

Graham pauses for effect, allowing himself a wintery smile.

'Well,' he continues, 'you can guess what I said to that. With an ex-wife like mine, I ain't got money to lend. But even if I had… well, fuck me… you may as well flush money down the porcelain as lend it to Carl.

'And then, because I wouldn't sub him personally, he asked me for an advance on this month's wages. But you all know he ain't been selling cars, so he was asking for an advance on fuck-all, even if I could have swung it with head office.'

'So where is he now?' asks Kate.

'It all came out after that,' Graham replies. 'I asked him why he needed the money, and so he told me how much trouble he's in – and, believe me, he's over his eyes with the debts he's run up.'

Rudi reiterates Kate's question: 'So where's he gone?'

'I've given him a day or two off, to see what he can sort out.'

It's not like Graham to allow someone time off to sort out their shit, not when they're underachieving so badly in the job. And only yesterday Graham was talking to me about sacking Carl. I must look surprised, and so must Kate and Rudi, because Graham suddenly flashes an angry scowl around the table.

'Well, what would you lot have done?' he demands. And when no one supplies the obvious answer, he adds, 'I wouldn't sack him when he's got so many problems, not this fucking close to Christmas. Not unless he gave me no choice.'

Quick as a flash, Rudi replies, 'What about that kid from the Underwood Estate? You sacked the little twat on Christmas Eve.'

'Well…'

'You wouldn't even let anyone drive him home.'

'That's right,' Kate chips in. 'It was sleeting and blowing a gale, but all you kept saying to him was, "Bus stop's that way."'

Graham breaks into a grin, and we all start laughing. 'Alright, you fuckers,' he says. 'You've got me there. But that Underwood kid, what was his name?'

'Robbie,' I remind him.

'That's it. Robbie the fucking jobbie. And yeah, alright, I sacked him on Christmas Eve, but the kid was a liar and a shithead, and he had it coming. Now look,' – Graham's face turns serious again' – 'I know Carl's another shithead, but he's our shithead, isn't he? We four and he go back a bit, so I'm giving him a couple of days to try and get sorted.'

There's a moment of silence. Rudi brushes some imaginary dirt from the lapels of his jacket. He asks Graham, 'Do you really think Carl can get sorted in a couple of days? It sounds like he's got the world on his shoulders. What's he supposed to go and do?'

'Get some professional help.'

'You mean one of those debt management companies?'

'Doesn't have to be a company. They charge you for their help, which is the last thing you need when you've already got a ton of debt. There are debt charities that help you for free. I've given him the name of one.'

Rudi, Kate and I exchange wary glances before Kate says, 'You sound well informed about how it all works.'

'I am,' Graham replies, his tone of voice softening. 'Not everyone comes out the army and does as well as me. I know plenty of lads with debt – blokes who can fight and march and strip a rifle, but haven't the first idea about holding down a decent job on civvy street.'

'At least Carl's in good company,' says Rudi. 'How much debt has he got, do you know?'

Graham doesn't respond immediately, and his eyes narrow while he appears to consider his reply. 'North of twenty grand,' he finally answers, and the belligerent look on his face says: *Don't ask how far north. It's not your business.*

Rudi doesn't push it, and Graham adds, 'Look, I've told you more than Carl would thank me for. But we are a team, and those of us in this room have worked together a good long while. If Carl's going to be off for some time, I want you to know why.'

'Thanks,' says Kate.

'No problem. And if anyone else asks, tell them his granny's ill or something. Alright?'

We tell Graham it's alright, and then he says, 'So now to business.' He gets up briskly from the table, and picks up a slither of paper from a message pad on his desk. 'Reuben Fitzgerald,' he says, squinting at the paper, holding it far enough away to suggest it's time he got some reading glasses. 'Anyone heard of the bloke?'

'Don't think so,' replies Kate.

'Unusual name,' I say. 'Not the kind we'd forget.'

Rudi smirks. 'Sounds like a posh fucker.'

'Comes across on the phone that way,' says Graham. 'Very well spoken. Phoned a short while ago to complain about Carl – specifically about how Carl looked after him yesterday. Or rather failed to look after him, by the sound of things.'

'Oh, yeah,' I reply, as the penny drops with me. 'If he's who I think he is, then he was here late afternoon. It was getting dark and I was dealing up on the Astra. The bloke was extremely well dressed. Didn't get his suit at the penny arcade.'

Rudi's nodding to indicate that he remembers Reuben Fitzgerald too. To Graham, I say, 'Carl was looking for you to stack a discounted deal, but you weren't having it because the bloke was in a hurry and not giving Carl any commitment.'

'Oh yeah,' says Graham, slowly nodding. 'I remember. You're right – it was late on, wasn't it?'

'What does he want?' asks Rudi. 'Apart from to complain.'

'He wants to buy a car, apparently, if I can only put him together with a salesman who won't dick him around or talk bollocks.'

Rudi gets up, hand outstretched for the slip of paper. Graham sidesteps him neatly and puts the note down in front of me. Rudi looks instantly pissed off – Graham likes a hungry salesman, and the first one to ask for an available lead will normally be given it.

'Jimmy's worked the hardest at scraping windscreens,' says Graham. 'And he ain't been smoking on my fucking pitch.'

'Looks like you were spotted,' Kate teases Rudi. She glances at the whiteboard on the wall. 'Jimmy could catch you today. Eleven each for the month.'

Rudi doesn't simmer for long. 'It's no great sweat,' he says to Kate. 'I'll soon see Jimmy off, even with the boss feeding him leads.'

'Game on, then,' says Graham. 'This bloke Fitzgerald should be here for eleven. I've already told him to ask for you, Jimmy.'

I check my watch. Eleven o'clock is only seven minutes away, so it looks as though my call to Isabel will have to wait. Meanwhile, Graham's desk phone starts ringing. He picks it up and says, 'I said no calls.' Then he listens for a moment, his expression growing weary. 'Alright,' he says. 'I suppose you'd better put her on.'

There's a pause while the call gets connected, and then Graham says hello and introduces himself. He makes an effort at small talk, but the caller's having none of it and pretty soon Graham's doing all the listening. Now and again the caller draws breath long enough for Graham to say "hang on" or a "just a minute", but mostly he's on the receiving end, shaking his head in exasperation at his failure to get a toehold in the conversation.

I look to Rudi for clues, but he just shrugs back, apparently nonplussed. In contrast, Kate won't let me catch her eye, but she has a knowing look on her face – it's almost as if she can hear what the caller's saying.

Graham's finally had enough. 'Just shut it!' he snaps. 'Shut it and calm down!' Even then he has to listen some more before he gets to speak again. 'That's why Carl's not here,' he eventually explains. 'I've given him leave to try and sort things out.' After that, the caller rabbits on some more while Graham holds the phone with one hand and his head with the other. After a while, he manages to get another word in. 'I've no idea where Carl is, but I'll come round myself. No, I will. Right now. Don't go anywhere.'

Graham puts down the phone and slips into his jacket. Next second, he's heading for the door.

Rudi asks, 'What's going on?'

'Carl's missus, that's what. She's in pieces because the fucking bailiffs have turned up and Carl isn't answering his phone. Their kid's upset, and the bailiffs sound like a gang of bully boys. I'm going round to see what I can do.'

'I'll come with you,' I tell him.

Graham pauses in the doorway. 'You've got a punter arriving,' he reminds me.

'Then I'll come,' says Kate.

'I can look after myself.'

'I know,' she replies, 'but it's not you I'm worried about.'

Graham looks ready to argue, but then he sighs and shrugs his shoulders. 'Whatever,' he says, huffily. 'I suppose it might help having another woman there.' He turns and hurries from the office. 'Come on, then,' he calls over his shoulder. 'We need to get a shift on.'

Graham moves quickly, weaving between Rudi's desk and the sleek blue Sirocco we currently have displayed in the showroom. Kate, who put her heels back on when she came indoors, can't keep up with him and loses even more ground by diverting to her desk for her handbag. Rudi and I keep step with Graham, ready, if needs be, to stop him driving off without her.

'Rudi,' says Graham, without breaking stride, 'try phoning that twat and see if he'll answer. Tell him his wife and kid need him urgently.'

'Already on it,' says Rudi, who does indeed have his phone out. 'Straight to voicemail.'

'Keep fucking trying.'

We're nearly at the showroom door, Graham in the lead, Rudi and I just behind, Kate scurrying to catch up, when I see Emma and a tall, slim guy coming the other way. They reach the door just before we do, and as much as Graham's in a hurry he steps back to let them in. Emma is pink-nosed and red-cheeked from both the cold and, presumably, the effort of clearing the remaining screens. The tall guy I recognise from yesterday. He's no longer in his super-smart suit, but still looks expensively dressed in dark tailored jeans and a fawn-coloured trench coat.

'Jimmy,' says Emma. 'This gentleman's here to see you.'

'Hello again,' says the tall guy, offering his hand and a confident smile. 'I'm Reuben Fitzgerald. I believe you're expecting me. And if it's no trouble, I'll have that coffee from you this time.'

2.4) Reflections on Times Recently Past

It's after seven in the evening before I finish work, and the weather has gotten really cold. An icy wind is billowing the pitch-side promotional flags and sending little scraps of litter scudding across the forecourt. I crank the Mondeo's heating up to maximum, and before pulling away I drop Charlotte a text reminding her that I'll be late home because !'m meeting Ash for a drink. That done, I put my foot down and get gone, happy to be away from the place. I've worked the last six days on the bounce, some of them for ten hours or more, and I'm relieved that tomorrow's my day off.

I'm meeting Ash in the Alnwick Arms, on the other side of town. Thinking about it, we could have picked a better venue. Although the rush hour's long since over, plenty of people go late-night shopping in December, and tonight the queues for city centre parking have backed up onto the ring road. Sitting in a tailback, staring at a fog of brake lights and exhaust fumes, I tell myself that Ash and I will need to make better decisions once our company is up and running.

At least the delay gives me chance to think about the business ideas Reuben Fitzgerald shared with me after I'd sold him a Toyota Verso. Dealing him up on the seven-seat Verso was straightforward enough. He knew what he wanted to buy, and was out to get it for as little money as he could. What with Graham charging off to play Lone Ranger at Carl's house, Rudi stood in as acting sales manager, and he authorized a discount of just under two-hundred quid. (I thought it was good of Rudi to play fair with me, considering he had wanted the deal for himself.) Although Reuben Fitzgerald tried to chisel me further on the price, he was happy enough to pay a deposit once I'd made it clear there was no more money off.

The bloke who lost out in all of this was Carl. He dealt with the initial enquiry, only for me to finish up doing the deal and claiming the commission. It would be easy to feel sorry for Carl, especially as Graham refused to let him have what Rudi then gave me, namely a discount to close the sale. But that's the way this business goes: it isn't fair and nicey-nicey; it's a tough and ruthless trade. So bollocks to Carl – fuck him, in fact – because I'd be in the wrong job were I to start feeling sympathy for the bloke. One thing's for sure: had the boot been on the other foot Carl would have been rubbing my nose in it. ("Yeah, Cooter, I sold your bloke a car after you fucked it all up. Got any more hot leads that you've tragically mishandled today?")

Anyway, it's not as if we make much money out of the Fitzgerald deal. Our margins are slim once the discount is deducted, especially as our well-groomed punter didn't take out a finance agreement nor buy any extras. Commission wise, I'll make around fifty quid before tax – hardly the kind of money to have helped Carl with his debts had he managed to get the deal done yesterday evening. What will help Carl with his debts, however, is a decision I made earlier this afternoon: a decision to hand him a big fucking chunk of cash. He doesn't yet know about it though, and I can barely bloody believe it myself.

Meanwhile, the traffic's still moving slowly. When it comes to a complete halt, I glance around for cop cars and then pick up my phone to send Ash a quick text saying I'm running late. That done, I slide my phone away and think some more about Carl, asking myself whether I'm doing a good thing by giving him money or whether I'm just a bonkers fucking idiot. A text pings back from Ash. He's also late, stuck in the same bloody traffic. We're a pair of Muppets, I reckon.

My reasons for bailing Carl out are less to do with him than they are his son, who I reckon will be aged seven or eight by now. I met the kid once, when Carl brought him to the showroom a couple of years back. I remember his bright smile, good manners and the carefree way he dashed around our pitch, his scruffy fair hair poking out from beneath a New York Yankees baseball cap. I liked him a lot, but once he'd gone home I pretty much forgot about him until this afternoon, which was when Kate and Graham came back from Carl's house and Kate told me what had happened there.

Plenty of what Kate told me was really sad. But a couple of things were just plain weird, especially her claim that Carl's missus hadn't known a thing about her husband's debts until the bailiffs knocked the door this morning.

'Is she thick or something?' I asked Kate in reply to that revelation.

Kate looked at me severely. 'No, she's not thick. She's a pharmacist. Her name's Dawn, and she's a nice lady.'

'That's as maybe,' I replied. 'But the woman must have known something. There must have been phone calls to the house, mustn't there? And demands for money through the post, all marked "URGENT" in big red letters?'

'No,' said Kate. 'Apparently not. It seems Carl managed to hide everything from her really well. The poor woman was in shock. Couldn't get to grips with what was going on.'

'I can't believe that people are so easily fooled by their partners,' I replied. But even as I finished the sentence, I remembered that Isabel had fooled me easily enough. Turns out she'd been shagging Lee the Shithead Lawyer for at least two months before she and I actually split.

And Kate, whose shoulder I'd cried upon loads at the time, was clearly having the same thought. Her look alone said: *Oh, really? James, you dumbass.*

I felt myself blushing. 'Alright,' I backtracked hurriedly, 'you don't have to say anything. I suppose I can believe it.'

Kate shrugged. 'We all get fooled sometimes, James. Love is blind, after all.'

'True – and I reckon you'd need to be blind to put up with Carl.'

'Maybe so. But only this morning you said I was the one being brutal.'

'Fair point,' I answered. 'Anyway, about Carl's wife – I suppose there wasn't much you could do for the woman.'

'You suppose right.' Kate shook her head sadly. 'Graham made the bailiffs show some manners, but that was about all. We couldn't stop them taking anything, as everything was legal and above board. It was their kid I felt most sorry for.'

'I'm surprised he was even there. Didn't think the schools had actually broken up yet.'

'Don't know about that. But whatever, he was there alright, watching it all. Big, grim-faced men in black bomber jackets, walking off with the TV, the stereo, the iPad. His mother beside herself, too hysterical to explain what was going on. His excuse for a father nowhere in sight, not even answering the phone to Graham. When I see Carl, I'll… oh, I don't know. What's the fucking use?' Kate shrugged, clearly tired, her eyes flaring with anger for a moment and then lapsing into resigned sadness.

A moment's quiet passed, during which I thought about a fair-haired boy in a Yankees cap charging around our pitch. Then I said, 'I suppose the kid was going frantic too.'

'You suppose wrongly, James. I don't know if he's used to watching his mother go off the rails, but he was a picture of calm compared to her. He simply stood there with a little sad look on his face and watched it all happen. Sure, he looked disappointed, but when he went to his mum – which he did, a couple of times – it seemed to be because he thought she needed him, rather than him needing her.'

Kate shook her head and mustered a thin smile. 'He was trying so hard to be brave, and there was nothing I could do for him. Then Graham told him he'd make a fantastic soldier when he was older, and the little fellah shook his head as if to say Graham was stupid. When Graham asked him why he didn't fancy the army, the kid just kept on shaking his head and telling us he was going to play tennis for a living.'

'Cool dream, at least,' I said. 'What's the kid's name again?'

'Sammy. His mum calls him Samuel.'

'Sammy – that's it. I remember.'

And that wasn't the only thing I was able to remember. I could remember vividly what it felt like to be seven years old and get let down by your dad at Christmas. Mine walked out on us on a cold December day over twenty years ago, so that he could take up with another woman. He sent us money afterwards, but the feelings of loss, rejection and deep, deep sadness lived with me for years. I can remember thinking that somehow it was all my fault, and I can also remember the half-empty bottle of aftershave he left in the bathroom. For months after he'd gone I used to take the top off the bottle and sniff the musky aroma that seeped out, because it was the best I could do to recapture the feeling of having him around. I don't know whether my mum knew what I as doing, or whether she doing the same, but it took a fucking long time for her to throw that bottle out. Naturally, she was in bits about it all, and there wasn't much I could do for her except try to be brave, just like Carl's kid tried to be brave for his mum today.

That's my justification, such as it is, for giving Carl a fuck-load of money. That little bit of common ground with a seven-year-old kid is what's at the heart of it all. Or, if I'm totally honest, it's the main reason for my generosity, at any rate. I may actually have a secondary motive, but it's one I won't yet admit to – not fully, anyway. Not even to myself.

While I've been thinking things over, the traffic has moved slowly on, and by now I'm third in line at some lights, waiting for them to turn green. The road ahead looks clear, but queuing here has cost me at least fifteen minutes. There are no good, strong, sensible reasons why Ash and I still meet up at the Alnwick Arms, not unless habit and nostalgia count as good, strong or sensible.

The Alnwick is round the corner from Frank Kinning's old workshop, which is where Ash and I both started out as mechanics. But the workshop's a pet supplies store now, and Frank has retired to Tenerife, where he plays golf, gets drunk and more or less lives the life of Riley. Meanwhile, Ash and I both live and work on the opposite side of town.

It dawns on me that whether he's arrived at the Alnwick or is still sitting in traffic, Ash won't be thinking like I'm thinking. He won't be having a word with himself and questioning our choice of venue. The only word he'll be having will be over the phone, with his wife Suki, while she baths their kid and Ash grumbles good-naturedly about the heavy traffic. Easy-come and easy-go, that's my best mate Ash, and if the two of us are going to start making better decisions it's going to be me who makes it happen.

The lights go green and I'm through. There's a dawdling old Ford ahead of me, and I have to tuck in behind until a gap appears in the lane to my right. Finally I pull out and zoom past. I'm shifting now, and ought to reach the Alnwick in ten minutes.

There's a reason why I'm obsessing about time tonight. It's that I let the day go by without phoning Isabel. Although I was genuinely busy this morning, I frittered away the afternoon. I spent too long nattering with Kate for one thing, and then, once word came through that Ann and Rob – my punters from yesterday – had passed their credit checks, I called them back in to sign their finance documents so that they can collect their car on Friday. That was all well and good, but once they were here I wasted another hour letting them tell me about their plans for Christmas.

It was getting dark by the time Ann and Rob left. I saw them out the door, then got myself a coffee to drink at my desk. To anyone asking, I was checking my emails, but mostly my mind was elsewhere, giving myself a round of fucks for having got through the afternoon without phoning Isabel. There was still time, even then, to call her up, because Shithead Lawyer Lee wouldn't yet have arrived home from his high-powered, high-paid, high-rolling job. I could have taken my coffee and my phone to a quiet corner and just dialled Isabel's number. But I no longer had any appetite for the call. I no longer felt as positive about it as I did this morning, and so when Wes materialised, wanting to natter with me, he offered me the perfect excuse to put Isabel off for the day.

I say "natter", but I could tell straightaway that it was a serious talk Wes wanted. He's got a face which is easily read – a definite handicap in this job – and when he eased into one of my chairs he could have picked up a pencil with the furrows in his brow.

I finished skimming an email. I looked across my desk at him. 'What's up, mate?' I asked.

Wes looked left and right, checking to make sure no one could overhear. Quietly, he asked, 'You got a minute, Jimmy?'

'Course I have.'

He looked around again. 'I think I've upset Emma.'

I waited for him to tell me more, but he didn't come up with the goods. He just sat and cringed, looking at me like a man might look at his doctor when waiting to hear the results of his tests. Eventually I asked, 'How've you upset her, then? Doesn't sound like you, Wes.'

'I've gone and asked her out,' he replied.

'I see.' I hoped my poker face was better than his. I hoped it wasn't apparent to him that I'd already heard his news. 'Well done, Wes. It was about time you asked her.'

'How do you mean?'

'Well, it's been obvious for ages that you fancy the girl.'

'Seriously?' he asked. 'You are joking, aren't you?'

I answered with a sympathetic look and a swift shake of my head.

Wes let out a tiny groan, and again went through the rigmarole of looking around for eavesdroppers. No one was any closer than Emma herself, and she was sitting at her own desk on the opposite side of the showroom.

'Chill out, mate,' I said. 'Nobody can hear us. And even if Emma could read my lips, your silly fat head's in her line of view.'

He just looked at me in horror. 'Really, Jimmy, has it been that obvious?' he asked.

'Only to me, mate,' I fibbed. I knew that Rudi, too, had sussed things out, and I'm sure we weren't the only ones to have noticed. I found it hard not to laugh, really. Here was Wes: young and fit, sleek and cool – envied big-style by loads of other blokes – but naïve and flustered when it came to women, or at least when it came to Emma.

'Anyway,' I continued, 'how come you reckon she's upset?'

'She didn't say yes when I asked her.'

'Well, did she say no?'

'No, she didn't. She said she'd think about it. But Jimmy, she's hardly spoken to me since.'

'Just relax,' I told him. 'Asking out a woman isn't a crime. Don't be down on yourself just because you've yet to get the answer you want.'

'So what should I do?'

I didn't answer immediately. Instead, I got to my feet, having picked out a glimmer of movement in the darkness beyond the showroom. There was someone on the pitch, just outside the front door. A punter, most likely. A chance to do a deal.

But Emma was faster than me. She was up and heading for the door before I could get clear of my desk. Resigned to losing out this time, I sat back down and spent an idle couple of seconds admiring the swing of her hips beneath a tight little skirt. Emma glanced back and grinned, but that proved a mistake because Rudi nipped out from the Admin entrance and waltzed through the front door half-a-step ahead of her. Although Emma then tried to speed up, Rudi closed the door in her face, and that was the end of that.

Wes had been oblivious to the whole chain of events. He simply sat and looked at me, waiting expectantly for my advice. That was because I'd just given him hope, and now he reminded me of a cute little puppy waiting to be thrown a bone. He must have thought I could do magic or something.

I glanced at Emma as she returned to her desk. She smiled at me grimly while shaking her head. I didn't know who was causing her more despair – Wes or Rudi.

'Wes,' I said, 'how old are you, again?'

'Twenty-two,' he replied, after a second's hesitation. 'A year older than Emma.'

'In which case, mate, the time has come.'

'It's come for what, Jimmy?'

I picked up the plastic cup on my desk and turned it upside down to demonstrate that it was empty. 'Time you got me a coffee. Then we'll have a little chat about women – a little chat about Emma, if you like. No promises, Wes, but I'll tell you some stuff to improve your chances.'

Wes glanced left and right again. The look on his face was wide-eyed and panicky. 'Jimmy, I appreciate your help, but any chance of keeping your voice down? Please, just a bit?'

'White, no sugar,' I told him, leaning back with my hands behind my head. 'And in the Spiderman mug, please, if the thing doesn't need washing.'

2.5) Another Crowded Boozer in December

While we're waiting at the bar, I tell Ash about my day and he tells me about his. It takes a while for us to get served because there's only the landlord working, and he has to go and change a barrel before we can have our beer.

Eventually, we get to sit down with our drinks at a table in the corner, and it's here that Ash commits a schoolboy error – the kind he'd have had to pay for with a drinking forfeit in the old days. He has a question to ask me, but in his eagerness for answers he hunches forward and rests an arm on the table. The furniture in the Alnwick Arms has seen better days, and the floor of the pub is uneven anyway, which is why the table lists to one side when Ash leans down on it. Our pint glasses wobble, and beer gets spilt. Ash has to postpone his question while he attends to the puddle.

'Bollocks,' he says, tamping a couple of beer mats over the spilt lager in an effort to soak it up. 'The number of times we've sat here, we should know by now.'

'We should,' I reply, fishing in my pocket for the tissues I acquired with a take-out coffee on my way to work this morning. 'It's got to be dozens of times,' I add, helping Ash to mop up. 'Hundreds, even.'

I'm not certain my mate heard that last part, because he's taken another beer mat, folded it in three, and leant down to wedge it beneath a table leg. 'There,' he says, sitting back up and testing the table's stability by gently trying to rock it with his hands. 'Works every time.'

'Well done,' I tell him. 'I remember us fixing a few cars using similar technology.'

'Too right,' he replies. Then an expectant look settles over his face as he returns to his aborted question. 'Okay buddy, what was your grand plan?'

'Plan?' I smile and shrug, and sip from my pint. 'Mate, I didn't have a plan. Definitely not a grand one.'

Ash grins right back at me. 'Come on, Jimmy. You of all people didn't have a plan? Yeah, right.'

'Why would I have a plan, Ash?'

'Because you make plans,' he says. 'It's what you do. And because you're a genius with women.'

'Fuck off. Since when was I ever that?'

'Since as long as I've known you.' Ash is laughing now, his smile wide enough to reveal the gold insert which replaced the tooth knocked out by Ben Isherwood in this very pub, several years ago, in a drunken argument about fuck-knows-what. 'Come on, buddy. You think I've lost my memory? Or maybe you've lost yours, and can't remember all the women you've had.'

Still laughing, Ash takes a big gulp from his pint and wipes froth from his lips with the back of his sleeve. Then he sits back, folds his arms and awaits my response, his stupid big grin fixed firmly in place. Setting aside his brown skin and rapidly greying hair – he's far greyer than Rudi, and long since gave up trying to mask it – Ash reminds me a lot of myself, or at least of how I used to be. He's a dad these days, but still seems the carefree young bloke of a dozen years ago, while in comparison I reckon I've changed. That's partly because I'm no longer a mechanic who'll wipe his lips on his sleeve or hang up a girlie calendar at work, but other events have changed me too. Events like Isabel getting gone from my life.

'Ash,' I say, gently shaking my head, 'I haven't forgotten that stuff, but it is ancient history. And anyway, when it came to all those women, well, there wasn't a lot of thinking going on. Cunning maybe, but not thinking. I just a kid, acting on instinct and hormones. When it comes to wrapping up my experience into neat parcels of advice for the next generation – calling it a plan, if you like – well, I wouldn't know where to start.'

Ash looks at me gone out. 'History?' he asks. 'Next generation? Jimmy, buddy, you make you and me sound like fossils.'

'Well look at us, mate. You've been married six years, and as for me – this supposed great womaniser – there have been two women in about a decade. Isabel and Charlotte – no one else. Well, apart from you-know-what, but we had to pay for that, and so it doesn't count.'

'Okay, okay,' he replies, still laughing. 'I suppose you have a point.'

Neither of us dwells on the shameful high-point of his stag weekend, and I don't let on about the shabby, consolatory sex I had with Tara, the temporary receptionist at work, in the aftermath of Isabel walking out. Nor do I tell him that I tried it on with Kate around about the same time, and got slapped round the face for my trouble.

Instead I tell him he's right to admit I have a point about our age, a point I emphasise by mentioning the bar Rudi and I were in last night – the one where we must have looked like someone's parents checking up on them. 'I mean, Ash, look at you,' I continue. 'Married, with a son already at playgroup. And bloody hell, mate, grey hair really suits you, but you do look like a fossil. Sorry, it's true.'

'Yeah, yeah, yeah.' Ash runs both hands through his hair and then studies his palms, as if expecting the gray to have rubbed off. 'Okay,' he admits, so we're not youngsters anymore. But we're not that out of touch either. You could still have given this kid the benefit of your experience.'

'Which I did.'

'There you bloody well are. You did have a plan.'

'No,' I reply. 'What I had could hardly be called a plan. I simply let him know my opinion.'

Ash drinks more beer. 'And your opinion was what, exactly?'

I glance at my watch. I want to deal with this quickly because I want to move on and talk about other things. Specifically, I want to talk about a concept called Triple Bottom Line, the basics of which were explained to me by Reuben Fitzgerald in the showroom this morning, and which makes me more excited about starting a business than at any time since I won the lottery. But even though Ash knows this – what with me having set the scene while we were waiting at the bar – he seems keener to find out about the advice I gave to Wes concerning Emma. Ash's attitude underlines what I already knew – that I'll have to be the leader when we're in business. Although he's a hard worker and a great mechanic, he needs someone to tell him what to do. In effect, he needs a boss. I reckon he's the living, breathing proof that that the stereotypical Asian entrepreneur is exactly that – a stereotype, and therefore subject to exceptions.

'Okay,' I say, 'what I reckon about Wes is that he's probably scaring Emma off. He's needy and possessive around her, and women don't find that sort of behaviour attractive, as you and I both know.'

'So you told him to play it cool, yeah?'

I take another look at my watch, but if Ash senses I'm dropping a hint then he doesn't let it show. Of course, the easiest way to finish up with this would be to confirm to Ash that I told Wes to play it cool. But actually, playing it cool isn't what I told Wes to do, and it suddenly feels important, for reasons I can't properly explain, to be precise about what I actually said.

'Not quite,' I tell Ash. 'You see, that's what Wes thought too. He actually used those same words. He said, "So you think I should play it cool, Jimmy?" But no, I was trying to say something else.'

'Which was what?' asks my mate.

'Well, to play a something cool is to act indifferently about it – to pretend that it isn't all that important. But we do know that Emma is important to Wes. Whether she accepts his offer of a date is a big deal to him, right?'

'Right.'

'Okay, but she knows that too. So if he suddenly starts to play it cool – to play it indifferently – well, that just looks false. The point is, Wes isn't cool or indifferent where Emma is concerned. For him to act as though he is would just be game-playing, and that will put her off just the same.'

'I'm with you.' Ash drains the last of his pint and glances towards the bar. He's hoping to catch the landlord's eye, but there's no chance of that. The Alnwick is filling up, and even though more staff have come on, there's a big queue of people waiting to be served. 'So come on, Jimmy. What did you tell him to do?'

'I told him that he has to be true to himself and to the way he's feeling. He has to behave as though her answer is important – for the simple reason that it is.'

'Sure.'

'But also – and this was the important bit – Wes has to have enough about him – enough confidence in himself, if you like – that it isn't the end of the world if she says no. In other words, be eager and honest and genuine, but not the desperado he's been acting. He needs to let her know that he'll be disappointed if she turns him down, but that he'll deal with it if she does. That was my advice to him, anyway. It came out sounding bollocks, just like it sounds bollocks now, but I didn't have a better way of putting it across.'

'Buddy, it doesn't sound like bollocks,' says Ash, his big, insolent grin coming back. 'Or at least no more like bollocks than usual. And I agree with you about what the kid needs to do. But it's a tough thing to get right.' He picks up his glass and gets to his feet. 'Another beer?'

'Just a soft drink, mate.' I drain my pint and slide the empty at him. 'You're right. It's a difficult balance, and Wes will need to think about how he carries it off.'

'I'm sure you're right, Jimmy. You usually are.'

The Alnwick is crowded by now, and Ash is eyeing up his best route to the bar. Maybe I should just let him go; maybe I shouldn't bother telling him what's on my mind. But after a moment's thought, I decide to press on. He can just stand there and wait a minute.

'It's something I've been thinking about quite a bit,' I tell him. 'That kind of attitude shouldn't just apply to Wes and how he approaches Emma. I think that if you're going to try anything in life then you have to take it seriously and give it your best. But whatever that something is, you mustn't let it mean everything to you. It's okay for it to mean a lot, but not absolutely everything, otherwise you may be afraid to ever try. You have to be ready for it not to work out, to dust yourself off and try again – or try something else.'

I'm struggling to put my thoughts into words that make sense – if Charlotte were out with me she'd translate all this malarkey into something that would hold Ash's attention. As it is, he only makes a few polite noises before he goes to the bar. While he's queuing up, I tie myself in mental knots, trying to think up a better way of saying what's on my mind, but my thoughts are interrupted by the arrival of three loud and leery lads, who rack up the balls on the pool table and begin to play badly. They hit a load of rubbishy shots, and each miscue provokes a mini-pantomime of swearing and name-calling. 'Useless wanker,' sneers one, when his mate hits a crap one. 'You do better, cunt-face,' comes the reply.

The Alnwick's hardly a posh pub. It sells beer and peanuts to people who mostly have blue-collar jobs. Nobody comes here for canapés and cocktails, and if the landlord banned swearing he'd soon go out of business. But there are basic standards of behaviour, and the three idiots round the pool table aren't adhering to them. They're *too* loud, and there's *too* much swearing. The pub has filled up, and there are women close by, having to listen to this filth. I'm thinking of having a word, of asking these guys to tone it down, when one of them, maybe reading my mind, gives me a hard stare, as if to say, *Come on then. Come and have a fucking go.* In truth, I don't want to have a fucking go. I had my fill of aggravation last night, and anyway I don't fancy three-against-one, especially when they're the ones holding the pool cues.

So I look away. But when I look back, a moment later, the bloke is still staring, and so is one of his mates. There's bother brewing, and I'm relieved when Ash reappears. He's clearly figured the situation because he says, 'Come on, Jimmy – come over here,' before leading me away to a quieter corner. And maybe he's also been thinking about the half-arsed lecture I just gave him, because he hasn't bought beer – just a Coke for each for us – and he's keen to talk business once he sets down the drinks. 'So, tell me about this bloke you met earlier today,' he asks. 'And this business idea. Triple Bottom Line, did you call it? What does that mean?'

'Yeah, that is what I called it.' I'm pleased Ash has remembered the name. 'It's not a new idea, but the first I heard of it was the morning, when my customer explained it to me.'

'Go on, then. What's it all about?'

'Alright, I'll tell you.' I watch Ash lean forward, and I pause to see if the table wobbles. When it doesn't, I say, 'So this posh bloke came in today. Reuben Fitzgerald, he's called.'

'Certainly sounds posh.'

'Sounds posh, is posh. But he's not a snob; nice bloke, actually. Anyway, he came in and bought a seven-seat Toyota. When people want seven seats they've often got a big family, but it turns out he's gay with no kids.'

Ash sips his Coke. 'So why seven seats?' he asks.

'Because the car isn't for him. He's giving it away, to some local charity, one which takes underprivileged kids on day trips and holidays.'

'Fair play to the fellah. What did it cost?'

'Nearly twelve grand.'

Impressed, Ash leans even further forward. 'He must have a few quid.'

'He seems to have. Apparently he has a successful business, some sort of IT consultancy. But you see, mate, he runs it on the principle of Triple Bottom Line.'

'Which is what, exactly?'

'Well the first bottom line is the traditional bottom line, the one that's always mattered in business: namely, how much money you make. The second is about the environment; it's about how green your business is. And then there's the third, which is about what your business is doing for society. It's how much you are giving back when the business is doing well.'

'Like how many seven-seaters you can buy for local charities?' Ash's smile has developed a wonky, sceptical slant, and his eyes have narrowed too.

'Something like that,' I reply. 'Don't get me wrong, mate. I want us to start a business, not a charity. And I want us to make money for ourselves. But this could take us to another dimension.'

'Like on *Star Trek*, or something.'

'Yeah, whatever – fucking funny. Look Ash, Triple Bottom Line gives us more reasons to be in business than self interest only. Other reasons, bigger reasons. But there's something else, too.'

'What's that?'

'It gives us an edge in how we market ourselves. Everything else being equal, you'd buy from a company that said it was going to give, say, three percent of its profits back to the community, wouldn't you?'

Although Ash tells me he would, there's a frown on his face which says he's not actually sure. To reassure him, I say, 'Alright mate, I know I've sprung this on you a bit.'

He says nothing, stroking his chin and rocking gently on his stool. There's a far-away look in his eyes, and he seems oblivious to the hustle and bustle around us as the crowd in the Alnwick swells. Half-a-minute must go by without a word from him, and I eventually decide enough is enough. 'Earth to Ashok,' I say jokingly, waving my hand in front of his face. 'You in there, Ash?'

He seems to make up his mind about something. 'Listen Jimmy,' he says, his eyes focusing again, 'when you said you wanted to start a business, and you wanted me to join you, I was excited about it. I believed in you, and I still do. But look, you're suddenly talking about giving money away.' Ash glances around and leans in closer, lowering his voice for what's coming next. 'Buddy, you've got well over three million quid. If you want to help the community, why not just do it? Why open a car lot first?'

He's asked a tough question, similar to those I've dwelt on while staring at lists in my den at night, and I'm not sure I've got any good answers. Nor am I certain that it's Ash I'm trying to persuade, or simply myself. I only know that I need to be doing something with my life – "floating rudderless in a morass of luxury" doesn't do it for me.

'Look,' I tell him, 'I wanted to start a business before I ever came into the money, you remember?' He nods at that, and then I add, 'Well I still want to start one, because otherwise… well, what else is there to do?'

Ash looks at me like I've got my head up my arse. He says, 'I can think of lots of things for you to do.'

I'm really struggling tonight with big thoughts that I can't express fully. 'I know what you're saying,' I tell him. 'But what I mean is this: I wanted to start a business to succeed in business. I wanted to prove something to myself, and I still do. If I don't have a go I'll regret not having tried, however much money I've got. And as for Triple Bottom Line – that's an extra motivation, not the be-all-and-end-all. Plus, as I said, it's another way of positioning ourselves, of marketing the business.'

I reckon Ash gets all the fulfilment he needs from being a husband and a father, and maybe, just a little, from being a bloody good mechanic. I don't think he has any motive for joining me in business other than to give his family a better future. He hasn't got any points to prove, but perhaps I've made him see that I have, because he finally says, 'Okay, cool, I get that.' Then he chinks his glass against mine and says, 'Let's do it then.'

'You're sure?'

'I'm sure,' he replies.

'Right then. Game on.'

Ash takes a sip from his Coke, and then looks disdainfully at the glass. 'Sorry buddy,' he says, 'but I'm getting another pint, even if you're not.'

I tell him I'm not stopping him and I reach for my wallet, but he's away to the bar before I can come up with the price of his beer. While he's away, I think some more about the things I've just said. I do want to prove something to myself – that much is true. But I'm well aware that I want to prove something to Isabel as well, and to the high-earning, high-flying bastard she dumped me for. Deep down I know it's corrosive and dangerous to feel that way, but knowing something is one thing and changing it is another.

When Ash comes back he has a fresh pint for each of us. 'Don't drink it if you don't want it,' he says. 'Only it's a big queue over there, and I thought you might want one when you saw mine.'

He has a point, actually. I had been sticking to one beer because we had business to discuss, but I don't think that conversation is going much further tonight.

'We both have to drive,' I remind him.

'Well, I spilt most of my first one.'

'Is this the weak stuff?'

'The weakest,' he laughs. 'Total piss.'

I push my coke aside and clear my throat to say what I think needs saying before we get much more alcohol inside us.

'So, in principle,' I ask, 'do you like the idea of Triple Bottom Line, if I do some more work and make a plan around it?'

'You're the one with the business head. And you've explained your thinking. So… yeah, I'm happy.'

'I can show you a proper plan next week, along with some new financials now that we're not borrowing from the bank.'

'That's fine.'

'And those premises I texted you about – the unit on the Barthwick Business Park – I think it's still available. What about I have a look tomorrow, while I'm off work?'

'Absolutely,' he replies, before knocking back a third of his pint in one hit. Then, from the pocket of his jacket, he produces a packet of crisps – one of those trendy flavours I don't like – and opens them out on the table. 'Help yourself,' he says, getting stuck in like a man who hasn't eaten all day.

'I'll be fine,' I tell him.

I'll have to be fine, too, doing all this work. It would have been great if Ash had said, "Tell you what, take a look at those premises during my lunch break. That way I can come too." But I remind myself that that's just not his way. He'll work hard all day to fix cars, but business initiative? Forget it. And actually, that may not be a bad thing. If only one of us is making decisions we'll get ahead faster.

Through a mouthful of crisps, Ash manages to say, 'Talking of financial projections… '

'Yeah?'

'Who else knows by now?' He leans closer, lowering his voice. 'About your new-found wealth?'

That's another awkward question. I shuffle in my seat before replying, 'Nobody. Not yet. Not unless you've said anything to Suki.'

'Buddy, you're fucking bonkers,' he tells me, his eyes boggling like they did the night I told him I'd won the money. 'I don't know how you've kept it to yourself for so long.'

'I haven't kept it to myself. I've told you about it.'

'You know what I mean. And by the way, since you ask, no, I haven't told Suki. But on Christmas morning, when I tell her that she and I and little Balbir are off to the Caribbean, she will want to know how we're paying. And she won't believe me if I say I've been putting overtime money aside. She knows that ain't been happening.'

'I know, mate. I know.'

'Man, I can't believe you haven't told Charlotte. Are you still thinking of leaving her?'

'Maybe. I'm just not sure right now.'

'It would be a shame if you did. It's none of my business, I know, but she is a great girl.' He shovels the last of the crisps into his mouth and adds, 'You got some other bird on the go?'

I tell him that I haven't, but I can feel my face reddening, and he'll think I'm either lying or that I've at least got "some other bird" in mind. If I were to tell him it's Isabel, I reckon he'd have me sectioned.

Straight-faced, Ash says he believes me and that he understands that it's difficult with Charlotte. 'But what about your mum,' he asks. 'Why haven't you told her about the money?'

'I've got my reasons, Ash. It's complicated.'

'Try me.' Having knocked off the crisps in less than two minutes, he now runs two fingers round the lining of the packet so that he can lick off the crumbs. 'I've got a brain in my head. I can do complicated.'

I've half a mind to tell him to fuck off and keep his nose out. Trouble is, he's my best mate. I've entrusted him with news that I've kept from everyone else, and I suppose he's entitled to ask these questions.

'Okay, look,' I begin. 'About the money, and setting aside the amount we'll use to start up the business, I've got some big decisions to make about what to do with the rest. How much of it I give away, for instance, and to who.'

'Course you have. I understand that.'

'And there are people I'll look after – you know I will. Charlotte, whether I leave her or stay, can count on me. You and Suki will benefit. Then there's my mum – and also Stuart, of course. He and I probably exchange two-dozen words a year, but he is my brother when all's said and done.'

'Sure.'

'But while they can share in the cash, I don't want them sharing the decisions.'

Ash is giving me a *what-the-fuck* look. 'And that stops you telling them?' he asks. 'For this length of time?'

'It does. Because I can guarantee two things that will happen as soon as I tell my mum about the money.'

'Go on.'

'The first is that the rest of the world will know about it roughly seven seconds later.'

Ash starts laughing. 'Okay, fair point,' he admits.

'The second is that she'll start coming up with names of people needing financial help. And there'll be loads of them.'

'Serious?'

'You bet. She'll be coming to me and talking about some ex-neighbour she hasn't seen for twenty years, but whose husband has been made redundant from his foreman's job in a pork-pie factory somewhere, and suggesting we slip them a few grand to see them by.'

The Alnwick's getting full to burst by now. A big, loud, high-spirited group has turned up over the past few minutes, all of them wearing their glad-rags. It's some firm's Christmas do, I reckon, and they're probably meeting here before moving on elsewhere. In the meantime, they've become jammed in around our table, causing

Ash and I to work ever harder to make ourselves heard. It's only when Ash sits back to scratch his chin and think about my last remark that I realise we'd moved almost into snogging range just to talk to each other.

'I do see what you mean,' Ash says, leaning in again. 'Your mum's always been a very generous woman.'

'She has. Think about all the times you ever called round for ten minutes and ended up staying for dinner.'

'That's the only reason I ever came round.'

'Sure it was. Dickhead.'

'Well alright, that and to steal your smokes.'

We both fall quiet. We drink our beer and spend a minute just absorbing the noise around us – the banter and the laughs, the bitching and the bellyaching, the casual flirting and the casual cruelty; it's all the stuff of office life, exported to the pub in its party clothes. And eventually there's a minor abatement from the noise when two of the women standing closest to our table go off together to the toilet, and in turn two of the blokes who'd been trying to impress them slope outside for a smoke.

Ash takes his chance to renew the conversation. 'I do understand you, buddy. But look, it's a month since you bought me a holiday, two months since you first let me in on the news, and I reckon nearly three since you found out for yourself. Sure, I need something to say to Suki about the holiday, but for your own peace of mind you need to start telling people. You will go nuts, otherwise.'

'I will tell people,' I reply. 'Soon. I just need to figure out where I'm at with Charlie.'

Ash knocks back what's left of his beer and then studies his empty glass, his keen mechanic's eyes watching the suds as they slide slowly down the sides. 'Soon can mean many things,' he says without looking at me.

'Just give me a week or two to make my plans.'

'So I can tell Suki? At Christmas? About who's paying for the holiday, and how.'

I finish off my own beer, buying myself a moment to come up with an answer. Christmas is nearly on us and I don't feel comfortable with my news breaking so soon. Suki's a chatterbox like my mum – once she knows, everyone will.

'Look mate,' I eventually reply. 'Meet me next week so I can talk through a business plan. And by that time I'll have worked what you can say to Suki and when you can say it. If needs be you can say I've won the holiday as part of a sales incentive, but haven't got time to go.'

For a moment I think he's going to argue, but the noise level around us is rising again. It looks and sounds as though the sweary lads round the pool table have started a row with a group of blokes from the firm's night out. The kings of foul language might regret kicking off, because they're clearly outnumbered and they're up against some big fuckers. But Ash and I don't hang around for the outcome because it's getting time for home.

It's bitterly cold outside, and that icy wind is even stronger than before. Even though we're keen to be in our cars, we both have something to say before going our separate ways. I tell Ash I want the business up and running quickly, and that he should be ready to quit his job in January. He initially looks startled at that, but then recovers himself and says that's fine. For his part, Ash tells me to be selfish with the other decisions I'm facing. 'Just remember,' he says, 'it's your life, and your big pile of dough. Do what's right for you, buddy, and not for anyone else.'

I'm not sure whether he's talking generally, or whether he has something specific in mind. And I don't bother asking him to explain because it's freezing out here and I'm feeling knackered by now. But in the car, on my way home, his words are echoing around inside my head. And the words don't go away. They're still there later on, when I'm lying next to Charlotte and only she can sleep. I toss and turn, listening to the wind gusting against our window, and watching time slide away on the face of the bedside clock. Eventually I lie still, and try to put Ash's advice into effect: I try to work out how much of what I'm planning to do is really for me, and how much is for someone else.

I'm thinking of Isabel when I finally fall asleep.

3) Thursday

3.1) Ghosts in the Kitchen

I wake up feeling tired after a rubbishy night's sleep. In spite of that, though, I get up quickly and head downstairs to the kitchen, sliding into my Thursday morning routine the way I'd slide into a favourite old coat.

Along with alternate Sundays, I have Thursdays off, and my Thursday mornings follow a regular pattern. I get up, make a brew, and take Charlotte's tea upstairs, leaving it on the dressing table while she's in the shower. After that, I return downstairs to drink my coffee and watch a few minutes of breakfast news on the kitchen TV.

Next up is to cook Charlie's breakfast. I start when I've finished my coffee, and I aim to be serving up by the time she's got dressed and arrived downstairs with her work face on. Cooking Charlotte a good breakfast on my day off is something I've done for as long as we've lived together – I suppose it's one of those rituals which cement a relationship in place.

Today, my routine starts off normally. I make the drinks, take Charlie's upstairs, and come back down to watch the news. My coffee tastes like coffee does. The news headlines, it turns out, are bland and ordinary. It's pretty dark outside – there being barely a week to the year's shortest day – but there's just enough light in the sky to see that the overnight wind has blown our patio furniture around the garden, and I'll take that as an urgent, overdue reminder to get it stored away for winter. Otherwise, it's a normal Thursday morning and everything about my routine is… well, routine. There's nothing going on to interfere with the idea that this is a regular day off.

But after a few minutes, once I've started cooking, something changes. The something that changes is my mood.

I've got bacon under the grill and I'm beating eggs around a jug when the thought hits me, completely out of the blue.

Today could be the last time I do this.

Today could be the last time I make breakfast for Charlie on my Thursday off. Her school finishes for Christmas tomorrow, and she may want to lie in next week. Even if she chooses to get up, things won't feel the same if she's not heading out to work. And after the Christmas holidays? We might be together, or we might not – I can't say for sure either way. I'll finally be phoning Isabel later this morning, and who knows where that could lead, or what thoughts the call might conjure in my head.

Fuck me. So much for one of those rituals which cement a relationship in place.

Of course, today doesn't have to be the last time I do this at all. It's my choice, and so I could choose to stay. I could decide to remain with Charlotte, and to stop obsessing about bloody Isabel. Trouble is, I know I'd be feeling bored, and like I'm missing out on something.

Wrapped up in my thoughts, I haven't heard Charlotte come downstairs, but as I'm pouring the beaten eggs into a pan I suddenly realise that she's here in the room, standing right behind me.

I whirl round. An empty kitchen yawns in my face. Turns out I was fooling myself, because Charlotte isn't here at all.

Then I catch sight of our friends-'n'-family photo montage, pinned to a cork board on the far wall. My mum's photo is there, and there's an old one of my brother and his wife on their wedding day. In comparison, there are more pictures of Charlotte's family than mine. There aren't just her parents, brother and sister, but also both sets of grandparents, plus a posse of aunts, uncles and cousins. In fact, there are so many of the fuckers that I can't even name them all. But this morning the people in Charlotte's family photos all have one thing in common: their faces look accusatory, each pair of eyes appearing bitter and hard where once they looked warm and friendly.

I shudder a little, and return to my cooking, but it feels as though those eyes are tiny lasers, burning dozens of holes in the middle of my back. I'm so disturbed that I completely fail to notice when Charlotte really does arrive in the kitchen.

'Timing off, sweetheart?' she asks from over my shoulder. I'm so surprised that it's small wonder I don't jump six fucking feet in the air.

'Sorry,' I reply, turning hurriedly and trying to hide my fright behind a smile. 'I am a bit late. But don't worry – I'll soon have this plated up.'

I can't help noticing that Charlotte looks fantastic. She's wearing dark slacks and a white cotton blouse, while her make-up runs to no more than a smidge of blusher and lip gloss. Her hair is casually pinned up in a kind of loose, tottering bun – from which a few stray strands have wandered away – and she's added a touch of casual razzmatazz with some big, loopy earrings and a dark suede waistcoat which put me in mind of a glamorous gypsy. She looks truly amazing. The woman I'm thinking of leaving totally rocks the house.

'Are you alright?' she asks, placing a hand on my arm. 'Your face is so white. It's as though you've seen a ghost.'

I think: *I've seen fucking several.*

I say: 'I'm just tired. So don't go worrying. Here, sit down and I'll serve your breakfast. Would you like more tea?'

Charlotte doesn't want more tea, preferring juice from the fridge. She pours herself a glass, sits down at the little kitchen table, and tucks into her food. A couple of minutes pass with no conversation other than her appreciative murmurings about my cooking.

I make myself another coffee before joining her at the table. She says, 'You should go back to bed if you're so tired.'

'Maybe I will.'

'How are you fixed for lunch today?' she asks.

I don't answer immediately. Today's going to be busy. I've got premises to view, business plans to write and an ex-girlfriend to call up on the phone. But Thursday lunch is another shared ritual – another one we might never do again.

'I'm fine for lunch,' I finally reply.

'You're sure?'

'I'm sure.'

'You took your time answering.'

'I'm fine for lunch.'

Half a minute's silence ticks by, and then I say, 'Sorry if I sounded arsey. I really am just tired.'

'It's okay.' Charlie reaches across and gives my hand a little squeeze. 'I was tetchy too. And I know that you've got a lot on right now.'

'Not so much that I can't have lunch with my beautiful girlfriend. I'll take you to Ringo's.'

'Flatterer. But thanks. Flattery's nice when it comes from you.'

Although she hasn't finished eating, Charlotte sets down her knife and fork to ask her next question. 'Now that lunch is decided, can I talk to you about another subject?'

'Of course. What is it?'

'I know you're busy, and that I've told you to go back to bed, but might you find time to have a look in the shops today?'

'What for?'

'Come on, you know what for. You can work that one out.'

'You mean for Christmas presents?'

'You know full well I mean for Christmas presents.' She laughs, but it's the laugh of someone trying too hard to make light of a subject they consider to be serious. 'I thought that this year you might try starting your shopping before Christmas Eve.'

'Alright. Well, we'll see.'

Charlotte throws me a sceptical glance and picks up her knife and fork to resume eating. 'I know what that means,' she says. 'It means, "No, Charlotte, I won't be going to the shops today. I prefer a panicked, last-minute dash when everywhere is closing."'

'Don't be angry when I've made you breakfast.'

'I'm not angry. And breakfast is great, by the way. I just get exasperated sometimes, and I'm trying to reform your errant, blokey ways.'

'Well, Christmas shopping would be much easier if you'd let me buy you that car.'

'Sweetheart,' she protests, 'I'm not talking about me. You know I'm easy to buy for. I'm talking about everyone else.'

The flaw in her thinking is that "everyone else" doesn't amount to many people. Sure, Charlotte has a big family, but she buys the presents for them, while I just stump up half the cash once she tells me the cost. And after her side of the family are bought for, there's only my mum, my brother, his wife, their kid. I needn't panic – it's no great sweat to buy gifts for four people. Admittedly, I also need to get booze and fags for the people I rely on at work – namely the admin ladies, the mechanics and the valeters – but that's taken care of by fifteen minutes spent in a supermarket or off-licence.

When I point all of this out to Charlotte, she simply tuts at me and shakes her head. 'Even so,' she says. 'Even so.'

'Even so, what?'

'Even so, you should get your bloody shopping done.'

'Even so, you should let me buy you a bloody car.'

Charlotte pushes her plate aside and takes a moment to chew on her last mouthful of breakfast. She dabs her lips with a tissue and says, 'Alright, then. 'I've got an idea about this car. I'll come and see you on Saturday. Have you got an appointment free?'

'There'll be nine days to Christmas. The weekend will be flat. I'll pretty much have the whole day free.'

'Then I'll come to you for mid-morning.'

'So, you're actually agreeing to my idea? You're going to let me do this for you?'

She laughs and pushes back her chair. 'Down boy,' she says. 'It won't be that simple.'

'So why are you coming in?'

'You're the salesman. I'm going to give you the chance to sell me a car.' She smiles slyly. 'If you can persuade me to buy one, then I might also accept your very generous offer to pay for it.'

I think her suggestion over, and find myself liking it. 'Alright, Charlie. That's a date. That's what we'll do on Saturday.'

'But I'm warning you, sweetheart, this isn't a done deal.' She gets to her feet and loads her breakfast things into the dishwasher. 'I have to get to work now. You can start planning your patter for the weekend.'

'I don't do patter. I'm not that kind of salesman.'

'Then you can start planning whatever it is that you do instead of patter. It's time I was off.'

I get up from the table and dance round Charlotte as she heads into the hallway. 'I'll go and check your car,' I tell her. 'It may need defrosting.'

'You're in your dressing gown,' she says. 'You'll catch your death, you big idiot.'

'Maybe, but at least you'll be able to see where you're going.'

'Sweetheart, just stop.' Pulling on her coat, she catches up with me by the door. 'My car won't be frosted over. It's been too windy for any ice to go forming on the screen.'

I think about the gale that rattled our windows overnight, and threw our summer furniture round the garden. 'I suppose you're right,' I reply. 'Sorry, it was just a thought.'

'It was a nice thought,' she says. 'But I'm glad I won't have you getting pneumonia on my conscience.' She goes to open the door, but I get briefly in her way by stooping down to pick up our post from the mat. There's some promotional bumph from one of the phone companies, the sight of which reminds me to ask her a question.

'The other night, Charlie, while you were marking books and I was in my den – who was it that phoned on the landline?'

She points at her watch and gives me a look. 'You're asking now? When I need to go to work?'

'Fair point – sorry about that.' I open the door for her and move out of the way.

'Anyway,' she says, stepping past me, 'it was a wrong number, that's all. Just a drunk making threats.'

'Threats? Seriously? And you weren't going to tell me?'

'I said it was a wrong number, sweetheart.' Charlotte unlocks her car while I watch from the doorway in my dressing gown. 'He was making threats against someone called Hooter.'

'Hooter?'

'That's what it sounded like.' Charlotte opens the Clio's door and throws her bag onto the passenger seat. 'His voice was very slurred,' she adds. 'He could have said Hooter or Cooter, or Charles Flamin' Pooter – I don't think it matters overly when the caller's a drunken idiot dialling up the wrong number. I'm sure we won't hear from the moron again.'

3.2) Hey Baby, I'm your Telephone Man

I go to my den after Charlotte leaves for work, and I spend twenty minutes working up a sweat on the running machine. I haven't exercised enough lately, and in spite of my tiredness I push myself hard. Then, after showering, I pull on some jeans and a t-shirt, before going back downstairs, this time to fix my own breakfast. I eat quickly and then load the dishwasher, before making my third coffee of the morning. I sit down with it at the kitchen table, my diary and phone close at hand. There are people I need to call.

Not long after I've sat down, a low winter sun breaks through the clouds, casting its hazy pale light into my eyes. I shield my eyes with my hands rather than getting up to close the blinds, and I sip at my coffee while figuring out who to phone first.

In the end I decide to start with the easiest call – the one to arrange a viewing of the premises I discussed with Ash. I'm not expecting the agent to be busy in mid-December, and sure enough it turns out they aren't. A lady answers promptly, and is keen to help. After a few brief questions, intended to establish that I'm not a timewaster, she agrees to send someone to meet me on the Barthwick Business Park in an hour-and-a-half's time.

That leaves two more calls to make, and the easiest of the pair will be the one to my bank. But first I sit back, squinting into the sun, trying to decide for certain that I want to go through with this. It's all well and good my deciding to help Carl out, but do I still want to do that now I've learnt that he got pissed and rang up making threats the night I stopped him menacing Rudi for money? Really, I ought to let him twist in the wind, and for a few minutes I simply sit there, doodling in my diary and letting my anger with Carl wash over me. I realise, finally, that nothing has happened to alter my previous decision. I'm doing this for his kid's sake, after all – not fucking

Carl's – and little Sammy is blameless in all of this malarkey. Besides, there's also that other reason for helping Carl with his problems – the one that's more about me than anyone else and which I won't even face up to yet.

All of which means it's time to get back on the phone.

The bank holding my lottery winnings isn't any old bank. I did not deposit my cheque for nearly four-million quid in the same high-street branch where I've had my wages paid since I was sixteen. Discretion would not have been assured, and I reckon news of my winnings would soon have leaked. My mum's mate, Cheryl, is a cashier there, for one thing. And for another, Robert Farley – a kid with bad acne from my class at school – is now managing the bloody place.

Instead, on the advice of the lottery people, I opened an account at a high-roller's bank, a discreet and exclusive set-up that simply isn't like other banks. It doesn't have a long counter where you queue to be served, and there are no cash machines built into the walls. It does, however, have carpet deeper than some kids' paddling pools, and there's a lady on the front desk who could have stepped from the front cover of Vogue. Opening an account was like being vetted by MI5, but once over that hurdle I was allocated a personal banker by the name of Nathan Fortescue-Edwards, a man with all the breeding that his name suggests. He does not have acne – his face doesn't permit zits any more than the All England Club permits weeds on Centre Court.

I pick up the phone and make my call. There are no menu options to navigate, just an efficient bloke on the switchboard who sounds like a retired colonel, and he puts me through to my banker just as soon as I ask. Nathan Fortescue-Edwards sounds pleased to hear from me, and he claims he's been looking forward to my call, trusting that I've made some decisions about "the funds on deposit". I can feel his disappointment when I tell him that I haven't, knowing as I do that he's keen to start doing the sort of things with my money that he already does with other people's, namely move it around and make it grow larger. Although he tries hard to hide his frustration that I'm not ready to "issue instructions in the matter of investment", the mask slips and he admits to being "somewhat taken aback" when I want to make a swift withdrawal of thirty-thousand in cash. He blusters for a while about rules and regulations, telling me that my request is a hard one to fulfil at short notice. Adopting his formality, I thank him for his "prompt attention to my affairs", and then I throw the fucker a bone – I promise we'll have a meeting next week if he can pull his finger out and get the cash sorted today. He says he'll see what can be arranged, and promises to phone me back shortly.

When I end the call, I realise that I'm starting to sweat. It takes me between six and nine months to earn thirty grand selling cars, and here I am fronting up that sort of money for a shithead like Carl. I fucking hope it's enough, that's all. Graham said Carl owed more than twenty grand, and I took that to mean less than thirty.

After finishing my coffee, I try to clear my head. I've got one more call to make – the hardest of the three. I've got butterflies in my stomach, and so I dig out a bottle of scotch and pour a generous shot into my coffee mug. I knock it back in one, and while the scotch burns a fiery path down my throat I take my phone and begin dialling the number.

It's over three years since I last called Isabel. I no longer have her number stored in my phone, but I do have it stored in my head. I tap in the last of the digits and, just for a moment, I simply stand and stare at the number, asking myself what the fuck I'm doing. Then I press "call" and hold the phone to my ear. While I'm waiting for a connection, I walk to the window on legs that are wobbly and stare into the garden, using my free hand to shield my eyes from the sun.

I'm half expecting the anticlimax of an unobtainable tone or a message telling me that the number isn't in service. But Isabel's phone begins to ring. It rings twice, three times, four. She doesn't answer. I'm trying to imagine the look on her face if she recognises my number. It might be a look of contempt, or maybe horror. Worst of all would be pity.

Six rings, seven. I should have delayed my shower because I'm soaking in sweat again. I reckon Isabel will answer the phone any minute, but only for as long as it takes to tell me to fuck off. Or maybe Lee will be home, and she'll simply pass him the phone so he can deliver the good news.

Nine rings. I'm debating what message to leave if the call goes to voicemail, but I can't think of a suitable one. I'd have to simply hang up. In fact, I should fucking-well hang up now.

But then, suddenly: 'Hello?'

I feel frozen in time. There's sweat running down my forehead, stinging my eyes, and I'm suddenly unable to speak.

'Hello? Jimmy, is that you?'

'Yes,' I reply. And that's as much I can say because I've totally dried up. The inside of my mouth feels like old bones in the desert.

'So, how are you?' Isabel asks. She sounds relaxed and chilled, and surprisingly pleased to hear from me. That's a good thing, but totally unexpected.

'Hello, Jimmy? Are you there?'

I've got my mouth under the cold tap. After swilling some water I manage to say, 'I'm fine.' After swilling some more, my next words come in a rush. 'Look, sorry about that. For not answering straightaway, I mean. It's just you surprised me.'

She laughs, and her laugh sounds gentler than I remember. 'You phoned me, but I surprised you?'

'Only because you took a while to answer. I thought you weren't going to. I was about to hang up.'

'Sorry, only I was in the garden.'

I look out the window at so much winter deadness, and I think about summer barbecues in the old days. I think about Isabel wearing short shorts and sleeveless tops, and about her creamy skin and perfect curves.

'That's okay,' I say. 'I'm only pleased you answered in the end.'

'So, how are you?' she asks me for a second time.

'I'm fine,' – and that's twice I've replied with the most witless answer known to man – 'what about you?'

'I'm great, thanks,' she replies. A brief pause follows, during which I realise my heart is racing, and then Isabel asks, 'Jimmy, I suppose you had a reason for calling?'

I could begin by saying sorry for all the toxic phone calls I made to her during the brief, miserable weeks of our break up. If I remember rightly – and I might remember wrongly, given how much I was drinking at the time – those calls were roughly two parts pleading to three parts ranting and one part sobbing my eyes out. When I think about how pitiful I became, it's a minor miracle that Isabel even answered today.

But there's no point covering old ground now, not when she's asked me to get to the point. I take a breath and tell her my tale: 'I was up in the loft the other day, looking for some papers I needed for my solicitor. That's when I opened up an old case and found the trophy you won at college when you were learning to cut hair.'

I pause. Isabel doesn't reply. I decide to go for it: 'Iz, I wondered whether you'd like me to bring the trophy round.'

More silence follows, enough of it for me to realise I must sound like a chancing halfwit. Three years on from Isabel and I breaking up – a break-up more combustible than an arsonists' convention in an oil refinery – and here I am phoning up with the poxiest of excuses to see her again. I mean come on, would she really like me to come round with some worthless piece of shitty old tin from donkeys' years back?

But then she laughs that laugh again – the laugh that's gentler than her old one. 'I'd forgotten I won that trophy,' she says. 'I haven't thought about it for ages. Second place, wasn't it? I should have come first, but Michaela Thomas was shagging the tutor after class.'

'I remember you telling me.'

'Yeah, it's not like I'm bitter, is it?'

'You don't sound bitter now. Anyway, the trophy. I just thought I'd see if you wanted it. I didn't know I still had it, lurking up there in the loft.'

Silence again, during which I suppose she's constructing a version of "thanks but no thanks". She'll probably say that she has no interest in the trophy, that she's "moved on" – meaning, of course, that she's moved on from me. And that will be that. She won't ask me round, and there'll be no way back into her life. I could make this easier for both of us right now: I could offer to post the fucking trophy.

'It was sweet of you to think of me, Jimmy.'

I'm waiting for the "but" when I realise I've missed something obvious. Something I should have figured out from her explanation for not answering the phone any sooner than she did. She said she was in the garden when I rang. And why would she be in the garden at just gone nine-thirty on a bitter winter's morning?

Answer: she wouldn't.

And so the obvious something which I've missed?

It's that she doesn't live here anymore. She and Shithead have moved somewhere where it's hot in December. Australia, maybe? Or California? And if she hadn't kept her Facebook profile private, I'd have known that already. So now, no doubt, she's about to give me the bad news. I can't believe I've been so fucking stupid as to assume –

'Jimmy, are you even listening to me?'

'What? Sorry Iz, no. Just got distracted.'

'Fuck's sake.' (And that sounds much more like the old Isabel.) 'You're the one who phoned me. The least you could do is listen.'

'I know, I'm sorry. I just tuned out for a moment.'

'Bloody hell. So you didn't actually hear what I said?'

'Not exactly.'

'I asked if you had a pen. You'll want to write down my address, 'cause I've moved across town. When were you thinking of coming round?'

3.3) Where there's Muck there's an Ass

My potential business premises look dirty and ramshackle. They're badly in need of a good clean and a lick of paint, along with some new furniture to replace the old tat that's currently in place. But I don't let any of that put me off, because the place is the size and layout I had in mind. The slick, sharp bloke who's here to show me round tells me the site was once the warehouse for a regional newspaper company, and that their loss could be my gain. The big forecourt, he explains, was where vans used to load up with newsprint, and he's quick to suggest that it offers plenty of space for displaying cars.

He's right about that. He's on his game, the slick, sharp bloke. He reminds me a little of myself, except that he overdoes it, coming across as slicker and sharper than I'd ever want to appear. His teeth are too white, he's gelled his hair to excess, and he talks like someone who's overdosed on sales manuals.

I'd say there's space enough here for thirty cars and some customer parking. Meanwhile, the old warehouse is easily big enough for a workshop and valet bay, with room left over for expansion. The office area, in comparison, is actually pretty small, and that's no bad thing either – it's not like I'm planning to employ loads of admin staff.

So the place is of the right size, and in the right proportions. The location isn't bad, because it's in a corner of the estate and can be seen from the main road. Honestly, I'd have preferred somewhere on the edge of a retail park, somewhere where I'd get people browsing once they'd bought their bread and their beans or their wood and their nails. But an absence of casual footfall isn't the be-all and end-all nowadays. A car dealer's most important location isn't so much physical as his ranking in the architecture of internet search engines. If his cars are easily found and well presented online, then a bright future awaits him. He can get business done – and good business, too – from the corner of a 'seventies-built business park like this one.

The slick, sharp bloke knows this as well as I do. He can also tell that I'm very interested. He's looking at me with a glint in his eye – the kind of glint I recognise as the one we salesmen get when someone wants to buy what we're selling. And the man clearly isn't messing around. He's suggesting I sign a lease right here and now.

But I'm not ready to close on a deal, and this guy being a bit too slick and sharp isn't the only reason for that. Another reason, a bigger reason, is that I'm in no state to conclude important business when I feel like I currently do – namely mixed-up and confused, with my feelings strewn about as though a hurricane has passed through my head. The cause of my confusion is, quite simply, the guilt I'm experiencing over my phone call to Isabel. Although I'm excited about meeting her later, I know I'm an arsehole for the casual haste with which I've effectively betrayed Charlotte. I'm meeting Charlie for lunch in a couple of hours, and I feel sick with shame that I'll be going on afterwards to Isabel's house – although not so sick with shame that I'll be changing my mind about turning up there.

Torn as I am, I'm in no frame of mind to be signing contracts. And anyway, there are the terms and conditions to read first, and my business partner to consult. Ash probably wouldn't mind if I did sign without talking to him, but I reckon we should do things properly.

That's what I'm telling myself, at any rate. But the slick, sharp guy is thrusting a draft lease at me, telling me that properties like this don't come along often and that there are other people interested. He says I should act quickly to avoid missing out.

We're interrupted by the ringing of my phone. I excuse myself to take a call from my hard-pressed banker, Nathan Fortescue-Edwards. He tells me he can have thirty-thousand pounds available for me to collect this afternoon, and then asks if I can please confirm a date to meet up next week? I tell him I'll collect the money after lunch, and that we'll sit down this time next Thursday.

I hang up and thank the slick, sharp guy for his time. I ask a copy of the lease to take away so that I can read the small print before signing anything. He agrees, but he's huffy about it and that glint has gone from his eye. By the time I leave, he's looking less slick and less sharp and more like a sulky school kid who's been grounded for the day. I hope I don't look quite so gutted when my prospects walk without buying, but I suspect I probably do. We're all the same, us salespeople. We hate it when we can't close the deal.

3.4) The Sexiest Bird in the Place

As promised, I take Charlotte for lunch at Ringo's, which is probably our favourite place to eat, and definitely one of the priciest.

Some people call Ringo's a gastro-pub. Ringo himself calls it a boozer serving food. That's a bit of false modesty on his part – it's actually a boozer serving sensational food.

Ringo is really called Adam, and came by his nickname for the dual reason that he's from Liverpool and used to play drums in a band. He reckons he's a decent drummer and an excellent chef, and I'll happily vouch for the culinary aspect of that claim. It's also obvious that he believes people should pay through the nose for his excellence. However much money I've got nowadays, I still look at his prices and think: *fuck me*. Which is more or less what Ringo's doing, I suppose.

But I'm not the only one willing to pay what he asks – that much is clear from the place being packed out day after day. Ringo has about a dozen tables set aside for dining, and Charlotte always phones in advance because there's rarely one free on the off chance. And that's how it is today, with Ringo's waiting staff – crisp and professional in starched black and white – hurrying between lounge and kitchen as though they've got rockets in their heels.

Finishing my fishcake starter, I ask Charlotte if she'd like another apple juice. Food-wise, she's a couple of mouthfuls behind me, but her glass is nearly empty.

'Just water this time,' she replies. I begin to get up, but she looks around, waves me back to my seat and says, 'Don't bother. The bar's rammed. I can hang on for the waitress.'

'You're sure?'

'I'm sure.' She smiles, and adds, 'You could do with a top-up yourself. Have a beer if you want one.'

I pick up what's left of my Coke and examine it closely. By now it's more melting ice than carbonated soft drink. 'Thanks,' I reply. 'But I'm staying alcohol free. Busy afternoon coming up. Business plan, and all that.'

'Of course – you said.' Charlotte reaches across and squeezes my hand. 'It must be exciting, starting a business. And it's brave of you, too. Lots of people talk about it without ever taking the plunge.'

Her being nice makes me feel guiltier than ever. And I wonder how brave she'd think I was if she knew how much money I already had. I can't think of a decent reply, but a waitress comes to my rescue, swooping to fill the silence by removing our plates and taking a drinks order.

'Anyway,' I say, after the waitress has gone, 'I've been to the pub two nights running. It won't hurt to have a booze-free lunch.'

'Good point,' Charlotte replies. A few more strands of her hair have become unpinned since this morning, and she takes a moment to push one out of her eyes. Then she asks, 'Will you be going to the pub tonight?'

'Doubt it – I've got too much to do. Why? What are you thinking?'

'I know it will be three nights in a row, but would you have a problem if I went to the gym later?'

Although I don't have a problem – or at least shouldn't have a problem – the first thought that comes to mind is: *She's spending a lot of time at that gym.*

As if I'm the one with any fucking right to be suspicious.

Fortunately though, that thought stays unspoken, and then a different waitress arrives with our main courses. She sets down my shepherd's pie and Charlotte's grilled sole, before wishing us a *bon appétit*.

Once the waitress has gone, I tell Charlotte, 'Of course I don't mind you going to the gym.'

'That's great,' she says, pushing a fork into her fish. 'It's just been a crazy week over there. Tuesday's one of my regular nights, as you know, and then last night was Pilates.'

'Yeah, I remember you saying. And this evening?'

'Nothing special. There's a new girl who's recently joined. She specifically wants to go tonight, but not on her own, and so I said I'd meet her there.'

I hold a forkful of pie to my mouth. I blow on the pie because it's hot. 'So you're going to hold a newbie's hand? Make sure she buys you a wine afterwards.'

'I'm sure she will. Being new there, I think Izzy's keen to make some friends.'

'Izzy?'

'Yes, Isabel. It's the first time she's joined a gym, apparently, and so she likes having someone to – '

The way I'm looking at Charlotte stops her in her tracks.

The penny must quickly drop, because when she speaks again it's to say, 'Oh, come on now, sweetheart. It's an Isabel, not your Isabel.'

I put down my knife and fork. 'Can you be sure, Charlie? When you've never met her before?'

'Well… no, I suppose not. And it's not the sort of thing I've thought to ask.'

'Okay,' I say. 'So what does she look like?'

'Attractive girl, about my age. Blonde hair, blue eyes.' Charlotte fiddles with one of those big, bold earrings and throws me a begrudging look. 'Alright, very pretty. I'll admit that.'

'Sounds quite a lot like Isabel. Do you happen to know her surname?'

She shakes her head, appears to think, and then adds, 'But this Isabel does seem a really nice girl. Nothing like the evil whore you've described to me.'

In spite of myself I manage a laugh. 'She wasn't always an evil whore,' I tell Charlotte. 'And do bear in mind that I might be slightly prejudiced against her.'

We sit and look at each other. Our food is cooling on our plates, while all around us everyone else is presumably enjoying theirs.

'I won't go,' she says, after ten seconds of silence. 'I'll text her and tell her I can't make it.'

I don't know what the fuck to make of all this. Normally, I don't reckon I'd mind Charlotte and Isabel meeting up. But I do mind them meeting up on the very day that I've been back in touch with Isabel – I don't want the missus hearing that news from the ex. But then, on the other hand, what are the actual chances that this is the same Isabel, and that the two women will have that conversation? And here's another factor in all of this: I may not want the two of them meeting up, but nor do I want Charlotte to think I'm all that bothered if they do.

'Hang on,' I say. 'This is crazy. Like you said, there's a girl called Isabel at your gym. She's the right age to be my ex-girlfriend, Isabel. But that doesn't mean she is.'

'She matches your description of her, though.'

'Sure, but there's got to be more than one blonde, blue-eyed Isabel running round town. And anyway, suppose she is the same one. What major catastrophe is going to happen by you and her meeting up at a health club?'

Charlotte takes a few seconds to think about that one. 'Nothing, I suppose,' she eventually replies. 'I'm just a bit freaked out by the idea. So were you, a moment ago.'

'I was, that's true. But thinking about it, is it really such a big deal?'

'No, I daresay it isn't. It just means that I'll talk to the girl differently, that's all. I suppose I'll be more guarded around her.'

'Look Charlie, there's an easy way of figuring out who she is. Phone her now, on loudspeaker, to check that she's still meeting you later. If it's Isabel I'll recognize her voice.'

The look on Charlotte's face says she's not comfortable with the idea. 'Alright,' she says. 'But not in here. Let's finish eating first.'

'I'd be glad if you both would,' says Ringo from over my shoulder, his scouse accent bold, brash and unmistakable. Then he steps around and into view, a big man with a day's growth of stubble and a self-satisfied smile. His chef's whites are rolled up at the sleeves to reveal muscular forearms marked by football tattoos and a back-catalogue of kitchen burns. 'You pair,' he says, 'are a really bad advert for business, sitting there talking while your food goes cold. Is everything okay, or did I not put in enough arsenic?'

Charlotte returns his smile. 'Don't mind us, Ringo. The food's great. The conversation went *off piste*, that's all.'

'Just so long as it's not my cooking you're talking about, at least not in a negative way. You're free to say positive things, though. Compliments are always nice, and they'd certainly be appreciated.'

'Stop being so needy, you big lump,' Charlotte mocks him. 'We weren't talking about you. We've just discovered that I may have accidentally befriended Jimmy's ex.'

'The one you lived with, before?' Ringo asks me. 'The one you told me left you for some lawyer fellah.'

'That would be the one,' I reply.

'That was a happy day for you, Jimmy.'

'How do you mean?'

Ringo looks at me like I'm an idiot, and then winks conspiratorially at Charlotte. 'I'm amazed he needs to ask,' he says.

I catch onto his meaning very, very late. 'I get it,' I tell him. 'You mean my old girlfriend had to leave me before I got to meet Charlie.'

'Take a good look around you,' says Ringo, with a big sweep of his arm across the crowded dining room. 'I'm fully booked in here. And at least half my customers are women. But the sexiest bird in the whole bloody building is sitting with you. And I include my Alison when I say that,' – he pauses to wink at us again – 'being as she's in the kitchen and can't actually hear what I'm saying.'

I smile at Charlotte and reach for her hand, knowing that Ringo isn't wrong. Like me, he might flatter his punters from time to time, but here's the bottom line – when he says that Charlie's the sexiest woman in here, he's dead bloody right. And if I had any sense at all, I wouldn't be going round to Isabel's later.

But going round I am. I will be seeing Isabel. Fuck me – I must have bloody rocks for brains.

3.5) Gobsmacked

Isabel's new home is a big mock-Tudor spread, located in a modern executive development on the edge of town. It's the biggest house of five in a posh little cul-de-sac, with four large windows across the upper level and a double garage down below. Out front, even though the block-paved driveway could easily fit two big cars, there's still enough lawn for roughly half a tennis court.

I'm not surprised at Isabel having the largest house, but I am surprised at her having the scruffiest. The windows of her front room, for instance, where there are lights on inside, look streaky and filmy. They're badly in need of a clean, and then the lawn isn't tidy either. The grass has been left to grow long during the autumn, and so now, in winter, when it's too wet to cut, it looks a straggly mess.

The Isabel I used to know wouldn't have put up with an overgrown lawn or mucky windows. She was a great one for appearances, not only hers and mine (to the point where she'd trim my hair twice most weeks) but also that of the house. I wouldn't believe she was living here if it wasn't that her purple Nissan Juke is parked up on the driveway, flaunting its sexy contours and oversized wheels.

Sight of the Juke brings bad memories for me. I remember seeing it new, a little over three years ago, on the day I last saw Isabel. She had already moved out, but came back briefly for the last of her stuff. Emotionally I was in a bad way, and I felt even worse when I saw that Shithead Lawyer Lee had already bought her the car she'd been wanting for absolutely ages. I lost my rag watching her load bags and boxes into the Juke, so much so that I called her a festering whore. She called me a loser and a fucking arsewipe. Later, I drank half a bottle of vodka and cried myself to sleep.

I try to shelve the memory while I work out where to park my Mondeo – either next to the Juke on the drive, or outside by the side of the kerb. It would be a liberty to park uninvited on the drive, but I'm conscious that there's a manila envelope stuffed with thirty grand beneath my passenger seat, and I reckon the money is safer the closer I park to the house. Sure this is a nice neighbourhood, but cars in nice neighbourhoods do get turned over.

From the corner of my eye, I catch a glimmer of movement in an upstairs room. When I turn to look properly, there's no one there, but I can guess that it was Isabel, wondering what the fuck I'm up to, just bloody sitting here. I told her I'd arrive for half-three, but I got delayed at the bank, and it's now nearer four.

In the end, because I don't want to get off on the wrong foot, I decide to leave the car on the road. I consider moving the envelope to the boot, but that would only draw attention to it, and drawing attention to it is something that Nathan Fortescue-Edwards advised me to avoid, stressing that there were people "out there" who would cut off my hand to get the envelope if they knew what it held. I don't how much familiarity Fortescue-Edwards has with those kind of people, but I daresay he has a point. And so, leaving my big stash of cash under the seat, I get out and lock the car, using the last of daylight to discreetly check my reflection in the glass. I'm looking good, so far as I can see, but I feel like a nervous kid on his first date as I begin my walk up the drive.

I haven't gone far before I realise there's something else about the house which is bothering me. It's that there are no Christmas lights or decorations on display. Of course, we're only at mid-month, but I do remember that Isabel used to splurge on tinsel and illuminations, and was a first-of-December kind of girl when it came to putting them up. Walking further, I can also see that the flashy purple Juke looks sad and neglected when seen in close up. I pick out a spattering of unattended stone chips to the bonnet, and a couple of nasty scrapes to those big alloy wheels. And they're not the only things about the Juke which are troubling me. Something else is out of kilter, something I can't consciously identify, but which my hyper-critical car trader's mind has latched onto at some level or another. I stare fixedly at the Juke for a second or two, searching for irregularities in the panel fit or some minor deviance from the manufacturer's spec'. Spotting no such glitch, I resume walking up the drive, but can't shake the feeling that there's an anomaly with that car. Whatever it is might occur to me later, but for now I need my wits about me because I've arrived at Isabel's front door.

I push the doorbell. Not hearing a ring, I raise my hand to knock. But the door begins opening before I can make contact. I step back as it swings aside.

'Hello, Jimmy.'

'Isabel… Hi.'

'You look great,' she says'

'So do you, Iz.'

And she does too. But in a different way to how I remember. Her face has changed, and I don't just mean the purely physical stuff that comes with three years of ageing – stuff like those crows' feet forming round her vivid blue eyes. No, it's more than that – it's the *expression* on her face, one that suggests a changed woman inside. Isabel looks mellower and kinder than before – no less attractive, but somehow not so severe. I remember, as well, that she sounded gentler on the phone this morning, and I immediately think to myself that this is someone new.

For a few seconds we just look at each other, and then, without another word, she steps outside and hugs me tightly. I hug back, and to touch her confirms another impression I'd quickly formed: Isabel has bulked out and is bigger than she used to be. It's hard to say exactly how much bigger, because when she lets go and steps away I can see she's wearing so many bloody layers. She's got on a quilted body warmer over a zip-up fleece, and where that's open at the neck I can see a thick woollen sweater beneath. A stripy bobble hat completes the look of someone who's dressed for cold weather rather than high fashion, and this is also something new – something I wouldn't have expected. Only Isabel's designer jeans seem suited to the woman I remember.

She looks me up and down. Her eyes haven't changed – they're still piercing, like lasers – and I'm filled with this crazy sensation that Isabel can read my mind and memories. It's as though she can see what I've been up to these past three years: where I've been, what I've done and why I'm here. I even sense that she knows how much money I've got in the bank. Yes, it's a crazy, stupid feeling, but crazy and stupid somehow feel real when she looks at me like that.

Inspection apparently over, she offers me a bashful little smile. 'It's good to see you,' she says quietly.

'You too,' I reply. Feeling there are things I have to say, I take a breath and wind myself up. 'Isabel, about my behaviour, three years ago, I –'

'Enough, Jimmy,' she interrupts, holding a finger to her lips. 'All that bad stuff – forget it. It's history, and we don't need to talk about it.'

'Whoa, hang on. That's fine, but I wanted to apologise.'

'Okay, apology accepted. But now, like I said, forget it.'

'Just like that?'

'Just like that.' She sighs and adds, 'Jimmy, we had eight good years and a few shitty weeks. Fault on both sides. Let's leave it at that. Now, are you coming in, or what?'

Isabel leads the way. She's in stocking feet, but the heels of my shoes echo hollowly on polished floorboards, an echo which reverberates all the more for the hallway being nearly empty. There's just a coat-stand in the corner – bearing a single, full-length cashmere – and two taped-up cardboard boxes standing behind the front door. It's fucking cold in here as well. There's clearly no heating on, which would explain why Iz is wearing all those layers.

Don't mind the state of the place,' she says, matter-of-factly. 'We won't be here much longer.'

'I get that impression,' I reply.

'Come on through. It's warmer in the front room.'

'Lead the way, then.'

'But... Jimmy?' She halts at the door to the lounge and smiles at me nervously. 'Be prepared for a shock.'

Then she goes through, with me tagging behind.

It's much warmer on the other side of the door, and that's thanks to the fake-coaled gas fire which is roaring away. And although it's a big room, the lounge is also far more cluttered than the hallway. There are two big leather sofas, for starters. There's a huge TV and a tiny hi-fi. There's a paper rack spilling magazines onto the floor, and a TV cupboard overflowing with DVDs. An ironing board is set up near one wall, and there's a pile of clothes lying close by on one of the sofas. In the centre of the room, there's a thick rug bearing a hieroglyphical pattern which makes me think it came from the Middle East. On a different day, the rug might have been a talking point.

But not today.

The TV is showing cartoons. In the middle of the rug there's a playpen. There's a safety guard around the gas fire. And I suddenly realise what was bothering me about the Nissan Juke outside. It's that there was a baby seat in the back.

Kneeling in the playpen there's a blue-eyed young man – *very* blue-eyed and *very* young – playing with some soft rubber bricks in an assortment of sizes and colours.

He's clearly the shock I was told to prepare for. But I couldn't have prepared for him because I couldn't have imagined him – not in a hundred-thousand years. Isabel having a baby, becoming *someone's mum*? No chance of that. No fucking chance at all.

'I'm back, honey,' coos Isabel, producing a tissue from her pocket and leaning into the pen to wipe saliva from the kid's mouth. 'And I've brought someone new to see you.' She straightens up and gives me a look which seems to say many things. That she's ecstatic, for one. That she can't believe it any more than I can, for another. And also, for a third, that she's a tiny bit scared about the whole bloody business. 'So, what do you think?' she asks, pocketing the tissue. 'Isn't he great?'

I'm stunned, but I manage to agree that yes, he's great. Then I ask, 'What's his name?'

Isabel doesn't immediately reply, but reaches under the kid's arms and lifts him out from the pen. He makes a noise which translates to me as a grumble at being separated from his rubber bricks, and he comes out still clutching one of them, which he throws in a clumsy, straight armed motion so that it scuttles across the floor and finishes beneath a sofa.

Isabel holds him so that his face is six inches from hers and gives him a big smile. 'Don't be grumpy, Oscar,' she commands him. 'Come and meet your Uncle Jimmy. He'll say hello when he can get his jaw off the floor.'

She brings him over so he can peer at me with wide and curious eyes. He's got a cheery, bewildered little smile, and he gurgles at me happily when Isabel carries him close, his enforced separation from the rubber bricks apparently forgotten.

I'm awkward and rubbish around kids, even in normal circumstances, and these circumstances are a long way from normal. But I don't mind making an effort, and I put on a hushed, excited voice. 'Hello, Oscar. What about you then, big guy?'

He gurgles and squeals some more, and wriggles a bit in his mother's arms. Isabel nuzzles his ear and murmurs, 'You're right, Oscar. He does look scared of you.'

'I'm sorry,' I reply. 'I don't mean to be. It's just that, well…'

'It's just you don't know one end of a baby from another. And you're gobsmacked I've got one. Me of all people.'

'I am – that's true.' I laugh at my awkwardness, and then I say, 'You know, this morning, when we spoke on the phone and you told me you were in the garden, I wondered why you'd go out there on such a cold day, and then I got around to thinking that maybe you'd moved abroad. I could imagine you moving somewhere hot and glamorous – I could easily see you doing that. I could see you doing many things, Iz, but having a kid would have been a long, long way down the list.'

'Don't worry. You're not the only member of the lost-for-words club. It took me long enough to get used to the idea.'

'And you, Oscar?' I ask. When I reach out to him, he grabs my middle finger in his little hand and begins to squeeze. 'How old are you, then?'

'He's ten months,' say his mum. 'Sometimes, when he gurgles, it's nearly a word. He'll be talking soon, and walking as well. Look, see.' She prises his fingers off mine and then sets him down on his feet, facing his playpen and toys. She lets go of him, and for a moment he stands there, teetering and wobbling, trying to find some balance. Then he makes a sudden, ungainly lurch forward, and just at the point where he'd fall flat on his face Isabel sweeps him back into her arms. 'My big boy,' she gushes, kissing him on top of his head, before setting him down on his knees, back in the pen. He gurgles and giggles and looks at her in surprise, as if not exactly sure what just happened.

'He's awesome,' I tell her. 'You both are.'

'Well, he certainly is.' Oscar goes back to playing with his bricks, and Isabel just stands for a moment and watches, her eyes intent and devoted. Then, when I think she's about to tell me something else about him, she looks at me sharply and says, 'Coffee. You haven't changed, Jimmy, so you'll want coffee.' She moves past me, towards the door. 'Come through to the kitchen.'

'Will Oscar be okay?'

'Oscar will be just great. For five minutes at least.'

I follow her to the kitchen. It's another big room, and fitted out expensively. There are granite surfaces, brushed steel fittings and precision spotlights. But like the hallway, it's fucking freezing. And again there's an assortment of taped-up cardboard boxes in one corner. Although many things must have been packed away, there's a big red coffee machine on one of the surfaces. It's an expensive-looking Gaggia, standing just along from the kettle and toaster.

'Your packing's in full swing,' I say, with a nod at the boxes. 'When is it that you're moving?'

'Very soon,' is all Isabel replies. She casts an eye at the Gaggia, and even toys momentarily with its pans. But then, with an apologetic glance at me, she moves away and switches on the kettle, before retrieving a jar of instant coffee from a cupboard. Then she opens a drawer, takes out a glass ashtray, and sets it down next to me. 'I haven't packed everything away,' she says. 'Go ahead. I don't mind if you smoke.'

'Sounds like you've stopped.'

'When I found I was expecting.'

'In which case neither of us needs this.'

I slide the ashtray back towards her. She picks it up, smiles, and says, 'God, I thought you'd smoke forever – or until you died of it, anyway. Why did you quit?'

'I wanted to save up some money.'

'Good for you. For anything special?'

'This and that. The future, you know.' To get off the subject, I amble towards the window and gaze into the back garden. It's pretty dark now, but I can see that the rear lawn has grown long like the front. Also, one of the fence panels has come free of its posts. It's then been leant up against the rest of the fence, with a patio table pushed hard against it to keep it upright.

'Now you know what I was doing in the garden,' says Isabel, joining me at the window. The fence came down in the winds last night, and I was outside propping it up when you rang.'

'I pick my moments.'

'You always did.' She glances round, to where the kettle is doing its thing. 'Two sugars?'

'Just milk. I cut out sugar as well.'

She laughs at me, turning away to spoon coffee into mugs 'Saving more money, Jimmy?'

'More like trying to keep some weight off. It's not so easy since I turned thirty.'

'I know what you mean.' She pats her waist and frowns just a little. 'I'm still a bit mummy shaped, myself. But I've been working hard at getting my figure back. Get me the milk, would you? The cupboard nearest the oven is a fridge in disguise.'

I get the milk. Thinking back to lunch, and remembering that Charlotte never got through to her new friend Isabel, I ask, 'So, have you joined a gym?'

'No chance of that. I don't have enough time. But there's a cross-trainer in the garage, and one of those machines for doing crunches. I blitz them both when I have the chance.'

Isabel finishes stirring the coffees and hands me mine. I tell her, 'You're doing a great job. Of getting back your figure, I mean.' I pause then, unsure whether to say more, not knowing whether I'm treading on forbidden territory.

I don't think Isabel knows either. At first, she says nothing in reply, peeling away to put the milk back in the fridge. She takes her time about it, and the lull in conversation grows awkward to the point where I'm about to say something – anything at all – just to get us back on a safer subject. But then she closes the fridge and turns around to smile at me. It's that same bashful smile she wore at the front door, a smile which suits her new face far better than it would ever have suited the old.

'That's sweet of you to say,' she replies. 'But if I got undressed right here – just dropped everything on the kitchen floor – you'd see I've got some work left to do.'

'I doubt I'd be complaining, Iz. I bet Lee certainly isn't.'

Isabel sips her coffee, those blue eyes appraising me coolly over the rim of her mug. Then she says, 'Lee's not here anymore. He upped and left us.'

Frankly, her news doesn't really surprise me. I'd already worked out that something was wrong. It could have been the unkempt lawn which gave it away. Or maybe Isabel's evasiveness about when she was moving. And something else as well: there's no evidence around the house of Lee actually living here. Now that I think about it, that single cashmere on the stand in the hallway was definitely a woman's coat.

Still, I do my best to look surprised. 'I'm sorry, Iz,' I say to her.

'Don't be.' It's her turn to walk to the window and stare into the gloom. 'It's not your problem. And anyway, turns out he was a right wanker.'

I take a breath. 'Iz, can I ask what happened?'

She says nothing. Just stands and stares at the dark and the gloom.

'Alright,' I say. 'It's none of my business, I know.'

'No, it's okay,' she replies, turning away from the window. 'Come on, let's go check on my little man, and I'll tell you about it there. There's not a lot to say.'

Back in the lounge, Oscar greets us with a new bout of gurgling and by shaking the bars of his pen. 'What's the matter, honey?' says Isabel, her mood lightening in an instant. She lifts him out, holds him in the air, and then spins round and around. Three times they spin, then four and five, all the while scaring me that they're going to crash into something and fall over. But nothing bad happens, and in the end, with them both giggling, she sets him down on the floor, this time outside the pen, so that he's free to crawl around the room. While I take a seat on one of the sofas, Isabel produces a beanbag from the corner and sits down near the fire. 'Oscar has a way of getting past the fireguard,' she explains, removing both her body warmer and fleece. 'But there's no way he's getting through me.'

She takes off her bobble hat next. Her hair, as it spools out over her shoulders, looks a darker shade of blonde than I remember.

'So then,' she says, wriggling herself into a comfortable position against the beanbag, and stretching out her long legs along the floor. 'About me and Lee.'

'You're sure you want to tell me?'

'No problem. Happy to.'

But before she tells her story, first she glances at Oscar. He's stripping out the few remaining magazines from the paper wrack, and sliding them across the floor. Isabel rolls here eyes, but smiles tolerantly. Then she looks at me directly and says, 'Like I said, there isn't much to tell. We were only any good for about a year, really. After that the cracks began to show. Maybe I'd fallen for the money and the status more than the man, but it got to the stage where I'd get fed up with the long hours he was spending at work. And then, when he did come home, it wasn't any better. We were just too different. He didn't like what I liked, and I didn't like what he liked.'

'Neither of you liked me very much. You had that in common.'

She laughs at that. 'Come on, Jimmy. I still liked you, deep down. I'd stopped loving you, that was all.'

I think: *That was fucking all?* But I keep quiet because I didn't come here to rake up those old coals.

'At least,' she says, 'you and me had a good run. With me and Lee, things went pear shaped quickly. Looking back, he wasn't willing to work on our relationship, and neither was I. You know – make changes, compromise, all that stuff. Neither of us was willing to do it.'

'Iz, maybe you're being a bit hard on yourself?'

'No, Jimmy, I'm not. You know how selfish I can be. Or used to be, at any rate, before Oscar turned up. And Lee's just as selfish, or even more so. We were both too self-centred, and things reached the stage where the only place we made each other happy was in bed. Then we even stopped doing that.' She stretches, reaching for her coffee, and casts another watchful eye at Oscar. 'Mind you,' she laughs, 'the sex was great at first. He was a top shag.'

'Nice one, Missus. Thanks for letting me know.'

'Don't mention it.'

I lapse briefly into silence. Then I say, 'I can't believe you've just said that to me.'

She laughs some more. 'Come on, Jimmy. I don't need to spare your feelings. You had some moves yourself. Bet you still have.'

'Glad you think so. Is that a round-about way of coming on to me, Isabel?'

'Totally not,' she sighs. 'And you know it isn't. God, it's like there's two little boys in here right now.'

'Okay, okay. Just checking where I stand.'

'Where you stand is in a new relationship, or so I've heard. Don't go complicating this. I'm explaining why things didn't work out with Lee, and that's all I'm doing. You're the one who started asking me about it.'

'Alright, sorry I spoke.'

For a moment, there's an awkward silence. If Oscar's aware of it, he doesn't let it show. He's still skimming magazines around the floor, gurgling and giggling without a care.

'My fault,' I say. 'I didn't come here to cause a fight.'

'Fault on both sides, Jimmy.' She lounges on the floor and offers me a weary little smile. 'There's always fault on both sides. Like I said earlier, don't go worrying about it.'

There's that new Isabel again. Mellower, more chilled. Seemingly less likely to bicker about stuff. Maybe she won't mind my next question then.

'I have to ask – how did you know I'm in a relationship?'

She grins, readjusts herself on the beanbag, and says, 'Well for one thing, I could have guessed. It was only a matter of time, because you're not the sort of bloke to live on his own.'

'But you didn't need to guess?'

'No. I bumped into Ash, in Tesco, about year ago. He told me you were hooked up.'

'Ash? Seriously?'

'He didn't tell you, then?'

'No.'

'He probably thought that news about me wasn't what you needed to hear. Especially the news that I had a baby bump so big I could hardly push a trolley. Does it matter that he didn't tell you?'

I don't answer her straightaway. If I'm honest, yeah, it does matter. But this isn't the time or place to go on about it. 'I guess not,' I reply.

After that, we both fall quiet for a minute, the silence broken only by Oscar's low level gurgling and the cartoons on TV. Then I say, 'I can't imagine you with a big bump.'

'Hah! Nor could Lee. It freaked him out. The whole pregnancy thing did his head in.'

'So… Oscar wasn't exactly planned?'

'No chance. Sex had become a once-in-a-blue-moon thing when my little man was conceived. And I was still on the pill. But here he is, against all odds.'

'Does Lee see him much?'

She shakes her head with a passion, and an angry frown obliterates that chilled-out look. 'Lee's in the south of France, or was the last I heard. Cannes, or somewhere like that. He ran off with the wife of one of his clients – a film producer or something.'

'No. You're fucking kidding me.'

Her frown deepens. 'No, I'm not kidding, Jimmy. And I'm trying to discourage swearing in front of Oscar, by the way.'

'Sorry,' I murmur. 'Won't happen again.'

'It's alright,' she sighs. 'We'll let you off, won't we?' She glances round at Oscar, only to find him trying to strip the wicker from the paper rack, and that's enough for her to bring his adventures to and end. 'Hang on, Jimmy,' she says, rolling off the beanbag and getting to her feet. Next second, she has him separated from the paper rack and plonked back in his pen, but not before blowing a slobbery raspberry on top of his head. 'Enough of your sass,' she says to the kid, and just when I think he's about to cry she pulls a funny face at him through the bars of the pen, and that's enough to make him laugh instead.

'So yeah,' she says, returning to the beanbag, talking matter-of-factly. 'Oscar was six weeks old the day his dad left, and he hasn't seen him since. Lee never showed Oscar any love, and I can't forgive him that. He even accused me of getting deliberately pregnant, just to trap him in a relationship. He didn't think to wonder why the fuck I'd want to be trapped with an arsehole like him.'

'I get why you feel so strongly, Iz. But I thought we weren't swearing.'

'You're the one not swearing. I'm allowed to bend the rules. It's my house – for now at any rate.'

I smile at that. 'Fair enough,' I reply. 'Where are you moving, by the way? Where's the new house?'

'I'm moving back to Mum and Dad's. I've run out of money, and Lee isn't sending any.'

'None?'

'Jack shit. I don't know if he's even earning. I checked with his office and they haven't heard from him. They've taken him off the payroll and sent his P45 here.'

'The bloke's a scumbag,' I tell her. 'I mean, I know my dad left when I was just a kid, but at least he sent us some money.'

'I know,' she sighs. 'I never thought even Lee would just abandon his son. But he has, and now a girl's gotta do what a girl's gotta do. Mum and Dad's isn't ideal, but it will do while I sort myself out. I can go back to cutting hair, part-time at least. Mum says shell happily look after Oscar for a few hours a day.'

I look from one to the other: Oscar playing happily in his pen; Isabel reclining on the beanbag by the fire, telling me how things are and how they're going to be. I never imagined her as a mum, but she's much more than that. She's a terrific mum, if I'm any judge.

'Tell me to mind my own business,' I ask, 'but are you okay for money? I mean, I know things aren't great, but is your head above water?'

She gives me another of those disapproving looks. 'That first bit you said? About minding your own business? Well you mind it, Jimmy.'

'I know it's a private thing. But look, I'm concerned for you, that's all.'

She stares at me like I can piss off, but I continue to meet her gaze, and in the end she heaves out a big sigh and says, 'Alright, since you ask. I'm behind with the mortgage, and so we're moving out before they kick us out. The building society says they sympathise with my problem, but sympathy only goes so far. Then there's the other stuff,' she adds, counting off unpaid bills on fingers of one hand. 'The council tax, the gas bill, the phone – I'm way behind with all of them, even though Mum and Dad have lent me some money. That thing out there is barely drivable,' – she jerks a thumb in the Juke's direction on the driveway – 'because it needs an injector or something. Of course the warranty's just up, so that's three hundred quid I don't have. My little man here costs a fortune, and now the fence has blown down as well. And, oh yeah, it's Christmas.'

'Blimey,' I reply. 'You've got your plate full with that lot.'

'"Blimey" doesn't cut it, Jimmy. You can swear if you want.'

'Fuck me, then.'

'That's not happening. I've told you once.'

That's when she looks at me and I look at her.

And we both start laughing.

Laughing at the sheer fucking craziness of her situation. Laughing, because there's nothing else to do about it.

Except, that's not exactly true. There is something else I could do. I could do plenty if she'd let me. For starters, there's thirty-thousand quid in my car outside, and loads more where it came from.

'Isabel,' I begin.

'No,' she replies.

'No to what?'

'No to what you're thinking. I know you, remember. I can tell that you want to lend me money. Well, it's sweet of you to take an interest, Jimmy, but no thank you very much. Me and Oscar will manage.'

I take a deep breath. 'You're right, up to a point. I was going to offer you money, but I wasn't going to lend it. You see, I'm not short of cash right now, and I reckoned I could just… well, sort of give you some? You could think of it as a gift, something to tide you over.'

She stares at me hard. 'You'd really do that?' she asks. 'After all this time, and after everything that happened?'

'I would.'

'No strings attached?'

'No strings.'

'Not even a dirty shag?'

We both start laughing again, and I reply, 'No, not even that. Although, of course, if one was on offer…'

Isabel turns to the playpen. 'Oscar, it's official – your Uncle Jimmy is a sex pest.' Then to me she says, 'Listen, it's incredible of you to offer, but the answer's an even bigger no.'

'But, Iz, just think – '

'No arguing, Jimmy. I won't take your money.'

And before I can answer back, she adds, 'But look, there are a couple of things you can do.'

'Like what?'

'You could get Oscar a Christmas present.'

'Happy to do that. Anything in particular?'

Isabel looks at him, and then looks at me. 'You can choose,' she says. It'll be interesting to see what you get.'

'Consider it done.'

'Nothing too expensive, though.'

'Alright.'

'I'm serious, Jimmy. No spoiling him.'

'I get the message loud and clear. I won't spoil him. Now what else can I do? You said there were a couple of things.'

Isabel rearranges the beanbag and sits up straighter. 'Could you take a look at my car?'

'You know where that got us last time.'

She actually blushes, brightly too. 'God,' she says. 'I knew I shouldn't have asked.'

'Don't worry – I'm just teasing.'

'So, could you take a look, or not?'

'I'm out of practice. And short of time. But I can get one of the mechanics at work to sort it.'

'But that would cost you, wouldn't it?'

'There's no chance of it costing me. A couple of them owe me favours.'

I'm lying, of course, when I tell her that. Mechanics never owe salesmen favours – it's always the other way round. But Isabel doesn't need to know the truth. I can pay one of our blokes to fix the Juke, and she can think someone was doing me a good turn.

'Here's what I'll do,' I tell her. 'I'll pick it up in the morning, if you like. On my way to work. I can't promise to get fixed in a day, but we'll do our best.'

'Tomorrow? Are you sure?'

'It's no problem.'

She looks at me slyly. 'Maybe when you do collect it, you could bring me back that trophy – the one you said you had for me this morning?'

'Oh, yeah.' Remembering that the fucking thing is still in my drawer at home, I find it's my turn to blush. 'Sorry Iz, I've just had loads to do today. I'll remember next time.'

'That's fine, Jimmy,' she replies, that sly look still on her face. 'Next time's fine, and I know you'll remember. You wouldn't want me thinking you were just after an excuse to see me again, would you now?'

3.6) Beware of Greeks Receiving Gifts

I'm later leaving Isabel's house than I'd planned, but not so late that I can't complete a task that's been a work-in-progress all day. Having phoned the bank this morning and collected the money after lunch, there's enough time remaining for me to take thirty-thousand pounds round to Carl's house.

Of course, it would help if I knew precisely where Carl lives. But I don't have his exact address, and I didn't want to ask for it at work in case anyone queried why I needed to know.

Fortunately, I have a good general idea of where I need to be headed. It's to the address of Mr and Mrs Petridis, an elderly Greek couple who bought a car from me in the autumn. Carl's a near neighbour of theirs – I know that from the way he reacted to my clinching the sale.

'We go back, Mr Petridis and me,' he complained at the time. 'Silly Greek cunt only lives a few doors down. He should've seen me for a deal, Jimbo, not fucking you. No disrespect.'

I don't know whether Carl intended more disrespect or less when he called me Jimbo rather than Cooter. Nor do I know exactly what he meant by "a few doors down", but that's what I need to find out now, and it doesn't help that the street-lighting is so poor when I get close to the Petridis' house. The lamps in this tight little street are more or less relics; in fact, the Christmas lights in the residents' gaffes are about as much help.

But I find Mr and Mrs Petridis' place easily enough, quickly spotting their Golf on the narrow driveway. And it turns out that Carl lives six doors away, although on the opposite side of the road, which is why I end up driving another lap of the neighbourhood before I notice his current car, the sporty Focus RS which Graham has repeatedly threatened to take off him as a punishment for his poor performance, but which he's somehow clung onto by his fingernails. Fortunately, Carl has parked it on the driveway, so there's no debate about which house is his. It's also good that there are other cars lining the street, so my Mondeo won't stand out when I have to get out and leave it. That's a big relief to me, because I don't want to be noticed by the locals. I don't want Carl to know where his money came from, and I don't want anyone to know that I was ever here.

To make my final preparations, I drive less than a mile to a local supermarket, where I pull up in a quiet section of the car park, some way from the entrance. I take the money from the envelope and then carefully re-pack it, making the package as flat as possible, and taking care not to include the withdrawal slip or any other paperwork which would make it traceable to me. I reckon the end result is just about thin enough to fit through a standard household letterbox. Before sealing the envelope I slide in the typed note which I printed off before I left home this morning. It reads simply:

Your Lucky Day. One Time Only. Don't Waste It.

Once I've sealed the package I look around to see if anyone's been watching me. Satisfied that there's no one nearby, I restart the car. It's time to get this thing done.

It's also time to fully acknowledge why I'm doing this thing for Carl. Yes, a big part of it is the bond I feel with his kid, but being as

I've met Sammy just the once there has to be more to my reasoning than that. Which brings me back to my other motive, the one which keeps floating in and out of my thoughts. The motive that sounds fucking crazy, but keeps demanding to be heard.

The little part of me which is occasionally willing to believe in fate has a similar attitude to the concept of karma, and by "karma" I mean the idea that we get what we give, or that good deeds done attract good fortune back. And I reckon I've been looking for big karmic favours lately. Specifically, I've been looking for Isabel to answer my phone call and agree to meet up with me. And I dare say that in some way I see my payment to Carl as the price to be paid for enjoying success with Iz. In effect, this is some sort of deal I'm trying to strike with the gods. Sure, it sounds fucking stupid on any rational level, but we're not rational creatures for every minute of the day. I reckon this is how our minds work when they're operating in the one-percent zone. And some of our minds, mine included, maybe spend more than one percent of their time there.

But whatever. I'll go round the fucking twist if I over-think this thing. I just need to go and finish what I've started.

Back in Carl's street, I park in a space roughly half-way between the Petridis' house and his. Then I kill the lights and engine, and take a few moments to check the windows of the nearby houses. Again, I'm looking for prying eyes. I want to know if anyone's seen me arrive, and whether anyone's watching me now. I think my luck's still in, and that the coast remains clear.

Then I study Carl's house for a short while, reminding myself that this is a simple plan I've made. Walk up the drive, push the envelope through the letterbox, return to the car and drive away. It should all take less than two minutes, and the sooner I start the sooner I'll finish. *So get on with it, Jimmy*, I tell myself, realising that my heart rate is up and that there's a slick of sweat on my forehead.

I'm about to get out of the car when a light goes on in Carl's hallway, and a silhouette moves about behind the opaque glass panel of the front door. I'm not certain, but I think it's his wife rather than Carl himself, though from this narrow angle I can't see exactly what she's up to. I need to be patient now. I need to sit and wait. It would be too risky too approach while there's someone in the hall.

My attention having been on the front door, I've failed to notice anyone approaching the car. And so, when there's a flicker of movement close by, it comes as a surprise. Next thing, somebody raps twice on the driver's window, and I jolt in my seat like I'd received an electric shock.

I turn to look. It's bad news. Bloody bad news. Carl's outside, his face right by the window, staring intently in. He looks bewildered, and he looks pissed off.

I ought to go. I ought to get gone right now.

Carl tries the door handle, but I've kept the doors locked while I've been driving around with thirty grand. 'Cooter,' he wails loudly, too loudly – so loudly I immediately reckon the fucker's been drinking. 'Cooter, I know you're in there.'

I've got one finger poised over the ignition. I want to crank up the car and get the fuck gone. But this is a cramped little street, and by now Carl is hanging onto the mirror. He could damage the Mondeo if I try to drive off. He could damage his fucking self come to that. And from the way he's yelling, he'll bring people out of their houses in a minute. I might run the twat over in front of witnesses.

'Coooo-terrrrr! I can see you.'

I switch on the electrics and lower the window. 'Hey Carl, what's up mate?'

'Cooter!' he blurts. 'I knew it was you.' He leans closer, and yeah, he stinks of booze and cigarettes – I'd like to know where the money for those has come from.

'Yeah, Carl, it's me alright.' I try to sound casual, as though it's an everyday event for me to park up outside his house in the evening.

'Whatcha doin' here, then?' He takes a step or two away, so he can straighten up to look at me, and then he stands swaying in the road. 'Cunt Graham sent you here to spy?'

Although I came here to help him, right now I want to knock his lights out. I close the window, a movement which draws him back towards the car. But before he can get too close, and before he can say anything else, I open the door and slide out the Mondeo, bringing the big brown envelope with me.

For a moment we just stand in the road and face each other, like big kids who've fallen out over a goal scored in street football. Then I say, 'Back off a bit, mate. I need to go and see Mr Petridis.'

'Huh? Petridis? What?'

I wave the envelope and point towards the Petridis' house. 'Head office did a paperwork audit,' I tell Carl. 'They found documents in Mr Petridis' file which I didn't get him to sign at the time, and so I'm here to do it now.'

For a second or two he just stares blankly at me. But then some kind of penny drops – albeit the wrong penny – and he snorts, 'Head office wankers!' He sways about some more, and then, in a distorted version of what Graham told us yesterday – about Carl being declined an advance on his wages – he adds, 'They withheld my money.'

'Yeah, you're right,' I reply, still trying to sound cool and casual. 'Wankers, all of them, over there.' I step around Carl and begin to walk away. 'Anyway, Mr Petridis – I need to go and see him.'

I'm hoping Carl will head off home, but I don't hear his footsteps moving away. 'Petridis,' he says from behind me, slurring badly. 'Silly Greek, silly cunt. Should've bought from me, not you.'

'Carl, there's a car coming.'

'From me, Cooter. Silly cunt. Greek. Old cunt.'

I turn, grab Carl by the arm, and pull him onto the pavement. A big old Volvo cruises slowly past, its engine sounding smooth and silky for the age of car. Carl waves wildly in its wake and shouts, 'Slow down, Wellington. I'm here in the road.'

'Carl, you should get yourself home.'

'And you should get your paperwork done, Cooter. So you don't fail Cooter audits.' He laughs then, long and loud, doubling over like he's told the world's funniest joke.

There's a twitch of curtain from one of the homes in this no man's land between the Petridis' house and Carl's. A woman's face appears fleetingly at the window, her wary, watchful look comically uplit by the fluorescent smiling snowman on her windowsill. Maybe she'll call the police soon, and I reckon someone else will if she doesn't. When the coppers turn up they'll find a shambling drunk and a bloke with thirty grand in an envelope. Things will go awkwardly after that.

Carl's still doubled over, still laughing like a drain. 'Mate, you really need to get home,' I tell him. 'Before you rupture yourself, ideally. And I need to see Mr Petridis.' Then I walk sharply away, giving him no further chance to reply, stopping and turning round only when I've got as far as the Petridis' drive. I'm hoping Carl will have finally slunk off. If he has, then I can get back in my car and drive away.

But Carl's still there, still hanging round the Mondeo. He's finally straightened up, catching his breath and staggering about. Then he leans on the car to steady himself, and begins searching his pockets – I reckon for cigarettes. He doesn't look like he's heading home soon.

I need Carl to believe I came here to see Mr and Mrs Petridis. And so I walk up to the Greek couple's front door. They've got an illuminated nativity scene on their windowsill, and a sticker on the door which reads: *No Cold Callers*. I don't think they'll mind this cold caller, not when I give them the reason I've just invented for being here.

I ring the bell, and soon I hear movement in the hallway. Then the lights flick on, and the door opens just wide enough for Mr Petridis to peer out. 'Yes?' he asks. 'Can I help you?' He's a shortish bloke, maybe five eight, with a good head of hair that must once have been very dark. Now it's more white than grey, whilst his face is deeply lined and wrinkled.

'Good evening, Mr Petridis,' I begin. Sorry to disturb you at home. You may not remember me, but – '

His face lights up in recognition. 'Billy! Billy from the garage. How are you, Billy?'

'Jimmy, Mr Petridis. It's Jimmy from the garage. But Billy was pretty close. And I'm fine, thanks very much.'

'Jimmy! Yes, of course! But hold on,' – the smile falls from his face, and he looks past me at the car on his drive – 'is everything okay with my Golf?'

'Everything is fine, Mr Petridis. I'm just here on a routine errand. Sorry to disturb you, but could I come in?'

'Of course, of course.' He stands aside to let me pass. Before heading in I take a last glance over my shoulder. Carl is still out there. He's got a cigarette going and hasn't moved far. He's still looking my way.

Just as Isabel's hallway was bitterly cold, the Petridis' is sweltering hot. Even though I'm not planning to stay long, I'm happy for Mr Petridis to take my coat and hang it on a peg. Then, walking with a stoop, but full of energy and bustle, he leads me into the front room, where the festive spirit has certainly found a home. The walls are covered with Christmas cards, festooned together by trails of tinsel and glitter, and there's a strong smell of pine from what might be the largest Christmas tree ever crammed into someone's suburban semi. It dwarfs Mrs Petridis, who gets up from an armchair in the corner, muting a TV quiz show as she comes forward to greet me. Like her husband she's small and stooped, but moves less quickly, seemingly with more difficulty.

'Helena, it's Billy from the garage,' says Mr Petridis.

'It's Jimmy from the garage, old fool,' says Mrs Petridis. She might look frail, but her tone is tough and sharp, and her Greek accent has remained thicker than her husband's. 'How are you, Jimmy? Sit down. Some tea?'

'I'm very well, thank you.' I sit at one end of a plump sofa. 'But no tea, thank you very much.'

'Of course,' says Mrs Petridis, standing before me. 'You prefer your coffee. You like sugar, but you have given it up.' She gestures outwards with her hands to mimic a bloating stomach. 'So you can lose some weight, yes?'

I laugh. 'That's very well remembered. But no coffee, either. Thanks all the same, Mrs Petridis.'

'Helena, she remembers everything,' says Mr Petridis, sitting down at the sofa's other end. He produces a tobacco pouch and begins to fill an old pipe. 'Me, these days, I remember nothing.'

'Only the way to the pub,' Mrs Petridis cackles.

Mr Petridis shrugs and looks offended, but I can tell that it's a show for my benefit. 'Every day, she cuts me badly,' he complains. 'Cuts me badly with her tongue. Every day, for forty-six years. But not you, Billy – sorry, Jimmy. She says nothing bad about you. When we buy the car, she keeps saying what nice young man you are.'

While Mr Petridis has been talking, his wife has produced a whisky bottle from a sideboard. 'Something stronger than coffee?' she asks. 'You said you like your whisky, yes?'

'You have got a good memory,' I admit. 'But honestly, Mrs Petridis, no thanks.'

She looks disappointed, and sets the bottle down on a nearby coffee table in case I change my mind. 'Anyway,' she says to her husband, as she hobbles back to her chair, 'Jimmy is a nice young man – that's why I say so. What can we do for you, Jimmy? It's nice that you come see us, even though you don't drink our whisky.'

I lean forward, place the envelope between my feet, and begin to tell them the big lie I invented seconds before I knocked their door. 'It's like this,' I explain. 'Every Christmas we have a prize draw at the showroom. We enter the names of everyone who's bought a car in the past year, and the winner gets five hundred pounds.'

I await a response, but for once neither of them has anything to say. Her eyes are fixed on me, and he's staring at the envelope on the floor.

'Anyway,' I continue, 'getting down to business, so to speak... well, you've won. So here I am. With your money.'

Still no reply. I reckon they know I'm blagging.

It's Mrs Petridis who finally answers. 'Jimmy, that's nice,' she says. 'We never win anything except gout and the arthritis. You must thank your big boss. What is his name again? Graham?'

'That's right – Graham. Sure, I'll thank him for you.'

Mr Petridis adds, 'Yes Jimmy, you must.' He has his pipe filled, but is yet to light it. And he keeps looking from the envelope to me and back again. 'But you've brought the money in pound coins, maybe?'

'Ah-hah. I see why you'd think that, Mr Petridis, but it's in fifty pound notes. There's not just money in the envelope, but paperwork too – paperwork for some of my other customers. We were audited by head office, and I need to get some missing signatures once I've left here.'

Keeping the envelope angled away from them, I open it at one corner and slide out ten fifties. 'Which of you shall I give this to? Who's the big spender?'

'I'll keep it for now,' says Mr Petridis, holding out a hand for the cash. He looks halfway pleased and halfway plain suspicious, those lines on his face having deepened still further. 'But Helena – she's the one who'll spend it.'

'I'm the one who'll spend it because I won't waste it on drink,' she replies. Then she looks at a clock on the mantelpiece and says, 'Jimmy, they work you too hard. Must you visit these other customers tonight?'

'I must,' I lie, not wanting to stay for long. 'But I'll be quick about it.'

'You'll be very late,' she says. 'You should get home. Home to your beautiful Charlotte.'

'You've met Charlie?'

'No,' she replies. 'But you tell us so much about her that I feel like I have.'

I think back three months, to when Mr and Mrs Petridis came to the showroom. I remember that we got on well and we talked a lot. And I must have talked about Charlotte because Mrs Petridis, with her fantastic memory, can repeat what I told them pretty-much word for word.

'You told us that Charlotte is beautiful, Jimmy. And you told us that she's clever. Cleverer than you, you said. And I remember you saying you were lucky you met her when you did, because before that you were down and on your own. You told us that when you walk down the street with her and she is holding your hand, that you feel very lucky. And proud. Very proud, Jimmy – you said that as well.'

I look at them both in turn. Mr Petridis finally has his pipe lit, and he's sitting back, smiling, content to simply listen to his wife.

Mrs Petridis is looking at me curiously. 'You've forgotten you said these things, Jimmy?' she asks. 'It was only three months ago.'

She's right – it was only three months ago. But it feels like longer. If I have it right, the Petridis bought their car just a few days before I checked my lottery ticket. My world has turned on its head since then. I look at things differently these days.

Even so, those things I said about Charlotte were true at the time and they're true now. She is beautiful and clever. I do owe her a debt for walking into my life when it was a fucked-up mess, and I certainly feel proud when we walk down the street together. And so that's two reminders in one day of how lucky I am: one from Ringo over lunch, and one from Mrs Petridis now.

I should thank Mrs Petridis, but I'd feel even more like a hypocrite and a cheat than I do already. Sure, I'm going home to Charlotte this evening. But in the morning, so that I can pick up the Juke, I'll be heading back to Isabel's place. And while I hate myself for it, I'm really looking forward to seeing her again. Although Charlotte's beautiful and clever and more than I deserve, it's Isabel who's got my buttons pressed right now.

And yet, when I look at Mrs Petridis and she's looking hard and knowingly at me, that's when I start asking myself some tough questions. So what if I've got the hots for Isabel? If I chased every woman I fancied I'd have no time for a life. It's not like I'm seventeen any more, for fuck's sake. And I may have been obsessing about Isabel for weeks, but when everyone else keeps telling me how wonderful Charlotte is – and when they're so bloody right as well – isn't it time I at least gave Charlie a chance?

I clear my throat and get up from the sofa. All at once, Carl and the money and the lies I've spun in here seem trivial and unimportant. "Mrs Petridis, you're right,' I tell her. 'I shouldn't be working so late. So enjoy the money and have a happy Christmas. But I'm going to get off now. And I'm going to go straight home. Home to see Charlotte.'

From her crooked but approving smile, I reckon old Mrs Petridis is happy with my decision.

3.7) The Rich Really Should Sleep Better

I nearly told her. About the money, I mean. During the warm, dreamy moments after sex – those moments of holding and whispering and pledging – I nearly told Charlotte that I was fabulously rich. That we were fabulously rich.

But nearly is nothing. I can remember the days when I was new to the car trade and struggling to close deals – the days when I'd go into Graham's office and tell him I'd nearly sold a car. He would look at me pitifully. 'Nearly is nothing, Jimmy,' he'd say time and again. 'When you actually sell me a car I'll give you a *SOLD* sticker for the window. But get it into your head – there are no *NEARLY SOLD* stickers. Now fuck off until you've dealt someone up.'

I have no *NEARLY TOLD CHARLOTTE* stickers either, and so she fell asleep knowing nothing of my wealth, but maybe asking herself why I came home in a buoyant mood and clutching champagne, and also why my libido suddenly found top gear after weeks of dawdling like an old man's. When pushed for an explanation, I simply said, 'because it's nearly Christmas.' Charlotte said nothing, and she looked doubtful. I'm willing to bet her mind is still sifting things through on some level or another.

But if Charlotte's cogs are still turning, then they're doing so unconsciously. Her breathing is slow and rhythmic, her out-breaths producing the little low whistling noise she makes once she's fully sound asleep. I tried to talk to her once about the way she whistles softly like that – I wanted to know whether she even knew that she did it. I wasn't complaining, just making conversation and being affectionate (or so I thought), but she was prickly about the whole thing and so I let the subject drop.

I try to arrange myself so that I too can get some sleep. I alternate from my left side to my right, and when that doesn't work I move onto my back. But it's hopeless. Yet again I'm wide awake during the small hours. My mind is racing, but only around the same old loop, not to anywhere where it might find some rest.

I turn again in bed and study the silhouette of the woman sleeping by my side. I ought to be happy right now, but for all the good intentions I felt when leaving Mr and Mrs Petridis' house, I find myself lying here and wondering why this (*she*) isn't enough, and why it is I'm so looking forward to calling at Isabel's in the morning. Once again I ask myself the question I've asked countless times in the past few weeks: am I unhappy with Charlotte because I'm genuinely unhappy with Charlotte? Or is it the money talking, making me think there should be something (*someone*) more?

Some bonkers, scheming part of me thinks it would be great if I could simply forget about my winnings for a day. Forget about it, that is, while remembering everything else going on in my life. That way, I could have twenty-four hours to work out my true feelings for Charlotte, unburdened by the knowledge of my wealth. Briefly, I toy with the idea of finding a hypnotist who could actually make that happen, but then I give up the idea as delusional. Knowing me, I'd probably hook up with some rogue hypnotist who'd induce me to sign my money over to him, before permanently wiping my memory of ever having won it. That would be a great fucking entry on my personal *Pitfalls* list, wouldn't it?

I find that last idea pretty funny, and for a minute or two I lie there chuckling quietly to myself. The tension I'm feeling subsides as my laughter dies away, and I find I'm finally drifting off to sleep. But the thought isn't far from my mind that I'm no further forward than I was three months ago, on the night I found out I was a multimillionaire.

3.8) A Ticket to Willy Wonka's Place had Nothing on This

Buying a lottery ticket was all very well, but three months went by before I finally got round to checking the bloody thing. It might have sat in my wallet forever had Suzy Portlock not come to buy a car on that dank Saturday afternoon in the autumn.

Suzy was the pint-sized, heavy-smoking, big-talking younger sister of Gaby Portlock, one of my early girlfriends back when we were still at school. I hadn't seen either sister for more than five years, and then in came Suzy, looking for a car that wouldn't break the bank – 'a cheap car, Jimmy, 'cause the rent's gone up but my wages 'aven't.'

The cheapest car we had was an old Ford KA. The paintwork on the sills and arches was still okay, but I reckoned it would bubble and blister some time soon. Many KAs of that vintage are rusty, and I told Suzy she should look at something else. I suggested she cut down her smoking by one pack per week, and then add the money she'd save to her monthly instalment – that way she could do better than the ageing Ford. She could get a car which would hang together for a little while longer.

But cutting down by a whole pack per week was too a big deal for her. Besides which, she said she liked the KA - it was cute, apparently, and gave off a 'good vibe'. Suzy looked at me wide-eyed, and smiled like an innocent abroad. If I could get it her for a hundred pounds a month, she'd sign up there and then.

I felt like giving her a shake. For all her sass and all her front, Suzy was way too gullible to be car hunting by herself, and I wanted her to know that my having snogged her sister sometime back near the dawn of time was no grounds for trusting that the KA was a decent motor. Hoping that the loose, slappy wheezing of the engine would be enough to put her off, I insisted she at least drive the little Ford before signing anything.

Suzy's response to the loose, slappy wheezing of the engine was to turn on the radio and crank up the volume. She did so just in time to catch the regional news announcer advising that a jackpot lottery win remained unclaimed from three months back. Apparently the ticket had been bought locally, and the bloke suggested we all check our numbers.

'Just imagine,' Suzy said to me from behind the wheel. 'Imagine having the winning numbers and not actually bothering to claim. Imagine not getting your hands on all that money.'

'Yeah,' I replied, making a mental note to once and for all check the ticket lurking in my wallet. 'Just imagine it.'

So much for making mental notes. I'd still have forgotten all about the unclaimed jackpot if it weren't for my bloody fuel receipts.

That evening, standing in the hallway, waiting for Charlotte to finish getting ready for a night out with Ash and Suki, I slid my wallet into the inner breast pocket of my jacket. When I looked in the mirror, I noticed that the wallet caused a bulge, a consequence of it getting fat with fuel receipts. I put petrol in loads of cars, and so my wallet is always filling up with receipts – they normally add up to a tidy expense claim whenever I can be bothered with the paperwork.

I checked my watch and then glanced up the stairs. I could hear Charlotte's hair dryer at full throttle behind the closed bedroom door, and that told me I had time enough to clear out my wallet. I took it into the kitchen and disgorged its contents onto the table. There, among the receipts, lay my three-month-old lottery ticket, small and pink and all creased up.

Remembering the earlier radio broadcast, I checked my watch again. There was enough time for both jobs – I could sort out the receipts and check my numbers. I picked up my phone and began looking for the lottery website.

About fifteen minutes later, after checking once, twice, and again, I stood outside our bedroom door on legs which weren't quite steady. The hairdryer had finished its work and I could hear Charlotte humming a tune. It was Son of a Preacher Man – I remember the tune vividly, and I can hear it clearly, even now.

'Nearly ready,' said Charlotte as I walked through the door. She got up from her dressing table and turned her back to me so that I could zip up her dress. But once that was done, she turned around and read something in my face. A concerned look came over hers. 'Are you alright, sweetheart?' she asked. 'You look like you've been slapped.'

'I'm fine,' I said, sitting down on the bed. 'But you'll never guess what?'

Charlotte stood with a necklace in one hand and a curious look on her face. 'What is it?' she asked. 'Something you've seen on TV?'

I opened my mouth to tell her the news, but then I looked at Charlie and something made me stop. I had the sensation that I was about to release a genie from his bottle, and that once he was free I'd never get him back in. For some reason, I decided he could stay where he was for a day or two, while I got used to the idea that he was mine to let out in the first place.

'Come on, Jimmy,' said Charlotte. She unclasped the necklace and handed it to me. 'What on Earth's the big deal?'

'You'll never believe it,' I told her, placing her necklace on the bed and pulling the fuel receipts from my pocket. 'I've just been adding this lot up, and there's nearly two hundred quid's worth his time. That'll cover some drinks tonight, don't you reckon?'

4) Friday

4.1) Reading Between the Lines

'Who'd be texting you at this hour?' asks Charlotte in a sleepy voice.

I'm startled, because I hadn't noticed her waking up. It isn't yet light outside, and I'd been trying to leave her undisturbed by getting dressed more or less in darkness, with only the landing light switched on and the bedroom door half open. Two minutes ago, when I'd left her tea by the bedside, Charlotte was silent and still. But not anymore, not now I'd picked this moment to carelessly check my messages.

Not that there are any messages. There are none from Isabel, and none from anyone else.

'Nobody's texting me,' I reply, sliding the phone into my pocket. 'I just hadn't checked since early last night. You and I were pretty busy after that.'

Charlotte doesn't answer, but while I resume dressing she props herself up against the headboard, pushing hair away from her face. After a few seconds she reaches for her tea.

'Careful, Charlie,' I gently tease her. 'No spilling on the sheets, you sleepyhead.'

She doesn't reply, and I begin knotting my tie. I look at her silhouette in the big mirror. 'Last day of term,' I say. 'Got much happening?'

'I'm not sure right now, other than the prize-giving.' She draws her knees up, gathering in a clump of duvet. 'I really need to wake up properly.'

Charlotte takes a sip of tea and then sets her mug back down next to the bedside clock. 'You're earlier than usual,' she says. 'Any reason for that?'

It's too dark in hear to read the expression on her face, but from the undercurrent in her tone I reckon she's looking at me closely.

'I'm collecting a customer's car,' I reply. 'Taking it in for some work.'

'You don't do that for many customers.'

I fold down my collar and finesse the knot of my tie. 'I know,' I tell her. 'I'm doing someone a favour.'

A few seconds go by – a few seconds of me failing to fill in the blanks. Charlotte eventually asks, 'Who's the someone?'

I turn away from the mirror and peer at her through the gloom. 'Mr and Mrs Petridis. Old Greek couple. Thought I'd help them out as Mrs P doesn't walk so well these days.'

Charlotte's quiet and motionless for a short while. Then she slides abruptly out of bed and pulls on a t-shirt for the short walk to the bathroom. 'You're a nice man,' she says solemnly, ruffling my hair on the way past.

The whole conversation leaves me unsettled. Minutes later, driving away in the car, I admit to myself that I've made Charlotte suspicious. Despite the darkness of the bedroom, I reckon she spotted some of my tell-tale departures from routine, such as my putting on a better suit than any I'd normally wear on a mundane Friday in December. Then, to go with it, a favourite tie – carefully knotted, too – and Charlotte may also have noticed that I'd taken extra care with my hair. That's why she ruffled it, for fuck's sake – she never normally does that. And another thing, I laid on the Petridis story much too thick. Old fucking couple, and she can hardly walk! Yeah, I've gone and put Charlotte's antenna on alert, and it's no one's bloody fault but my own.

It's nearly light by the time I reach Isabel's house. The ex-missus is bright and cheery. Again in her body warmer, but without the bobble hat, she offers me coffee and asks if I want to come in and play with Oscar. I explain that I have to get going. I tell her I don't want to be late, as the later I am the less chance there is of getting her car fixed today. She accepts the need for hurry, but can't resist asking what's in the bulky brown envelope I've taken out of the Mondeo – it looks, she says, like a big wedge of cash. I laugh, and tell her that it's paperwork I had to get a customer to sign on my way home last night. Neither of us mentions that I've once again come without her trophy, and then Isabel hands me the Juke's keys, telling me to be careful driving the thing what with it misfiring so badly. I tell her I will, and I agree her request to phone and let her know if there'll be any cost involved. I think we both know that I won't be making any such call.

As expected, the Juke coughs and splutters its way across town. It stalls twice, and both times it's an effort to get it going. By the time I arrive at work and cajole Gareth, our best mechanic, into looking at it, I'm about five minutes late for Graham's meeting. Even then, I take a couple of detours. The first is to the valet bay: I need to make sure they're underway with Reuben Fitzgerald's Verso given that he's due to collect it in less than an hour. The good news is that the Verso's getting jetted off as I walk in, and so I remind the valeters that they've gone Ann and Rob's Astra to clean afterwards. They moan at me good-naturedly for creating work, and I joke with them that they don't know what real work is.

The second detour is past my own desk, so that I can lock the envelope containing nearly thirty grand in my bottom drawer. When I finally make it to Graham's office, the door is closed and the meeting well underway. I stand outside, looking through the thin strip of window in the door. Graham's in his usual place at the head of the table, doing most of the talking. I wait until he draws breath before I knock and enter. 'Sorry I'm late,' I immediately say. 'I agreed to bring a friend's car into the workshop, and it kept cutting out on me.'

'No problem,' says Graham. Thankfully, he sounds chilled out and even-tempered. 'Grab a seat, Jimmy. There's loads of room.'

He's right – there are plenty of spaces round the big table. Carl isn't back, whereas Emma and Rudi both have the day off. That leaves Kate and Wes sitting down one side, with Marlon and Kev on the other. Wes is wearing the hang-dog expression he usually sports in the mornings, and Kate appears to have caught his mood. I look at her and smile, but the glance she sends back is hard-faced and tight-lipped. I don't whether it's a problem with me that she has, or merely one with the world at large, but I make a mental note to find out later if I get the chance. In the meantime, I sit myself down near Marlon and Kev. As usual, Kev offers me a nervous little nod of greeting. Marlon's a rude fucker in comparison, and barely glances my way.

Marlon and Kev usually sit together. Different as they are, each is the closest thing the other has to a friend at work. They both started here on the same day, a little over a year ago, when Graham took on five newbies in an effort at breathing new life into the place. But the other three newcomers are long gone by now, and I reckon Kev's days must be numbered too. Being polite and helpful – and filling in as Rudi's bitch – only go so far. Kev needs to start selling more, otherwise he'll surely be toast.

Marlon, on the other hand, is a completely different story. He does enough to get by, but no more than that. I reckon he has the skill-set needed to be a good salesman, but he's a lazy scrote who's happy just to coast along. I don't like him for that, and I don't like him for the snidey way he looks down his nose at people. Nor do I like him for his pale, puffy cheeks, or the way his eyes sit too deep in his face, but I suppose the fucker can hardly be blamed for his own genetic make up.

I've just heard Graham ask, 'Male or female?' No one else is answering him, and when I look up I realise he's looking at me.

'Sorry, boss?'

'Your friend? The one with the broken car. Male or female?'

'Oh, yeah. Female.'

'Well you could do with selling her a new car rather than getting her old one fixed.' Graham leans back and points at the board. 'We had a good day yesterday. You lost some ground.'

I take a look at the whiteboard. They sold five cars on my day off, which is impressive for a weekday at this time of year. It looks like Rudi dealt one – I guess he would, wouldn't he? – meaning he's banged in a couple since I briefly pulled level, and now he once more has a two-car lead. Kate and Marlon also chipped in with one apiece, but the best performer was Emma, who dealt two for the day. She's now joint second, alongside me.

For the first time today, Marlon acknowledges my presence. 'This could be the month,' he says, smiling thinly and rubbing his hands together.

Although the others look puzzled, I know that Marlon's talking about the bet he and I made a few weeks back. We struck it after I pointed out that Emma, who'd only been with us for two months, was already outselling him, and that he ought to feel embarrassed about his numbers compared to hers. In his defence, Marlon replied that Emma was outperforming not only him, but also more experienced operators like Carl and Kate. It was a fair point, actually, but then he went too far by predicting that she'd kick my arse pretty soon as well. I wasn't having any of that, and I bet him fifty quid that she wouldn't outsell me in any one month during the next six.

And now, because everyone wants to know what he's on about, Marlon sneeringly explains our bet, managing to avoid mentioning that it came about because his own numbers were indifferent, but instead painting me as a loud-mouthed egotist. I can't be arsed with defending myself, but Graham sticks up for me instead. He rounds on Marlon and says, 'The point you're missing, Brando, is that Jimmy was willing to back himself – unlike you, you miserable splash of puke. Anyway, don't go counting your winnings just yet. Jimmy caught up with Rudi a day or two back. He's on pretty good form right now.'

The meeting winds up soon after that. There's some small talk and banter as we file out, but I'm not paying it much attention. In fact, I'm not paying much attention to anything at all until I smell Kate's scent as she falls in at my side.

'We need to have a word,' she says.

'Sure,' I reply, thinking that she might at least give me chance to grab a coffee. I tell her that I'm handing over a car in twenty minutes, and ask if we can talk afterwards.

'Don't leave it too long,' she warns me solemnly. 'It's important stuff we need to discuss.'

I'd ask her to elaborate, but she diverts to the ladies' room. Meantime, I need to get Reuben Fitzgerald's documents from the admin department. Kate's important stuff will have to wait a little while.

4.2) Sounds Posh, is Posh, Knows his Own Mind

Having taken final payment, I print Reuben Fitzgerald's receipt and slide his Verso keys across the desk. The paperwork is finished and he's free to take the car, but he appears in no hurry to leave. Although he's dressed like a man with places to go and things to do – he's wearing another great suit, this time with an open-necked polo shirt – he hasn't rushed anything since arriving. He took his time checking the Verso, and he took his time signing the paperwork. And now, with everything done, he's happy to use up a few more minutes finishing his second cup of coffee and telling me about some of the cars he's owned in the past.

When I ask if this is the first car he's ever gifted charitably, he shakes his head a little and tells me it's the fourth.

'Then you must have been doing this for some time,' I reply. 'I thought Triple Bottom Line was a fairly new idea.'

He looks at me like I don't know the half of it. 'It depends what you mean by Triple Bottom Line,' he says. 'The idea that you try to run a successful business while doing some good for your fellow man, and being mindful of the planet – that idea isn't new. Uncommon maybe, but not new – no Jimmy, not at all. I've been doing it for years, as have a few others. What's relatively new is combining all three into a coherent philosophy, and giving the philosophy a name, whether that name is Triple Bottom Line or something else.'

He finishes his coffee, but still he doesn't look desperate to leave, and so I ask, 'What makes you do it? Run a business like that, I mean. Is it that you want to be successful, or is it that you want to give away money and do good for others?'

'That's just the whole point,' he replies. 'The two aren't mutually exclusive. I want to do both.'

I daresay this is ground he's covered before – many times, I reckon – but he doesn't seem tired of explaining as he continues. 'I suppose, for me, a big part of it is about empowerment. We make our money and we pay our taxes. But if we bother to think about society, and how our government spends those taxes, it can drive us to distraction. Governments waste pots of money on lousy people and lousy ideas, while letting good people and good ideas go to waste. When I put money into people and projects of my choosing, I'm taking some control over my contribution to the world.'

'I see what you mean,' I say slowly. 'I hadn't thought of it exactly like that.'

He shoots me an appraising look and says, 'Jimmy, what makes you ask?'

'Honestly? Well, since you first mentioned Triple Bottom Line I've been thinking of doing something similar myself.'

'Be careful,' he says, quick as a flash. 'To start any business, a conventional one or one like mine, you have to genuinely want it.'

'Yes, I know,' I tell him.

'But do you though? Lots of people say, "Yes, I know." Lots of people say they want their own business. But most of them don't. Not really.'

I drain my cup and ask, 'How do you mean?'

Reuben Fitzgerald looks up at the ceiling, as if gathering his thoughts. Meanwhile, I notice that a punter has walked in. The bloke is big and round and bearded, and he's wearing only shorts and a t-shirt – which is nutty behaviour in December, even though this is a warmer day than many we've had. I watch as he walks round the racy blue Sirocco parked by Rudi's desk, examining the car's paintwork while pointedly ignoring Marlon, who's following in his wake and trying to make conversation. Marlon won't stick this for long. Faced with an awkward punter, he's likely to leave the bloke alone and fuck off back to his desk.

'There's a problem with us lot,' says Reuben Fitzgerald.

'Us lot?' I ask.

'The human race. There's a problem with us all.' He pauses and looks up again, his face thoughtful, as if he's picking his words with very great care. Finally he continues, 'The problem is that we often want things we haven't got or aren't supposed to have. And so we go out and get them, sometimes moving mountains along the way, only to find that once we've got that forbidden something we don't actually want it any more.'

'Meaning we don't know our own minds?'

'Maybe. Certainly, we don't know our own desires.' He lets out a little sigh and glances at his watch. 'Lots of people look at me, and at other entrepreneurs, and think that our life is the life for them. But then, if they choose to actually become an entrepreneur, they soon realise it's not for them at all.'

Having seen him check the time, I say, 'Sorry – I must be keeping you.'

'No, it's okay. I've got a little while.'

'So what you mean,' I press on, 'is that people don't see the hard work you have to put into a business. The blood, sweat and tears.'

'Well, I do mean that. But I mean more than that as well. Setting aside all the hard work, it's also this human thing of wanting something because you haven't got it got it, but then not wanting it once you have. How often do you see kids nagging their parents to get them something – a particular toy, maybe – because their friend has got one and they haven't. Yet then, once mummy and daddy give in and buy the toy, it hardly gets played with.'

I smile at the picture he's painted, but I ask, 'Don't we grow out of that, though?'

He laughs hollowly and says, 'I'm not sure we do. Take my partner, Keith, for example. He's no youngster; he's forty-two – I'd say that's old enough to have some self awareness. For years he's complained that we couldn't legally marry each other. Now that we can, do you think he'll walk down the aisle with me? "We're happy as we are, Reuben." That's what he says.'

'Tell me to mind my own business,' I ask, 'but are you? Happy as you are, that is?'

'Oh, I think so.' Again that hollow laugh. 'We make each other happy – mostly anyway.' He checks his watch again and picks up the Verso keys. 'I was only using Keith to make my point: my point being that we often want what we can't have only until such time as we can. That's when we find out we don't want it anymore. So before you make any life-changing decisions, Jimmy, make absolutely sure that you really, genuinely want to do the thing you're thinking of doing.'

What he says rings true. I think back to when I stopped smoking – to the days when I craved a cigarette not so much because I really wanted one, but simply because I knew I wasn't allowed them any more. We want we can't have. But if I'd actually lit a cigarette back then I'd probably have hated the fucking thing.

'Listen,' I say, reaching for my wallet, 'I know it's only a small gesture after you've bought the car, but let me get your charity a tank of fuel. No,' I add, as he begins to protest, 'I'd really like to do this. You've given me some good advice, and it's my way of saying thank you.'

Reuben Fitzgerald smiles at me. It's a big, gracious, winning smile. 'Have I changed your mind, then, about starting the business?'

'No, not really,' I reply, taking three twenties from my wallet. 'But you've helped me understand why I feel the way I do about someone. And only just in time, as well.' I slide the notes across the desk. 'This is a small price to pay for that, believe you me.'

4.3) This Close to Christmas as Well

I stand at the door and wave Reuben Fitzgerald away in the Verso. Once he's out of sight, I go back inside and check with the receptionist to see if anyone's phoned for me. Nobody has, and so next I check my mobile for messages. I've had a text and a voicemail. The text is from Isabel. It says Oscar thanks me for bringing his mummy's car in, and could I please let them know if there's any news from the workshop yet. Iz has attached a cute photo of Oscar kneeling up in his pen and smiling broadly at the camera.

I close down the text and listen to the voicemail. It's from the slick, sharp bloke at the property company, asking if I've thought any more about the premises he showed me.

I haven't thought any more about the premises he showed me. Instead, I've thought loads and loads about bloody women.

Charlotte and Isabel.

Isabel and Charlotte.

I reckon Reuben Fitzgerald was spot on. I reckon the only reason I want Isabel is that she's out of my reach. If that's true, then it doesn't say much for the buzz I feel when I think about her, because the buzz would likely fade if Isabel were actually available to me. And if I'm upfront about things, it's only that buzz which lends Isabel her appeal over Charlotte.

All of which means I've got two choices. I can chase after a mirage – a fantasy, if you like – or I can act like a grown up and do with Charlotte the things Iz admitted she and Shithead never did in their relationship: namely work on the stuff that's wrong to try and make it right.

But before I can do that, I've got a working day to get through, which means there's other, more mundane stuff to bother about. For one thing, I ought to find out why Kate was offhand at the meeting, and what it is that she's so keen to talk to me about. Trouble is, she's made herself busy these past few minutes, persuading the chubby punter in the shorts and t-shirt into sitting down at her desk. Succeeding where Marlon failed, she's managed to strike a rapport with the bloke and get him answering some questions. I walk past and offer her an admiring nod of acknowledgement, but receive only a cool glance in return.

Then I go take a look in the workshop. The Juke's bonnet is up and the engine partially stripped, with the cowl and the block's top half neatly arranged on Gareth's bench. But there's no sign of Gareth himself, and because I know better than to interrupt his tea-break I don't go looking for him. Besides, I have Ann and Rob's car to hand over next, and time is short. I text Isabel, saying yes, we're on with the Juke, but there's no news yet. After that I compose a text to Charlotte, thanking her for a great night last night. After wavering a moment, I add that I love her and that I'm looking forward to coming home tonight. I press send, and then, even though Ann and Rob are due, I mooch around at the back of the workshop, phone in hand, hoping Charlotte will reply straight away.

Two minutes go by. The only incoming text is from Isabel:

Gr8. Keep me posted please. Oscar sends hugs.

I put my phone away and go check on the valeters. I need them to be finishing Ann and Rob's car around about now, but when I get to the valet bay they're only just jetting it off. It's going to be twenty minutes, they say. I tell them to make it fifteen, and to stop pissing about.

I mooch about some more. Still no reply from Charlotte, and so I head back to the showroom. Ann and Rob, like Reuben Fitzgerald earlier, are bang on time. They're already waiting at my desk, Ann's fledgling baby bump appearing to have actually grown in the past couple of days. Rob is chewing gum, and from the smell on his clothes I can tell that he's just finished a cigarette.

'I can't believe we're buying a new car,' Ann tells me. She's excited, and can hardly sit still. 'This close to Christmas as well.'

'Well that's down to you, darling,' says Rob, rolling his eyes. He sounds averagely happy, but less upbeat than his wife. 'It was you who let Jimmy talk us into it.'

Ann digs her elbow into Rob's ribs. 'It was a joint decision,' she says.

'Yeah, right,' says Rob. He spreads his arms, rolling his eyes some more.

I could point out to him that he's the one who took the bait when I began talking about discount. But he's offered me an easier target than that by turning up in a hideous Christmas jumper – it shows Santa on a sleigh pulled by three reindeer; only the reindeer actually look like greyhounds with antlers.

I say to him, 'I think you should wind your neck in when you come here wearing that thing.'

To his credit, Rob blushes, while Ann has a good laugh. 'The sweater is down to me,' she says. 'We've been to my mum's and I made him put that on before we went. She knitted it for him last Christmas, and it's been sitting in the back of the wardrobe ever since.'

'Which goes and proves my point,' says Rob. 'The women are in charge. You only have to look over there.'

Rob's talking about events across the showroom, where Kate has marshalled Wes, Marlon and Kev into moving desks and cars, and got them sliding open the big showroom doors, all in order to get the Sirocco outside, presumably so that the man in shorts can take it for a test drive. The three of them are scurrying around while Kate stands near the door, pointing and commanding and directing. She may as well be cracking a whip.

'You go, girl,' Ann murmurs. 'Show them who's boss.'

'I think they already know,' says Rob.

'Bet she sells loads of cars,' says Ann to me.

I open my mouth to tell them the truth – the truth that Kate used to sell loads of cars, but that she's gone off the boil since her affair with the boss ended and the new girl put her nose out of joint. But Ann and Rob are looking at me expectantly, and they don't want to hear any of that stuff. They're here to collect their new car, after all; plus, it's nearly Christmas and they've got a baby on the way. All is well in their world, and what they want to hear from me is that I agree with everything they say. And anyway, to look at Kate today she's clearly bang on form, which does make Ann's assessment correct.

'Kate?' I say. 'She's brilliant. Sells more cars than I can count, and taught me most of what I know.'

'Thought as much,' says Ann. She shuffles her chair a bit closer and looks at me directly. 'Now then, Jimmy, where's our Astra? I take it it's got a full tank, like we agreed.'

'It certainly has. And the valeters are just finishing up with it, so it will look beautiful too. Let me get you a coffee, and while you're drinking it I'll take a walk to the valet bay and bring your car around the front.'

As I rummage in my drawer for change Ann says, 'Give Rob the money and he can get the drinks. That way you can bring our car round sooner.'

Rob leans back in his chair and sounds smug. 'Yep – my point again,' he says. 'Jimmy gets the car. I get the coffees. Ann runs the show.'

'That's your secret, then, you two?' I slide a handful of change across the desk and turn my gaze on Ann. 'Rob knowing his place and accepting you're the boss?'

I'm only chatting – going with the flow – and I'm expecting a quick-fire answer. But Ann pauses, and she reaches for Rob's hand. 'Don't get us wrong, Jimmy,' she says. 'Yes, I am bossy, and yes, Rob has to put up with that. But, really, he isn't nearly so henpecked as he'd have you believe. All the big things – like buying a car – we talk them through as equals.'

'We do talk,' says Rob. He looks at his wife, then back at me. He sounds thoughtful when he says, 'I suppose one of the reasons we work as a couple is that we talk the arse out of everything.'

I nod, saying nothing. I think back to the long minutes they spent outside on the day we did the deal. I remember them discussing the car in private, refusing to be rushed. Talking the arse out of everything, as Rob puts it. I'm starting to think there's much to be said for talking the arse out of everything. I may find it beats sitting alone upstairs, staring at lists and spreadsheets, over-thinking stuff and trying too hard to be clever.

'I'll get the coffees, then,' says Rob. 'If you could bring our car round, Jimmy, that would be great. I don't want to be rude, but time's getting on and we've got things to do.'

'We have,' agrees Ann, sounding excited again. 'We're both off work today, and we want to get the Christmas shopping done. Collecting our car's only the start.'

'Of course,' I reply, getting to my feet. 'I'll bring it round now.'

'That's lovely,' she says. 'We've a lot to buy. And don't think you'll get left out, Jimmy – not after all your help. We're going to get you something from Santa.'

I look at Ann as Rob lopes away to the coffee machine in the corner. 'You're way too kind,' I tell her. 'But if you buy me a jumper with mutant reindeer greyhounds, you'll be getting it straight bloody back.'

4.4) Unravelling all of Last Night's Malarkey

Despite their talk of things to do and shopping to buy, it's over half-an-hour before Ann and Rob drive away. Ann wanted a thorough talk-through of their new car's controls, and although I reckon Rob would have happily worked things out for himself, he was never going to overrule the missus on that score.

After they've gone, I drive their part-exchange – a tired and tatty old Fiat – round the back of the showroom, to the fenced-off compound where we park the ageing bangers destined for auction. Making a final check of the car, I find a forgotten CD in the player – a nineties compilation, mostly of Britpop. It can go into my desk drawer, for collection when Ann and Rob bring me my Christmas present.

Job done, I linger in the compound for a while. It's a cloudy day, and mild for December, warm enough for me to hang around out here while I make another check of my phone. This time there's some good news: Charlotte has replied to say that she too had great night, and she's sorry she was sullen this morning. She adds that, like me, she's looking forward to my getting home tonight.

I reply that I'll see her later, and that we can celebrate her breaking-up for Christmas. Then, pocketing my phone, I begin making my way back to the showroom. It's a big relief to me that everything's okay with Charlotte. It means we're in a decent place to start working on our relationship – a much better place than one where I've lost her trust. Tonight, when I get home, I need to tell her about the money. I'm going to take a cue from Ann and Rob, and bloody well talk the arse out of it.

By now I've made my way back to the forecourt outside the main entrance. I'm about to head inside when I spy a couple some way down the pitch, busying themselves around a smart little Micra. Although they're a good distance away, I can tell from her headscarf and his stooped posture that they're quite elderly. And my salesman's sixth sense says they like the look of the car. I watch as he leans to peer in through the driver's window, while she examines the Micra from a few paces away.

There isn't another salesperson in sight. And, as a rule of thumb, elderly couples are easily sold to if you treat them nicely. I can get a deal done here. I can close the gap to Rudi and reopen a lead over Emma. That would put Marlon back in his box, and his fucking predictions with him.

I take a step towards the elderly couple.

And feel a tap on my shoulder.

Wrapped up in my thoughts, I hadn't heard the click-clack of Kate's heels on the tarmac behind me. And when I turn to face her, she looks at me in the exact same pissed-off way she looked at me in this morning's meeting.

'We really need to talk,' she says.

I glance back at the elderly punters. They're still standing round the Micra. Still looking interested.

'It won't wait,' she adds.

The showroom door opens and Wes saunters out, heading the old couple's way. There's no urgency about him, but he's got the jump on me now.

I say to Kate, 'Those people might have been my only chance today.'

'Sorry James, but that's too bad. This is serious stuff we need to discuss.'

I shrug and ask, 'Okay, so what's up?'

'Why don't you tell me?'

'Because I don't bloody know. You're the one with the "serious stuff" to talk about.'

Kate rests her hands on her hips and tilts her head to one side. 'Seriously?' she asks. 'You really don't know what the problem might be?'

I ought to reply that no, I don't, and then ask her to get to the fucking point. But actually, I reckon I've worked out what's rattled Kate's cage. Thinking back to the days and weeks after Isabel left, when it was Kate's shoulder that I cried on all the time, I would have told her about Shithead Lee buying Isabel the Juke. And then, just this morning, Kate must have seen me driving the Juke into work. That was minutes before I came to the meeting and told everyone it was a friend's car. A female friend's car.

'Come on, Kate,' I say. 'It's not like I'm dating her again. We're not having sex. I've brought her car in for repair, that's all.'

But Kate looks nonplussed at that. She takes a step back and asks, 'James, what are you on about, exactly? Tell me, because I've got no idea.'

Fuck's sake – this is all going wrong. To avoid Kate's stare, I look across the pitch to where Wes is chatting to the elderly couple. I think, *Wes, take your hands out your fucking pockets.* He looks slovenly, and things like that will matter to punters like them.

'Oh, hang on,' says Kate. 'I've got it, now. I can't believe you sometimes. You're talking about bloody Isabel, aren't you?'

'Forget Isabel,' I tell her. 'I had the wrong end of the stick, that's all. Tell me what it is that –'

'Bloody Isabel,' she repeats. 'That cow. It's her car you've brought in for repair, isn't it?'

'Look Kate, I'll answer questions about Isabel some other time. Do you want to tell me what it is that you're so keen to talk about?'

'Do you want to tell me about Mr and Mrs Petridis?'

Her reply stops me short, and the surprise must show on my face.

'Yeah, that's right,' she says. 'Whatever you were trying to pull – well, you haven't got away with it, mate.'

I look around to make sure we're not being overheard. 'Kate,' I say slowly, 'please tell me exactly what's happened.'

Kate also looks around. She steps in closer. When she replies, her voice is hushed but seething. 'Exactly what's happened is that Mr Petridis phoned this morning, wanting to thank Graham for his prize draw winnings. Luckily for you, Graham was getting coffee and I took the call. When I told Mr Petridis that there must be some mistake – that we didn't do prize draws – he said no, there was no mistake, because that nice young man Jimmy had delivered the money himself. And five-hundred pounds was so generous of us, thank you very much. Well, all I could think to do was thank him for calling, and tell him that I'd pass the message on, and... and... James, if you don't stop smirking I'm going to fucking swing for you.'

'I'm sorry Kate, but it's actually funny. And not nearly as bad as you probably think.'

'Yeah?' She narrows her eyes. 'Well, you'll have to explain yourself before I'll bloody-well believe you. Even then, I'm not so sure.'

'Alright,' I reply. 'I will explain myself. First off, let me tell you what I reckon you're thinking. You reckon I've made a massive cock-up – one that I daren't tell anyone about – and that I've taken five-hundred quid to a customer's house to try and make amends. You're worried that I'm stirring up trouble, not just for myself, but for Graham and the firm. You want to know what the trouble is.'

Kate shrugs and tosses her hair. 'Okay,' she says. 'Something a bit like that.'

'Well, the truth's very different. And weirder. I haven't done a thing wrong, and last night I didn't need to make amends to anyone. It's just that Mr and Mrs Petridis live near Carl, and I wanted to give Carl some money, to try and help him with his problems. But I wanted to do it anonymously, so he didn't know it had come from me.'

I pause to see how Kate reacts. But she stays silent and her face is just a mask. Pushing on, I say, 'Anyway, before I could actually deliver the money, I bumped into Carl in the street – pissed out of his brains, by the way, for all his supposed poverty. To explain why I was there, I told Carl I'd come to get Mr Petridis to sign some paperwork. Then, to make the story really seem plausible, I had to knock the Petridis' door, and when the old boy answered I needed to offer him a good reason about why I was there, standing on his doorstep. I didn't actually have any forms that I could ask him to sign, but I did have quite a lot of money.'

This time I wait for a reaction. Kate looks at me for a long moment, then turns her back and walks a step away. 'Seriously?' she asks, turning back around. 'That's really why you handed over five hundred quid to the Petridis? It was supposedly for Carl, but you didn't want him to know that actually it came from you?'

'Exactly. And once I started making stuff up, everything just got away from me. I've never been much of a liar – I think you know that.'

'I'd say you're a brilliant liar, based on all of that,' she tells me. 'But you're also a bloody idiot. I can't believe you were going to give Carl all of that money.'

'Well, it was your fault, Missus. You and your sob stories about his wife and kid. Different story if it's just Carl – he can go fuck himself.' Kate nearly smiles at that, and then I add, 'Look, though, I am sorry. I can imagine what you thought when Mr Petridis phoned in.'

She looks away, down the pitch, and shakes her head a little. 'I'm sorry I jumped to conclusions. You are a bloody idiot, James Harris, but you're a nice man too. I should have known better.'

'Fault on both sides,' I tell her, remembering Isabel's choice of phrase from yesterday. 'No harm done, Kate – let's just forget about it.'

'No, James – I don't think so. Let's not just forget five hundred quid. Will you let me get it back for you?'

'How do you mean?'

'I could go and see the Petridis. Tell them it was a mistake.'

I have a laugh at that. 'Best if you don't,' I tell her. 'They might phone Graham again, this time to complain. I don't want to explain all of this to him.'

'But it's five-hundred quid. Bloody hell. You're really just going to wave it goodbye?'

'Looks like I already have.'

We lapse into silence while Wes walks up from the pitch with the elderly couple. Like Reuben Fitzgerald earlier, the old boy's rabbiting on about cars he's owned in the past, whereas his wife is telling him to "pipe down because the young man isn't interested." Wes just smiles and nods, and shepherds the two of them through the showroom door. It looks like his hands-in-pockets thing hasn't done too much harm to his chances of a deal.

When they're all inside Kate asks, 'Okay, will you let me give you half the money?'

'Of course I won't. It was my idea to try and help Carl, and everything that happened was down to me.'

'Well, what about I let you have the deal I've just done – the Sirocco to that fat bloke who came in dressed for the beach. It won't earn you very much by itself, but you'll be one deal closer to December's top-spot.'

I shake my head at her. 'Even if I agreed to the idea, I know Graham wouldn't. Look, what's done is done. I can live with the loss, so why don't you buy me a coffee and let's just forget all of this.'

Kate gives me a long look through narrowed eyes. She's telepathic, like Rudi, and she'll know there has to be a reason why I'm relaxed about losing all that cash – something I'm not telling her and which she'll try to figure out. But then, when I'm shaping up to handle a tricky question about money, she wrong-foots me with a change of tack.

'And Isabel? Come on, James. What the fuck? After everything that happened before...'

'Alright,' I admit. 'I phoned Isabel because I thought we might get back together. But that won't be happening now – I was having a wobbly moment, that's all. It means I'm left getting her car fixed for her, but that's the bloody end of it.'

'You're sure about that?'

'I'm sure.'

'Because phoning her again was one hell of a wobbly moment.'

'I know.'

'And writing off a big wedge of cash like you just have – I'd say that's a wobbly moment too.'

'Alright, it is. But like I said, it's done. What you want me to do about it?'

'Start, James, by telling me what's going on – why you're being so weird.'

'I'm not sure I can, you know.' I turn away from her, and begin the short walk to the showroom. Kate falls in step, keeping quiet and biding her time. We're nearly at the door when I come to a halt, my mind suddenly made up about something. 'Alright Kate, there's something I'm going to tell you – something about that five-hundred quid.'

I'm looking dead ahead, at our reflections in she showroom door. Kate is looking at me. We're both as still as statues.

'Alright,' says Kate. 'What about the five-hundred quid?'

I turn to look at her, realising I've reached a point of no return. 'Well, for starters,' I say, 'it wasn't just five-hundred that I took round to Carl's house. If I'm honest, I was going to give him quite a bit more than that.'

'Really?' she asks quietly. 'How much is quite a bit?'

I take a deep breath. 'A lot,' I tell her. 'An absolute fuck-load of cash. North of twenty grand, since you happen to ask.'

4.5) Just Try to Love the Woman

It's almost as if Wes is trying to disprove my theory that elderly people are easily sold to. He's having a right bloody struggle to get a deal done. More than twenty minutes have passed since he and his punters came back from test drive, and so far there's no sign of business getting concluded. It's not that he's rushed things – all told I reckon he's spent over an hour with the elderly couple. There were five minutes spent chatting on the pitch, ten more at his desk, twenty appraising their part exchange, followed by another twenty on the test drive. And since they all got back, he's spent twenty minutes more presenting three consecutive offers, all without getting closing the sale.

Sitting at my desk, Kate and I can't hear exactly what's being said, but we've got the general gist of it all. We've seen this happen before, many times and to many salespeople, but to rookies especially. The elderly couple will have objected to Wes's first offer because it contained too many optional extras such as extended warranties and tyre insurance. Wes will then have returned to

Graham for a revised offer – one with all the extras taken out – only to be hit with a further objection the minute he presented it. This new objection will most likely have centred on Graham's valuation of the couple's part exchange, and upon hearing it Wes will have scuttled back to the office for yet another set of figures – this one featuring a higher bid for his punters' current car.

Wes is now having to sit and listen while the pair of them reject his third offer. It's the bloke who's doing most of the talking, while his wife – still in her headscarf – is the more physically animated. She keeps pointing at the computer screen and then shaking her head – shaking it so hard I'm surprised it's still on her shoulders. Either they're still not getting enough for their old car, or they're expecting a monster discount off ours.

After working here for three months, Wes should be doing better than this. I'd have had it all wrapped up by now. I'd have handled things better, and more efficiently, by uncovering all of the elderly couple's objections after presenting the first offer. That way I'd have spent less time going back and forth to Graham's office, and I'd have kept tighter control of the negotiation. Rudi or Kate would have done exactly the same, and I'd expect Emma to have nailed it too. In the three months that she and Wes have been here, she's learnt the job that bit quicker and that bit better than he has. I reckon Graham won't mince words with Wes when he goes back to the office still without a deal done.

I'm about to say as much to Kate when she says, 'I still can't believe you thought about getting back with Isabel, not after she destroyed you last time. Bunging Carl several thousand quid is idiotic, even if it is only small change to you nowadays. But getting back in touch with that woman... bloody hell, James. That's double idiotic. Triple idiotic, even.'

I've spent the last hour explaining several things to Kate. Rather than explain or justify myself any further, I reply, 'Remind me where it was you learnt your diplomacy skills.'

She cuts me an acidic smile. 'Call my directness a coping mechanism. It's not everyday you find out that one of your friends has won the big one.'

'I suppose it isn't,' I reply, watching as Wes trudges into Graham's office with his head bowed.

'And anyway,' Kate continues, 'if you are going to tell me your plans, I'm going to tell you what I think of them. Thinking about it, I should charge you for consultation, shouldn't I? Now that you can afford to pay through the nose.'

'Kate, if it's money you –'

'Chill! I was joking. I don't want your money.'

'Okay, just checking. Because if you do –'

'I don't.'

'Okay, just checking.'

'So you've already said.'

'Alright.'

But she will want a cut, though. Of course she will. Carl's getting one, and I don't even like the fucker. In comparison, Kate's a proper mate, so she's bound to want her share. And, actually, that's okay, even if she won't admit to it – she is on my list for when I'm divvying up.

'But do you think I'm wrong?' she asks, after a moment's quiet. 'I know I'm being blunt with you, but seriously? Getting back with Isabel? Where the fuck was your head at?'

Meanwhile, as I reckoned, Wes has pushed Graham far enough. The boss emerges from his office looking exceptionally pissed off, and bustles his way across the showroom towards the couple at Wes's desk. But by the time he sits down and introduces himself, he's mustered a big, friendly smile, while Wes hovers behind like a sulky kid who's just had a bollocking – which, in truth, he probably has. This is something else Kate and I have seen before: Graham stepping in when a rookie's gotten himself deadlocked with a punter. Whatever happens next will happen quickly. Either a deal will get done or it won't, but either way it won't take long.

'Here's the thing with Isabel,' I say to Kate, 'You know what I went through when the two of us split up. But looking back, the grief wasn't all her fault. A lot of it was mine.'

'If you say so,' Kate replies.

'And whatever you think of her, she's still an attractive woman.'

'She's a cow.' Kate shakes her head vigorously. 'I've met Isabel – what? – twice in my life, and it's as plain as day she's a cow.'

'Alright, whatever. The main thing is we won't be getting back together. I had an idea that we might, but it's not going to happen.'

'I'll be holding you to that, Jimmy.'

'You won't need to. And as for Carl, like I told you earlier, it was you who put me up to solving his problems, telling me sob stories about his kid.'

'So it's my fault you went round there with probably more money than he's earned all year?'

'In a way, yeah,' I reply. 'What you said about his kid, Sammy, got me thinking about my childhood, and about how I felt when my dad walked out on us. So when it came to Carl's kid, well... I wanted to stop someone else being unhappy like I was.'

On the other side of the showroom, it looks as though Graham has saved the day. A deal has been done: it's smiles and handshakes all round.

Kate says, 'There's only so much you can do to stop the kid being unhappy. The poor fucker's still got Carl for a dad, and not even all your cash can fix that problem.'

I start laughing. And I'm still laughing when Kate wrong-foots me again. She asks, 'Do you think your dad walking out on you and your mum is the reason you've considered leaving Charlotte?'

'What?' I reply. 'No way. Bloody well of course not. What makes you ask a question like that?'

'There's a line of thought which says we justify the behaviour of our parents by trying to repeat it. Your dad walked out on you all, and so – without realising it – you're looking to validate his behaviour by doing what he did.'

'Kate, that's just mad.'

'It's behavioural science.'

'It's bollocks. I can promise you that I'm not trying to justify the way my dad behaved.'

'Not deliberately, James. I said you could be doing it without realising why. You could be validating him subconsciously.'

'No way,' I tell her, sitting back and crossing my arms. 'Not consciously, and not subconsciously. There's no way I'd do anything to back up what he did.'

Wes walks past my desk. Graham will have told him to get the chip-and-pin machine so he can take a deposit from the elderly couple. Kate smiles at him and says well done. He smiles back and says the deal was hard work. I could tell him he made it harder work than needs be, but I let it go this time.

Once Wes is out of earshot, I say to Kate, 'Anyway, I haven't said I'm leaving Charlotte. Most likely I won't. All I said was I'd thought about it, and that there are things I need to be sure about before I decide to stay.'

'That's your trouble, James, needing to be sure about things.'

'And what do you mean by that?'

Kate looks across to the reception desk, where Wes is collecting the chip-and-pin machine and the receipt book. 'Alright,' she says, 'do you remember when you were like Wes? When you struggled to sell enough cars?'

'Of course I do. I don't need reminding.'

'Well Wes struggles in a different way to how you used to. Sometimes, he simply doesn't know what to do, although to be fair he's still better than poor bloody Kevin. But you were different to the pair of them– after you'd been here a few weeks you usually knew what to do, but didn't always know when to do it.'

'Okay,' I reply. 'I sort of know what you mean.'

'Of course you know. You're the sort of bloke to remember these things. You can remember what used to happen when you were a rookie. We'd be moving cars around the pitch and a punter would walk on. The rest of us would fight each other to speak to them first, but you didn't want to talk to customers until you'd finished moving cars.'

I smile at the memory. 'It was the perfectionist in me. I didn't want to leave the pitch looking untidy.'

'Exactly. And these days you still don't like an untidy pitch. But you've learnt what's really important – that punters take priority. You'll drop everything to sell someone a car.'

'True.'

'Well then, here's my point.' Kate shuffles her chair closer and gives me a serious look. 'You have to get the perfectionist out of your private life as well. Right now you've got a whole load of money you can go and enjoy, but you're waiting to make sure everything is just so before you dare go and be happy.'

'Hang on,' I say. 'You're not being fair.'

'Bollocks I'm not. I'm dead right and you know it.'

I'm still trying to think of a reply when Kate adds, 'I can't say you'll be with Charlotte forever, but you can't say that you won't, and there isn't a formula you can use to work it all out. So just try to love the woman. Go and get on with it, James Harris. Try to live the life you want rather than worrying whether it will last.'

Part of me wants to argue, but I know she's got a point. And I'm certainly not short of advice today, one way or another. Reuben Fitzgerald; Ann and Rob; and now Kate. It's as though they're queuing up to offer me guidance, all of it pointing to one course of action, namely that I should stay with Charlotte and start working on our relationship. And perhaps this three-pronged intervention is the real payback for my choosing to help out Carl. Maybe my big karmic reward isn't, after all, the chance to get back with Isabel, but the insight to realise I'm already blessed to have Charlie.

'I should confide in you more often,' I tell Kate. 'And maybe you were right earlier – maybe you should charge for consultation.'

She sits back with a smug little look on her face, and takes a glance around the showroom. She swaps playful smiles with Wes, who by now is writing the elderly couple a receipt. 'You can buy me a drink at Christmas,' she says. 'Maybe even two.'

'I can only do that if you'll come to the pub with us.'

'Which I will,' she replies. 'Don't worry about that.'

'Even if Emma's there?'

'Even if she is. I don't have to talk to her, do I?'

'You don't have to, no. But look, what is it with you two?'

Kate makes a stack of the four plastic coffee cups we've emptied over the past hour, and then sweeps her hand across the desk, brushing away some crumbs left over from the customer-only biscuits we snaffled from reception. 'Nothing you need to know,' is all she replies.

'I know I don't need to know. I happen to care, that's all.'

'And I appreciate it that you care. Really, I do. But we're fixing your life this afternoon, not mine.'

I decide to press on anyway. 'Does your life need fixing, Kate?'

'Don't go there,' she says, smiling thinly. 'Not this afternoon. Not anytime soon. Go and sort yourself out first. And make it quick, James, for your own sake. Sort yourself out before you waste away wondering what to do with all your money.'

4.6) Anyone for Tennis in the Dark

Gareth has done a great job fixing Isabel's Juke. It's purring this evening, keen to surge ahead when it can, happy to idle placidly when the traffic's heavy. With its engine running well, the Juke's a pleasure to drive. More than a pleasure, actually: it feels alive in my hands, as if it actually wants to be out and about, ducking and diving on these dark and wintery roads.

But really that's all bollocks. We mechanics aren't supposed to talk about cars as if they're alive. We know they don't have desires, and that they aren't subject to changes of mood. We're aware that, just like bricks and shirts and toasters, they're not living, breathing things. The truth is that cars are metal and plastic; they're combustion cycles and the laws of physics. And yet the rational part of me, the part of me that knows these realities, feels overruled tonight by some deeper, roguish version of myself – a version I imagine speaking to me in a Celtic lilt when it takes me one side and whispers, *Sure Jimmy, cars do have souls, and the Juke's right now is full of joy.*

Soulful or soulless, the Juke has an errand to run before going home to Isabel. Carl won't associate this car with me if he sees it parked up near his house, and so I'm using it to finally deliver his money. There are fewer spaces in Carl's street than there were last night, but there is one bang opposite his front door, and as I reverse into it I remember that summer night when there was one space outside the off licence, and once again I find myself wondering about divine guidance and destiny. The Juke's interior lights flicker briefly on when I kill the engine, and for a moment I can't see anything outside the confines of the car. But once the cabin dims, I take a good look up and down the street. I'm as sure I can be that there's no one around.

There are lights burning in Carl's house – in the front room and upstairs – but the hallway is dark. I take a deep breath to steady my nerves, but already this feels easier than it did last night. My wealth won't be a secret for much longer, and once Carl knows I'm rich he'll surely figure out where his money came from. But I'd prefer not to meet him tonight, and that's because I don't want to be explaining matters just yet – certainly not in the street outside his house. Therefore, like yesterday, I'm trying to do this without getting spotted. I remind myself that it's an easy job, and that there are only four things I need to do: one, jog up to the front door; two, push the package through the slot; three, jog back to the Juke; four, get the fuck out of Dodge.

I take a final look around, twisting about in my seat to make sure the street is deserted.

Then I get going.

I climb out of the Juke, closing the door as quietly as I can, and then I run light-footed up Carl's drive, past the sporty Focus Graham should have had off him, and around a large ornamental plant pot at the top of the drive. All the while I'm expecting the hall lights to come on and the front door to open. But the hallway stays dark and the door stays closed, and soon I'm standing on the front step.

It's an old house with an old front door, featuring an old letterbox set at waist height, just below a panel of frosted glass. The letterbox has a metal flap that requires pulling outwards before I can push the package through. Shouldn't be a problem – it looks big enough.

I pull on the flap. It opens half-way, but no further. I try to push the package through, but it's too thick for the limited opening. And so I put down the envelope and try to force the flap open further.

There's nothing doing.

I can hear a TV on in the lounge – one they must have borrowed or scrounged, or somehow kept back from the bailiffs in the first place – but there are no other signs of life. I look around, to see if anyone's watching me from the street, and I'm relieved to see that the coast is still clear. I give one final heave on the letterbox flap, but it's jammed fast, and now I can't even close the fucking thing.

I could just leave the money on the doorstep, in the expectation that Carl or his wife will find it sooner or later. But then again, it could get picked up by some teenager posting flyers for the local pizza outfit – he'd have a great fucking Christmas after that, no doubt about it.

Or, another idea, I could leave the money on the step, ring the doorbell and do a runner. I might get spotted, but –

Suddenly, I hear movement – scampering footsteps from round the side of the house. Leaving the envelope on the step, I start to retreat down the drive, narrowly avoiding tripping over the plant pot. But it's too late anyway, because I've been spotted.

By young Sammy.

At first he and I just look at each other. We're standing outside in the dark, a year or two since he came with Carl to the dealership, and I've no idea whether he recognises me or not. He's dressed in jeans and a tracksuit top, but there's no Yankees cap this time, and his hair nowadays is cut short in a mop-top – a style not in fashion but which seems to suit his cheeky-looking face. In one hand he's clutching an adult's tennis racquet; it looks way too big for the kid.

My best plan right now must be to show him the envelope on the doorstep, and tell him to take it to his mum and dad. Then, while he's on with the job, I can make myself scarce. But before I can ask him to run that errand, he chooses to open the conversation. 'Hello,' he says. 'Who are you?' He sounds wary and guarded – which is hardly surprising in his current domestic circumstances – but not completely hostile.

I say hello back, and try to think about what name to give. I can't admit to being Jimmy, because that would raise a flag with Carl, who I'm sure would twig to "James" as well. In the end I don't give a name, because Sammy gets fed up waiting for my answer.

'My dad's not in,' he says.

'Really?' I reply. 'Your dad's called Carl, isn't he?'

He eyes me suspiciously, and answers only with a nod.

'So, is your mum about?'

The kid takes a step closer, and looks at me with solemn little eyes. He holds the racquet slightly behind and off to one side, as if ready to smash me with his best groundstroke. 'My mum doesn't want to talk to any more people,' he says. 'And she doesn't want me to talk to any either.'

'That's okay.' I look around, and there's still no one watching us from either the house or the street. 'I'm going to ask you for a favour, Sammy. It is Sammy, isn't it?' When he nods in reply I ask, 'Can you do something for me?'

When he doesn't immediately answer, I take a half step closer and squat down, so that we're looking at each other on the level. 'Sammy, can you tell you mum that there's a man at the door. He isn't here to cause trouble. He's got a parcel for her.' I point at the package on the doorstep and add, 'It's there, see?'

Sammy looks from the parcel to me, and from me to the parcel. He looks unsure what to do. Little wonder, what with all that he must have been through.

'Tell you what,' I say, conjuring my salesman's big smile. 'Here's the deal. I'll leave the package on the doorstep and go back to my car. Once I've walked away, you go and get your mum. Tell her there's a parcel for her outside. Are you okay with that?'

Still he doesn't answer, and so I begin walking down the drive. I stop near the bottom and look back. He hasn't moved from his spot. He's watching me closely.

I edge into the street. 'Sammy, can you do that for me, please?'

He stands and stares a moment longer, and then, without saying anything, he nods twice before turning to run, racquet still in hand, back the way he came.

I jog back to the Juke. The interior lights come on when I open the door, and I quickly kill them manually. Then I sit there in the dark, door closed and engine off.

Less than a minute goes by before the front curtains part and a face briefly appears, looking to see if anyone's on the doorstep. Seconds later, the hall light goes on and the front door opens. Given that Carl's never brought his missus to any of the meals out we've organised at work, I find myself looking at her for the first time ever. I don't know how I'd imagined her, but it wasn't like this. She's short and slim, and pretty too, to the extent that I can see her from this range. At first she peers into the street at large, glancing warily around, but then she stares straight into the Juke – directly at me, or so it appears. I force myself to keep still, knowing it's too dark for her to be certain that there's anyone in here.

Then she's joined in the doorway by Sammy. He's turned into a chatterbox now, finding far more words for his mum than he did for me outside, and I can see him pointing at the package with his racquet. She shushes him, and then stoops to pick the envelope up, handling it gingerly at first, as though it were a bomb – which I suppose it is, of sorts. She hefts it in her hands, seeming to gauge the weight, before holding it to her ear and giving it a little shake. Sammy tugs on her arm and points with his racquet into the street, jabbering on like seven-year-olds do. She shushes him again – but not too impatiently, ruffling his hair while she's about it – before ushering him back inside. Finally, with a last, inquisitive look in my direction, she takes the package inside and closes the door on the dark.

I stick around for a minute or two, curious to see if the door reopens. When it doesn't, and when the hall light finally goes off, I fire up the Juke and get on my way.

4.7) Liking those Big Lattes Sweet

I'm actually pretty nervous for five minutes after leaving Carl's house. I find that I keep checking the Juke's mirrors, half expecting to be pulled over by the cops and asked to explain why I've dumped the thick end of thirty thousand quid on someone's doorstep. Good job I'm not a fucking robber, that's all I can say – I can't imagine how anxious I'd feel if I'd actually stolen the thirty grand and were trying to get away with it.

But my nerves start to settle once I've driven a couple of miles without seeing blue lights, and that's when I realise I'm in a happy, upbeat kind of mood. I've been generous, after all – generous in a way most people can't afford – and I'm feeling not just good, but powerful too. Truth be told, I feel like some sort of god, and I appreciate needing to be careful of feelings like that one – it's the kind of delusion that could end up on a list of pitfalls put together by some future lottery winner.

For now, though, I decide to indulge that feeling of ultimate power. I try, for a few minutes, to see if I really can play god. And when I do, I look at things like this: Carl has financial problems and Isabel has financial problems. Carl has had twenty-nine-and-a-half thousand pounds from me, while Isabel's had the cost of a car repair. And because I like Isabel more than I like Carl, there's an imbalance there that I really should do something about. Although I've decided to stay with Charlotte – and try to fix the things that are wonky between us – there's no reason not to keep in touch with Isabel, especially when there's plenty I could do to give her and Oscar a helping hand. Just for starters, I could swap her Juke for a car that's less expensive to run. Then I could help with her out with her housing costs – that way she can stay independent and avoid having to live with her parents. And if she really wants to go back to cutting hair, I could actually set her up in a salon of her own.

By the time I swing the Juke onto Isabel's driveway, my mind is bubbling over with ideas about things I can do to help her. And part of me wants to discuss them with her right now. I want to tell Isabel just how great her future looks with my help.

But then, when I really stop and think for a minute, I realise that this isn't the time for that kind of conversation. Ash has known about my money for a month or two, and Kate for a couple of hours. Charlie will find out tonight, and I'll tell my mum over the weekend. But telling the people closest to me is one thing, and telling Isabel is another. We're just back on speaking terms after three years of no parley, and I reckon it's too soon to be bringing all this up. If I start offering her money right now, she's going to ask what I want in return. And after the way I came onto her yesterday, she's bound to suppose that I want is pretty obvious – frequent sex, preferably mind-blowing. Except that that's not what I want from Isabel any more, and I need to think carefully about how I'm going to tell her as much. Plus, there's the matter of what I want instead, which is, quite simply, to keep feeling as good about myself as I do right now – and I don't know how to explain that one without sounding like a basket case. And so I need to plan how I'm going to tell Isabel all this stuff. It's going to make for a complicated conversation.

And anyway, there are other, simpler reasons not to get into this tonight: it's getting late, and I happen to be knackered. Also, I really want to head home to Charlotte. I want to tell her about the money and then do what Kate told me to do, namely just try to love the woman.

I lock the Juke and walk up Isabel's driveway. I'm not sure from yesterday whether the bell works or not, and so I give the door a good knock – rata-tat-tat. A few seconds go by, and I'm about to knock again when I hear footsteps hurrying down the stairs. Then the hallway light comes on, the door swings open and there's Isabel, barefoot in a short, white, fleecy dressing gown, her hair damp and slick and shiny. 'Sorry,' she says, smiling. 'I was just drying my hair.' Then she looks over my shoulder, to where her car is sitting on the driveway. It may be dark out there, but it's easy to see that the Juke is looking buffed. 'Jimmy, you're special' she says, her smile widening. 'You've even had it washed.'

'And polished, ma'am.' I casually salute, at the same time trying to stop my eyes wandering where they shouldn't. Isabel's dressing gown is short enough to show off her legs, while higher up it's open just sufficiently to draw a man's gaze. 'You look great, Iz,' I tell her. 'Not very mummy shaped from where I'm standing.'

'Thanks,' she replies brightly. 'Come on in and I'll make you coffee.'

I'm about to say that I need to get off, but she's turned tail and slipped away towards the kitchen. Closing the door behind me, I head after her, noticing that the stack of cardboard boxes has grown since yesterday. Also, it's warmer in here now than then. Yes, it's been a milder day, but the heating's on as well.

'Been busy packing?' I ask, spotting that the Gaggia coffee machine still remains unboxed. It's actually plugged in and powered up, and has enough flashing lights to rival some pop concerts I've been to.

'I've been packing most of the day,' says Isabel. 'I didn't realise I owned so much stuff.' She waves me to the bench seat of a glass-topped breakfast bar, and then turns her attention to fixing me a coffee. 'Mum and dad's place won't be big enough for everything I've got.'

'I certainly realised you owned so much stuff,' I reply. 'It may have been three years, but I remember you're the world champion of stuff ownership.'

She smirks at me while getting milk from the fridge. Then, after a moment or two busying herself with the Gaggia, she asks, 'Was it the injector?'

'Say again?'

'My car. Was it a faulty injector, like the other garage said?'

'Oh yeah, it was. All fixed now.'

'That's really great. Thanks, Jimmy.'

I watch Isabel making coffee. She concentrates hard when grinding beans and steaming milk, which tells me she isn't used to working the Gaggia's controls. She's getting it right, though, or so I reckon – I can see the illuminated gauges from here, and she looks to be getting the correct pressure through the grinds. Trouble is, I'm finding it hard not to stare at her legs; so to take my mind somewhere non-horny, I say, 'I was thinking about what you said yesterday – about getting Oscar a Christmas present.'

She pours steamed milk into a large mug and says, 'He'd love one – I'm sure he would. But he's too young to understand it all, so don't feel you have to, Jimmy. Especially since you just got my car fixed for me.'

'Didn't cost me anything. Like I told you, a mechanic owed me a favour.'

'If you say so,' she murmurs, while adding fresh espresso to the milk. 'Still no sugar, by the way?'

'Still no sugar, thanks, Iz.'

'Not even in real coffee? You started drinking big lattes extra sweet. I remember that guy you work with – Rudi? – he got you into it.'

'Rudi still drinks them. And he hasn't put on weight.' I suddenly remember that I like the syrupy taste of sugar in a latte. 'Tell you what, then. Maybe just a spoonful. Maybe I deserve a treat.'

'Maybe you do.'

Isabel adds sugar, then gives the coffee a stir and sets it down in front of me. I ask her, 'Aren't you having one? Shame to fire up the Gaggia for a single latte.'

She casts me the same bashful smile as yesterday, and then tightens the belt of her dressing gown. 'I'm going to have a proper drink,' she replies, taking a bottle of Jack Daniels from a cupboard near the oven. 'I don't drink a lot these days, but it's Friday night and nearly Christmas.'

'And you've got your car back. I think that calls for a JD.'

She reaches down a tumbler, pours a good slug of bourbon, and mixes it with Coke from a can which she finds in the fridge. Then, after adding some ice, she reaches for a second glass. 'Have one with me?' she asks quietly.

Isabel doesn't set the second glass down. Instead, she hovers it at shoulder height, inches from its place on the shelf, as if to say that this is my choice and she can soon put it back if I don't want to join her. But although I should be getting home, there's a look in her eye which says she'd really like me to stay for a drink. I reckon she won't have had much adult company lately, and I don't want to look like I'm being mean. What the hell – I'm already late anyway, so a quick JD can hardly do any harm.

'Alright,' I tell her. 'But a small one, please. And we should take them to the lounge, shouldn't we?'

'Why's that?' she asks, pouring a measure far too generous to be anyone's idea of small.

'To check up on Oscar. Based on yesterday's performance, he could have torn up the room by now.'

She cuts me the bashful smile again. 'I wondered if you'd think of that,' she says, bringing over the drinks and sitting down next to me on the long bench seat. 'Here, I'll let you add your own Coke.'

I mix my JD with all the coke left in the can. Latte with sugar; JD with coke. I'm going to be wired on sucrose and caffeine.

'Anyway,' she adds, 'my big boy isn't home. So the lounge is safe for now.'

'Oscar's not here? How's that, then?'

'My mum's looking after him for a few hours.' She lifts her tumbler and swirls the contents gently. I remember that Isabel likes the chinking sound of ice against glass.

Then she adds, 'I've asked Mum and Dad to have him because I've got a date tonight.'

Having just picked up my latte, I put the mug down again without taking a sip. 'That's great, Iz. I'm pleased for you. Anyone I know?'

She doesn't answer. She sips her JD and looks at me out of the corner of an eye.

I say, 'You don't need to be sitting here for the sake of being polite. Why don't you finish getting ready?'

Isabel swivels towards me. She gives me one of her full-on, laser-eyed looks. Suddenly, the bashfulness has gone. 'Jimmy,' she says, 'don't be so thick. And please don't make this harder than it already is. You're my bloody date.'

'Me? I... '

'Seriously, did I get you all wrong?' She eases closer, smelling clean and fresh and sexy, and reaches out to put a hand on my leg. 'Did I really misread you? I thought this was what you wanted.'

I should leave at this point. Of course, I should show some diplomacy and tact – and somehow be a gentleman about the whole bloody thing – but I seriously ought to get gone through the door. Trouble is, my ex looks gorgeous and I've got a top-ranking hard on. Instead of getting up and getting gone, I find myself cupping her face.

'Isabel,' I ask, 'what's brought all this about?'

'You did, Jimmy. You brought this about – coming round here, being sexy, being funny, being kind.' She moves her lips closer to mine and asks, 'What the fuck did you suppose was going to happen?'

'So this is down to me?'

'Oh, yeah. Absolutely it is.'

Then we kiss, softly at first, before I feel her tongue pushing harder. I respond in kind and she breaks off, just once and just briefly, and looks at me with something close to disapproval. 'Just remember,' she says, 'that this is totally your fault, Jimmy. Make sure you remember that. Remember you brought all this on yourself.'

5) Saturday

5.1) Sometimes, Life can be Seriously Hard

I'm at home, sitting in the kitchen and pushing cereal round a bowl when the text message finally arrives. For ten minutes I've only toyed with my breakfast, not so much eating it as moving it with a spoon, all the while waiting for Isabel's text to come in. Waiting, that is, with a big fucking sense of dread. Now the text is finally here.

I reckon there are corpses with healthier appetites than mine right now. I move the bowl aside to reach for my phone, already having a pretty good idea how the text will read. Isabel will be asking questions and wanting answers. She'll want to know when she can see me again, and where we go from here. She may or may not raise the matter of my leaving in an indecent hurry after we'd finished shagging on her kitchen floor. Whatever questions she asks, she'll be full-on and demanding about the whole bloody business. And although I'm not ready for full-on and demanding, I will have to reply, even if it's only to stall for time.

Except that the text, as it turns out, isn't even from Isabel. It's from Ash. He tells me he needs to talk to me for ten minutes. He knows I'll be working today, but wants to know if he can drop by the showroom for a short while. Apparently, this thing my best mate wants to discuss is important. He says he wouldn't bother me otherwise.

There's nothing light-hearted or jokey in Ash's message, and that's unusual coming from him. It must be genuinely serious stuff that's on his mind. I type him a reply: *No problem. What's up mate?*

But I stop and think before pushing the send key. Suppose Ash is contacting me because Isabel has contacted him. Suppose she's requested the latest from him on the state of my relationship with Charlotte, and asked whether he thinks I'm ready to ring any changes. I don't want him texting me back about shit like that – Charlotte isn't the type to read my messages on the sly, but there's always a first time and I don't want to take a chance that she will.

And so I edit my reply to read: *Sure, mate. Come for half-nine if you can.*

If I had to guess what Ash most likely wants, then I reckon he's going to back out of joining me in the business. He said some things the other night – the gist of them being that I can afford to fail because I've got money in the bank – which made me wonder whether he was getting cold feet. And then there's the way his jaw dropped when I talked about him quitting his job as early as

January. It would be a shame if he's not coming in with me, but not the end of my world. No, the end of my world is something else. The end of my world is that once I'd decided to stay with Charlotte, I went round to Isabel's house with all my defences down and ended up fucking her like I was just out of prison.

Charlotte arrives downstairs just as I'm sending my reply to Ash. Still in her pyjamas, she's thrown a cardigan over her shoulders and pulled it tightly around her. She pauses in the kitchen doorway, leaning against the frame and eyeing me with the kind of suspicion normally owed to a man with a blacked out face and a bag marked "SWAG", caught shimmying up a drainpipe at midnight.

I say good morning and I try to smile. But I feel like a fake, and Charlotte just stands there silently, looking pale and gloomy and stressed all to fuck. Which is pretty much how I happen to feel at the minute.

I ask, 'How're you doing?'

She ignores the question, but has one of her own: 'Who were you texting?'

'It was Ash.' I pull out a chair and gesture that she should sit down next to me. 'I reckon he wanted to catch me before I left for work. He needs to come and talk to me at the showroom today.'

The chair goes begging. Charlotte doesn't move from the doorway.

I clear my throat. 'I think Ash is getting cold feet. I think he might want to pull out of the business.'

Charlotte finally sidles over and sits down on the edge of the chair. She pulls her cardigan even tighter around her. When she speaks she doesn't look at me, and her voice is flat and distant. 'Yesterday, at Ringo's, when I told you I was meeting a girl called Isabel, you reacted like a scalded cat. Why was that, Jimmy?'

'Charlie, you know why. I thought she might be my ex, and the idea of the two of you meeting up freaked me out a bit. That was all.'

'It freaked you out an awful lot. More than it ought to have. The shock was etched on your face.'

'So what do you mean by that?' I reach out and tug at her cardigan, shaking it gently until she looks me in the face. 'What are you trying to say?'

'I think you know exactly what.' Then, before I can reply, she gets up and goes to the sink, where she starts loading the dishwasher with cups and plates from last night. Except that loading isn't the right word for it – she's more or less throwing that crockery into the machine.

'No, Charlotte,' I reply. 'I don't know exactly what. And, by the way, you're going to break something in a minute. You tell me what you're talking about.'

Charlie slams the dishwasher closed. 'Jimmy, for God's sake don't be so obtuse. I'm saying you're seeing Isabel again.'

'Hey, come on, what's made you think that?' Getting up and going to her, I try to put an arm around her waist, but she twists aside and reels away from me. 'Look, if I were seeing Isabel, I'd have known if she was a member at your gym. I wouldn't have looked so shocked, would I?'

'Nevertheless,' she replies, shaking her head at me and continuing to back away.

'What do you mean, never-the-bloody-less?'

It's then that I realise I'm shouting, and that Charlotte's looking scared. I stand still, with my arms apart and my palms open. I also make an effort to lower my voice. 'Look, if I were seeing my ex-girlfriend, would I have told you to phone your gym buddy to see if they're one and the same woman? Would I have told you to keep your date with her, running the risk that she might let slip the news?'

Charlie's circled fully round the kitchen, and is now back near the table. 'And just now?' she asks. 'You were really texting Ash at eight o' clock on a Saturday morning?'

I point at my phone, which is inches from her hand, next to my bowl of barely-eaten cereal. 'Go ahead,' I tell her. 'Go ahead and take a look.'

In the end leaves the phone where it is. Instead she sinks into a seat, rests her elbows on the table and holds her head in her hands. 'God!' she sighs, running her fingers hard through her hair. When she lifts her head, she looks like she's stuck her fingers in a light socket because her hair's sticking up in short spiky clumps. Another time and place and we'd laugh about it, but humour's in short supply round here this morning.

I look at her. She looks at me. I think back to what Isabel said last night: *Just remember that this is totally your fault.*

Charlotte asks, 'So what is your problem?'

'There is no problem, Charlie.'

But she doesn't reckon that's true, and I know that it isn't. Of course there's a problem. A huge problem. A dick-ruling-the-brain problem. A problem of betrayal and guilt, and of recriminations still to come.

Things weren't supposed to pan out like this.

How things were supposed to pan out was that I'd come home last night and tell Charlotte we were rich. Then I'd tell her I still wanted to start a business – one which would make us richer still. Once we'd finished talking, I was supposed to take her to bed. And then, this morning, with both of us happier than pigs in shit, I was going to buy her a new car. I'd thought that tonight we could put up the Christmas tree and then open some champagne.

But instead I returned home in a filthy mood, so ashamed that I could hardly look at Charlie, let alone talk to her. I spent fuck-knows-how-long shut away in my den, claiming I needed to work on my business plan, but really only staring into the black night outside. Finally, I went to bed very late, undressing in the dark so that Charlotte wouldn't see the scratches on my back or the bites on my shoulder.

'Jimmy, you can't say that there isn't a problem when you're acting this way.'

I don't answer because I don't know what to say. Charlie is pissed off with me and utterly confused. And after the hurried, embarrassed, pants-up-and-go manner of my leaving her house yesterday, I reckon Isabel must be too.

'I just don't know what to make of you,' Charlotte continues, again running her fingers hard through her hair. 'Yesterday you were sending the sort of text messages I'd expect from a love-struck teenager. But then, last night, you could hardly stand my company. And now this morning, look at the state of you.'

'Meaning?'

'You look exhausted, stressed... worried sick. If I've made a wild guess about you seeing Isabel, it's because my imagination's running riot. It will do if you won't tell me what's wrong.'

I sit down next to her, avoiding her gaze and wondering how to reply. I could, I suppose, simply come out with the truth.

I mean, I could tell Charlie everything.

I could tell her all that stuff about me winning the lottery and us being rich, and how we'll get richer still by going ahead and starting the business. Then I could tell her that the happy ending has a twist – a twist called Isabel – and I could come clean about last night. Then I could do my best to tell Charlotte that it was purely a one-off, and I could beg for forgiveness.

I'd be making a clean breast of everything. And it would ease my conscience.

But I reckon it would fucking kill her.

Or at least that's what I tell myself would happen. Maybe, actually, I just don't have the guts to front up.

Either way, I revert to my default lie. 'Charlie, I'm sorry. There's nothing wrong, not seriously. I've got some issues with the business, and I've let them get on top of me.'

She looks at me coolly. 'They must be flamin' big issues to bend you this far out of shape. Come on, Jimmy, what else is wrong with you?'

'Seriously, genuinely, honestly – there isn't anything else. I'm behind with my business plan, there aren't enough hours in the day, and now I'm worried that Ash is going wobbly on me. Like I just said, I reckon he's having second thoughts.'

Charlotte lets out a shiver. Again, she pulls her cardigan tight around her midriff. I go to put an arm around her shoulders, but stop short when I remember how she turned away from me a couple of minutes back. 'How about I make you some tea?' I ask.

'Never mind tea.' She shakes her head like I'm an idiot. 'How big a problem is it if Ash walks away from the business?'

I glance through the window, at the grey dingy dawn and meagre streaks of emerging sun. If I were to tell Charlie the truth, it's that I could cope easily enough without Ash. I'd just need to employ a good mechanic, and I know a few of those.

I say, 'It's a big problem finding someone with the right level of commitment. It most likely means there'd be a delay. In think that's what's really pissed me off, Charlie. I was getting ready to rock 'n' roll, but this could put me back a month or two.'

I know my explanation sounds fucking flimsy, and the look on Charlotte's face says she knows I'm holding something back. But when she speaks, she at least sounds like someone trying to give me the benefit of the doubt. 'Sweetheart, we can't go on like this. I appreciate you've got pressures and problems, but who hasn't? If you shut yourself away without even talking to me, what chance have we ever got?'

I get up and switch on the kettle, despite her saying no to tea. I tell her, 'Charlie, I'm really, really sorry. I'll make this up to you – honestly I will.'

'Is it about money?' she asks. 'Are you sure you've got enough? This idea of buying me a car – look, it was a bit impulsive of you. Do you still want me to come to your showroom this morning? It's no problem for me to stay at home and forget about it for now.'

I turn away to get tea bags from the cupboard, and to think about her suggestion. I'm in two minds whether to agree. On the one hand, I like the idea of her not coming to look at cars, because all I want to do today is hide from the world. But on the other, I reckon I'm in for a tough day, and that hiding won't be an option anyway. Keeping Charlie as close as I can for as long as I can gives me my best chance of controlling events – I dread the idea of Isabel coming round here and talking to her while I'm out at work.

While I'm waiting for the kettle, I sit down again at the table and reach for Charlie's hand. 'Look,' I tell her, 'I absolutely promise you that I'm not short of money. I want you to keep your appointment at the showroom.'

She shivers again. Her eyes betray how doubtful and worried she is. I hate myself like a big fucking bastard for what I'm putting her through.

'Charlie, believe me, it's true. I'm fine for money. More than fine.'

(*Remember you brought all this on yourself.*)

'Alright,' she eventually says. 'I believe you about the money.' She casts a weary glance at the clock on the wall, and then another one back at me. 'So, should I still come at ten-thirty?'

'Or earlier, if you like. Ash should be gone by ten.'

'You're absolutely sure?'

'Never been surer about anything. Come for ten, and I'll start making amends to you.'

And that's one thing I know I can do: I can start making amends. But whether I can ever make enough of them... I reckon that's a different fucking story – a story I'm not sure can ever end well.

5.2) Thoughts about Getting a Porsche

After leaving for work, I nearly crash the Mondeo less than two hundred yards from the house. My near miss occurs when, with my mind all over the place, I turn right at the end of the street without noticing a Hyundai Coupe coming from my left. The driver has to brake for me, and then sounds his horn after I've pulled out ahead of him. When I look in the mirror, he's tapping his head and calling me names that aren't nice. I raise my hand in apology. I never saw him coming.

The Hyundai isn't the only thing I've been blind to. I should have reckoned on the consequences of picking up the phone to

Isabel. Sure, I had the idea that we might get back together, but I always saw it as a long shot, and I certainly didn't think we'd be shagging within thirty-six hours of my call. I never expected that, and never wanted it either. Had I decided to leave Charlotte, I wanted to be civilised about it – I didn't want to cheat on her beforehand. Not like Isabel did to me, going back three years.

Now there are consequences to deal with, and I don't know how I'm going to do that, although I do have one idea when a black Porsche Carrera pulls alongside while I'm waiting at traffic lights on the ring road. It looks mean and sculpted, and when the lights go green it powers away, covering a hundred yards before I've managed fifty. Watching it surge into the distance, I actually feel a smile forming on my lips. I could buy a Porsche like that, and then simply disappear in the thing. I could do that dead easily. I'd just need to write some short letters and some big cheques to the people who matter, and then take myself off to a new life in a different corner of the country. A new life, with whatever's left of my cash and a sexy black Porsche.

I daydream the rest of the way, and only when I'm parking up at work does Isabel's text finally come in. It's a short one. She asks: *RU32 talk?*

I think back to the aftermath of last night's adventures on the floor of her kitchen. I cringe when remembering how awkward I felt when the sex was over– how I didn't know what to say or do, or even where to look. I remember my muttered excuses and speedy departure, with my latte gone cold and my JD barely touched. I also remember the look of hurt on Isabel's face as she stood bewildered in the hallway, having thrown her robe hurriedly back on.

It isn't only Charlotte I've betrayed.

I text Isabel back: *Sorry Iz. Just starting meeting. Will speak later – okay?*

I lock the Mondeo and make my inside. Although I've arrived on time, I'm still last into the meeting, and it's crowded round the big table because everyone except Carl is in today. Graham's reading silently from a sheet in front of him, leaving the others free to chat in small groups. I try to squeeze in between Marlon and Emma, but Marlon pays me lip service when I ask him to nudge up, moving no more than a miserly couple of inches. The mood I'm in, I could easily tip him backwards from his chair and stamp on his fucking face.

Emma makes room for me by squeezing up the other way. I haven't seen her for a couple of days, and we manage a high-five as I sit down. Then I turn and stick an elbow into Marlon's unguarded ribs. 'Sorry, Brando,' I say. 'Complete accident, mate.'

'You're just a sore loser,' he replies. 'Do you want to pay me now or would you rather keep dragging this thing out?'

I feel like dragging him out. When he turns away to talk to Kev, I'm sorely tempted to throw another elbow, only harder this time. Emma leans in from the other side and says to me, 'I've been hearing about your bet.'

'Yeah,' I reply. 'The dickhead reckons you'll beat me this month.'

She looks pleased. 'How much have you had with him?'

'Fifty quid.'

'Wicked,' she says. 'I'll pay him off when I kick your ass and Rudi's. I'll have a thousand to play with.'

'No chance of that,' says Rudi to Emma, from across the table. 'You might beat Jimmy to second, but regarding first place, it's me who'll be kicking ass, not you.'

'You're bound to,' I reply, 'if you keep on fluking it like you do.'

'Says the man relying on Carl's deals, given him by Graham.'

Rudi has a point, and I could do with Emma's help in shutting him up. But Emma has suddenly zoned out of the banter, and her gaze has swung to where Kate and Wes are nattering away at the far end of the table. The two of them have their heads together, and Wes looks happier than I've ever seen him this early in the day. When Kate touches his hand, the soppy fucker's eyes light up as though someone's plugged him in.

Emma sends Kate a stare cold enough to make the sun freeze over and fall from the sky. Kate notices, and smiles cattily back. When Emma glances furiously away, Kate fires a little wink in my direction. Then she mouths a one-word question at me: *Well?* She's asking how I got on last night with Charlotte.

And somehow, I'd forgotten. During a few seconds of shit-kicking, I'd briefly forgotten the fuck-up I've made of my life. But now it all floods back, and the expression on my face must give the game away because Kate's smile turns down at the corners, and the look she now sends is one that says: *What, Jimmy? What the fuck...*

I stare back. I give a tiny shake of my head. The disappointment on Kate's face seems to grow and grow.

'Right then,' says Graham, looking up from the document he's been reading. 'I've had a right riveting email from Head Office.'

'Makes a change if it is,' says Rudi.

'Oh, it's riveting alright,' replies the boss. 'Although I didn't say smart or intelligent. I'll tell you more in a minute, but meanwhile how is everyone? We've had a good couple of days for the time of year. Are we up for selling a few today?'

A collective murmur of assent goes up, and then Graham singles a few of us out for mention: 'Emma, good week so far; Rudi, careful because she's catching you; Kevin, I don't expect very much in December, but a virgin birth looks likelier than a deal from you. You need to start showing me something, or we'll be having an awkward conversation come New Year. You catching my drift?'

Kev says he's catching Graham's drift. As ever, he blushes under scrutiny. There are two seconds of silence, during which someone could speak up for him or offer an encouraging word. But none of us says anything, which is a shame because he's a nice kid and a hard worker who'll happily do the drudge work round here. And yet here's the bottom line: Kev doesn't sell enough motors and he's way too timid, never having imposed himself in a workplace where, in the end, the timid always get found out and shown the door.

The spotlight moves quickly off Kev, though. Graham is looking at me.

'Jimmy, are you alright?' he asks.

'I'm fine, boss.'

'You sure? Because you look like you lost a pound and found a penny. And then the penny gave you fucking cancer or something.'

I feel everyone's scrutiny crank up a notch. 'I'm just a bit tired,' I announce to the room. 'I didn't sleep that well.'

'Best get an energy drink from the fridge,' says Graham. 'You need to do some deals to get back in the race. You did have Rudi worried, but I'd say Emma's the bigger threat now.'

I feel like laughing – loud and long and hysterically – at the notion that I'll feel better after an energy drink. Marlon starts to make some wise-ass remark, but Kate shuts him up and I'm grateful for that.

Thankfully, the conversation moves on. Someone changes the subject, and I step back from it all for another wallow through my guilt and misery. I think about Charlotte and I think about Isabel. What the fuck have I done? What the fuck am I going to do?

Shorty afterwards, I notice that Graham is talking again he's telling us about that email from Head Office. It's no longer enough, he complains, for the suits and bean counters to hassle him from Monday through Friday. They're now emailing him on Saturday morning to ask him how many customer appointments we've made for the weekend.

A groan goes up around the table. We'd all been enjoying the seasonal respite Graham allows us from the joyless task of cold-calling past customers and old contacts. But what with this shit from head office, it looks like the respite is over.

'I know what you're thinking,' says Graham, his hands for once raised submissively. 'And I happen to agree with you all. Cold calls this close to Christmas are a waste of fucking breath. But the jobsworths and the arse lickers at HQ – people who know as much about selling cars as I do about mending the Hadron Collider – they still want their pound of flesh.' He sighs, and shrugs his shoulders expansively. 'You know how it is – the more we give them, the more they want. Feed the machine and it only gets hungrier. So now, less than two weeks from Christmas, when every fucker is queuing for John Lewis and the Apple Store, Head Office wants to known how many appointments we've got for today and tomorrow.'

'I've got one,' says Rudi. 'It's not from cold-calling, though. It's just a bloke who was here during the week but didn't have time to test drive.'

'It's still an appointment,' says Graham, hovering his pen over the printed email. 'What's his name?'

'Collins.'

'And what time?'

'Half-ten.'

Emma says, 'I've got one too.'

'Well done. Name?'

'Padley. Half-ten as well.'

Graham writes down both names and casts a steely glance at me. 'Careful,' he says. 'You'll be falling further behind if both their appointments turn up and deal.'

'Well, we'll see,' I reply. 'I've also got an appointment, since you ask.'

'That makes three, then. The email warriors had better be happy with this. What's his name, your punter?'

'Her name. It's Hibbs. Charlotte Hibbs. You know, Charlie, my girlfriend. She fancies something newer.'

'Newer car or newer bloke?' retorts Graham. 'I hear Brando's available if you're not measuring up.'

Everyone laughs. Marlon says he doesn't want my cast-offs, and Kate tells him he should take what he can when he can, because she doubts he's spoilt for choice. More laughter follows, and then there's a knock at the door. The Saturday receptionist sticks her head round the corner and says there's a bloke here to see me.

'Another appointment?' Graham asks me.

'Only my mate, Ash. He just needs to talk to me for ten minutes, if that's okay?' When Graham nods his assent, I add, 'Tell you what, boss. Put him down as an appointment if it will make HQ happy.'

'Good idea,' says Graham, as I get up from the table. 'I'm glad you've learnt the rules of the game.'

'I know the rules, alright,' I tell him. But on my way out the door, I swap helpless looks with Kate. It's one thing knowing the rules, but they're no guarantee of playing a good game.

5.3) Fancying a Cigarette After all this Time

It's been two-and-a-half days since I sat with Ash in the Alnwick Arms and made the point to him that neither of us are kids any more. If I needed to prove that point right now I'd just take a photo of him sitting at my desk, and then wave the photo under his nose. He'd be shocked alright, because December's low, milky sun is refracting through the showroom windows at just the right angle to make his hair look even greyer than usual.

I don't know why he's gone so grey in only his early thirties. It can't be genetics, because his dad's hair is darker than his. And as for worry and stress, Ash just isn't one of life's worriers. I never used to be, either, but I've spent a lot of time worrying just lately. I think about Ash's parting words on Wednesday night – his advice to make my big decisions in my own best interests – and then I picture myself fucking Isabel on her kitchen floor. I worry about whose best interest that one was in.

There's not much point me telling Ash about Isabel right now. I could talk to him about women, football, or the decline of the Ottoman Empire, and he'd have forgotten everything within a couple of minutes. That's because he's seriously distracted this morning – his mind is away in some other place. Since I woke up, both Charlotte and Graham have told me I look awful, but my oldest mate – the one least likely to mince words with me – hasn't said a dicky bird. Which means this thing he's come to talk to me about must be weighing really heavily on his mind. Ash may not normally be among the worriers, but it looks like he's helping them out for the day.

Whatever it is he's bothered about – and I reckon it will be one of two things – he's slow and jittery about getting to the point. He sits at my desk nursing a cup of tea, making half-hearted small talk about the aggro he's having at work over some tools he's leant out and not had back. He casts nervy, skittish looks at anyone passing by my desk, especially Graham, who pushes a large, cold energy drink into my hand and blithely tells Ash he looks like he could use one himself.

With respect to Ash, I haven't got all day, and I've got problems of my own. Eventually, when he won't get to the point at my desk, I take him outside and walk him round the back of the building. Rudi and Emma are smoking there, but they're just stubbing out when we arrive, and once they've gone I look at Ash and say, 'Alright mate, what's up?'

It's not especially cold today, but he zips up his fleece and blows into cupped hands before he finally replies. 'Thing is, buddy, I've been doing some thinking.'

'And you don't want to come into business with me.'

He smiles, nervously, and asks, 'Was it that obvious?'

'Pretty much,' I tell him.

And yeah, it was pretty obvious alright. I remember how panicked he looked the other night when I said he should quit his job next month, and then, when I read his text this morning, I suppose I knew that he was getting ready to bail out. Either that, or he was finally going to ask me for some of my cash, and I'm glad he hasn't gone down that route. Although, like Kate and a few others, he'll be getting his share in due course, it's good that he hasn't come to me with his hand out.

'I'm really sorry about this,' says Ash.

On another day I'd try to change his mind. But my life's so fucked that I can't be arsed. I put an arm round his shoulders and tell him things are okay – that we're still mates. 'It will be harder without you,' I say. 'But I respect your decision.'

He looks relieved. 'You're sure it's no problem?'

'Don't get me wrong, Ash – I wish you were still involved. But you're better out than in if you're not sure it's for you.'

'You're right,' he says.

'What changed your mind?' I ask, still curious, despite the shit storm brewing in my life. 'Why this decision?'

Ash blows into his hands again, and makes a meal of rubbing them together. He answers without looking me in the eye. 'Thing is buddy, you're already rich now. The business could fail, and it wouldn't matter to you. But for me it would be a disaster.'

'The business won't fail,' I reply.

'I know, I know. I'm just saying... if it did... '

I shrug my shoulders – I can't help it that I've won the fucking lottery. I tell him, 'Fair enough, mate. I do understand.'

But I'm a bit pissed-off by his lack of faith, and Ash must see that because he tries to explain things further. 'Left to me, buddy, I'd still be in. But it's Suki who's said no. She says it's too risky.'

'Does that mean you've told Suki about my money?'

It's his turn to shrug. 'I had to. She was making plans to see family over Christmas, at the same time we're due to be away. I had to tell her about the holiday, and about how we're paying for it.'

'What about the story? The one that I won the holiday. Couldn't you have used it?'

'I could have, but I didn't. Look, buddy, does it really matter?'

'I suppose not. I just didn't want Charlotte finding out second-hand.'

'Then tell the woman.' Ash has found some safer ground, and suddenly he's on the offensive. 'Jimmy, it's your life, but people are going to have to know in the end. And when I say people, I mean Charlotte. Whether you're staying with her or not, it's high time she knew.'

'I know. I was going to tell her last night.'

'Then why didn't you? Bloody hell.'

This time it's me who avoids eye contact. 'There was just other stuff going on,' I tell him.

And now the tables are turned. I can sense Ash's disapproval when he says, 'It must be high priority, this other stuff, when it gets in the way of you giving life-changing news to the woman in your life.'

I could choose to tell him exactly what the other stuff was. I could tell him all about the madness of last night. Time was when I would have done, and without question. But something has changed in the last couple of minutes, and I feel a bit let down by the bloke. I also remember being shocked at learning that he'd bumped into Isabel in Tesco without mentioning it to me. Suddenly, I have the strong sense that although we're still mates, Ash and I aren't quite the mates that we were.

'Yeah, fair point,' I say. 'I just need to get on with it and give Charlie the news. You keep telling me that I should, and you're right about that.'

He smiles at me. It's the first time he's smiled all morning. 'You know it makes sense,' he says.

Of course it makes sense, or at least it makes sense if you happen to be Ash and you've got yourself a stable family life. But my head's all over the place, and I've got no idea – fucking none at all – what I should be doing for the best regarding Charlotte, Isabel, or any other fucker walking the earth. I look across to where Emma and Rudi were standing and smoking a moment ago. Our smoking area, which amounts to a pile of old fag ends in a sand-filled oil drum, looks filthy and disgusting, but I actually fancy a smoke right now. Although I haven't lit up in over a year, I reckon I could really use a cigarette.

I notice Ash looking at me strangely. 'Are you alright, buddy?' he asks. 'I've just realised you look fucking awful.'

'That's a popular opinion this morning,' I reply. 'And who am I to argue? One thing I can promise you, mate – money's a nice thing to have, but it's no immunity against feeling like shit.'

5.4) Okay Mate, So you Think you've got Problems?

I walk Ash to his car. We share a man hug and a handshake before he goes home to Suki. Afterwards I just mooch about for a minute, seriously minded to cadge a cigarette from Rudi. But in the end that's one temptation I manage to resist, and what helps me is the memory of how pitiful Carl looked a few nights back when he was trying to scrounge smokes in the pub. Instead, I get a clipboard from my desk and a coffee from the machine, before taking myself off to the far end of the pitch. If anyone asks what I'm up to, then I'm checking that the cars are priced correctly and have accurate point-of-sale material in their windows. In truth, I just want to be alone for a few minutes. I need some time by myself before Charlotte gets here.

Not that I made a song-and-dance about it, but Ash has pissed me off by telling Suki about my money. I gave him a perfectly good cover story to explain away the Caribbean holiday, yet he chose not to use it. If he can avoid telling his wife that he had paid-for sex with two expensive whores on the second night of his stag weekend, then I'd have thought he could keep his best mate's biggest secret under wraps for just a little while longer. Yes, I'm sorry he isn't joining the business, but I'm just as disappointed that he wouldn't tell a white lie to buy me a few short days of breathing space.

The far end of the pitch is where we keep our cheapest stock — it's where I bring my punters when they can't afford the car they really came to look at. It's also that part of our display which everyone neglects in terms of appearance and upkeep — litter and fag ends accumulate here, even on windless days like this one, and the pitch valeters are slower to pick up the debris than they would be if it turned up among the cars outside Graham's window. We salespeople are equally culpable in not only accepting the valeters' lower standards, but also letting them rub off on ourselves, with the result that the cheap-'n'-cheerful motors end up looking cheap-'n'-fucking-nasty. This morning, without even trying, I spot a middle-aged Citroen with no point-of-sale in its window, and two cars down there's a Fiesta so dirty we should never have allowed it onto the pitch because it looks like it's been cleaned by a blindfolded man using water from somebody's fishpond. I give a little sigh and take out my pen. Although I didn't really come here to work, I write down the registration numbers of the two problem cars, and make some brief notes about what needs doing with each.

It would be great if it were as easy to sort out my life. There's fat chance of that, though, because grief and heartache are coming for sure. I know I won't be able to keep the Isabel episode from Charlotte forever. I do know that I'll have to tell her the truth eventually, but I can't face doing that at the minute, not when I'm only managing half-truths for my even my oldest mates like Ash. And I'm not sure what he'll have made of my parting words when I walked him back to his car and more or less begged him to make sure Suki told no one else about the money.

'She'll keep quiet about it,' he promised. 'I've told her not to spill the beans.'

'Ash, just make sure she doesn't. Please, not for a couple of days — not while I sort things out.'

'Trust me, buddy. She won't tell Charlotte.'

'Anybody, Ash. Make sure she doesn't tell anybody.'

And that was as close as I came to telling Ash that I was worried about his gossipy missus saying something to Isabel. Frankly, I was less bothered about the chances of Suki talking to Charlotte. That's because the two of them aren't that close, only making an effort to be friends because Ash and I are mates already. But Suki and Isabel used to really get on, and I'll be in serious trouble if Suki gets hold of Iz and tells her about the money. That's because Isabel, quite naturally, will be that much harder to shake off if she finds out I'm loaded. Not that I've changed my mind about helping her and Oscar financially – it's just that after last night's shenanigans some dust has to settle first. A whole fucking world of dust, when I stop and think about it.

I finish my coffee and check my phone. Fuck – here's another text from Isabel, one she sent over half-an-hour ago and which I never heard coming in. She wanted to know whether my meeting was over and if I was free to talk. I wasn't then, and I'm still not now. That's because I can see Charlotte's old Clio pulling in to the customer car park, its dented bumper just another reminder of my capacity for fucking things up. Hurriedly, I cobble Isabel a reply: *Sorry – need an hour. Maybe two. With customers. Will call – promise I will.*

When I look up from my phone, I see Wes lurking close by. He's also got a clipboard and a pen – Graham must have got him doing what I'm pretending to do, namely check prices in car windows. But setting aside that we could pass for council inspectors, there aren't many similarities between us right now. I'm stressed and miserable, while he's got a huge big smile on his face. He comes loping over when I put away my phone.

'You alright?' I ask.

'Awesome, Jimmy.' He clenches his fist and gives the air a little punch. 'She's only said yes to me, hasn't she?'

'Nice one, Wes. I assume you're talking about Emma.'

'I am. That date I suggested – she's said she'll go out with me.'

'Well done,' I reply. 'That's great news. But I'm in a hurry, mate, so walk with me if you want to talk about it.'

I head towards the showroom with Wes bounding alongside. He's barely able to contain himself, almost as if Graham had foisted a dozen energy drinks on him and then bet he couldn't drink them in ten minutes. 'It's tonight we're going out,' Wes says, still beaming like a bloody big kid. 'After work. Don't know where yet.'

'Like I said, great news.'

I'm hardly mirroring his mania, and because of that, or maybe because he picked up on my mood at the meeting, Wes suddenly asks, 'Jimmy, are you okay? I mean really okay?'

'I'm fine,' I reply. Briefly, the two of us have to walk single file through a narrow gap between a pair of Peugeots. Once we're through, he comes back alongside and I fob him off some more. 'I'm just tired, Wes, that's all. But everything's fine, thanks.'

He nods, but doesn't exactly sound convinced. He says, 'Let me know if there's anything I can do. One good turn deserves another.'

'Yeah? What was my good turn for you, then?'

'Your advice about how to play it with Emma?' He looks at me sharply. 'You remember telling me how to handle things?'

'Do you think it was my advice, mate, or her reacting to you and Kate getting so friendly in the meeting?'

Wes slows down, but I've got Charlotte waiting and so I don't break stride. Seconds later, he's back in step with me. 'I wondered if you'd spotted that,' he says.

'Wes, it wasn't hard to notice.'

'It wouldn't be to you,' he says. 'Do you think Emma noticed as well?'

'I know she did. You and Kate may as well have taken out an advert.'

'Ahhh, shit.' Wes is suddenly back down from Cloud Nine. 'Do you think that's why Emma's agreed to go out with me?' he asks. 'To get one over on Kate?'

'You can look at it that way if you want to. That's if you want to be negative about it. Or you can choose to think that Emma fancied you – I mean, what woman wouldn't? – but that she was acting hard-to-get, and then you getting matey with Kate was just the hurry up she needed.'

We walk on in silence for a short while. Then Wes says, 'Thing is, Kate's been really friendly to me since yesterday, when both of us sold cars. And she's asked me out for a drink as well. She asked me last night, before Emma said yes.'

'And you agreed to go?'

Wes slows down again as we near the showroom entrance. This time, in spite of myself, I do too. 'Yeah,' he says. 'I agreed to go. I mean, you would, wouldn't you?'

'Maybe I would, Wes. But it's you who actually has.'

I look at anguish on his face, and nearly laugh wondering how he'd cope with women problems on the scale I've got them. Wes has gone from blissful bloke to tortured soul in the space of two minutes. 'Mate,' I ask him, 'what are you going to do about it?'

'I could go out with them both, Jimmy.' He's looking at me now like he's seeking my approval. 'I mean, after all, it's just a drink.'

Quickly, briefly, I shake my head at him. 'If you're looking for someone to sign off on that, you need to look elsewhere. I won't be endorsing your behaviour. Whoever you go out with, it will mean more than just a drink.'

I head away from him. He follows behind. I'm about to open the showroom door when he asks, 'Jimmy, what should I do?'

I turn back and lower my voice, feeling awkward about the bare-faced piece of hypocrisy I'm about to churn out. 'Go and talk to whichever one of these women you'll be letting down,' I tell him. 'I reckon I know who that is, but it's your call, obviously, Wes. The point is, go and see her as soon as you can, and let her know you've changed your mind. Say sorry, and be as nice as possible about it, but be to the point as well. Don't leave her with any lingering hopes. And Wes, get it done ASAP. Don't piss about.'

Then I open the door and motion for him to pass through. Once we're inside, I lower my voice even further. 'It won't be an easy conversation, but I know you'll handle it.'

'Thanks for your confidence,' he murmurs back. 'I wish I felt the same.'

'Look at this way, Wes – better to have two hot women after you than none at all.'

'I suppose so,' he replies, but he sounds daunted and out of his depth, like a fourteen-year-old who's never even dated before. Then it suddenly dawns on me that maybe he hasn't – not ever. For all his good looks, easy cool and magazine physique, maybe, just maybe, women really are a brand new world to Wes. And if that is the case, then I really should give him more time and effort than I'm putting in right now, for all the problems of my own.

I'm about to suggest we talk later, over a coffee, but he suddenly steps closer, his gorgeous big smile easing back into place. 'Talking of hot women,' he whispers, 'what about the cutie over there, talking to Rudi? I'd give Kate the elbow, and Emma too, if I could take that one on a date.'

It's only talk of course, but I can see where Wes is coming from. There are less than two weeks to Christmas, and it's very quiet here in the showroom. Some salespeople are trying to look busy, others are yawning at their desks, but a couple are simply gawping at the only punter in here – the "cutie" that Wes fancies so much he'd cast Emma aside, even after two months of damn' near stalking the girl.

Charlotte is certainly looking the part. She's wearing her favourite leather coat over a dark woollen dress, together with the suede boots I bought for her birthday last March. Her hair is pinned up in the loose, tottering style I liked so much the other day, and she's given another outing to those big gypsy earrings. Her lipstick's a dark, vivid shade of fuck-me red, and from the way he stands and stares I reckon Marlon, for one, would be very happy to oblige. Same goes for Rudi, I reckon. Having met Charlotte a few times, he's gone over to make small talk, but his laid-back chat can't hide a serious case of the hots – I know Rudi's mannerisms, and it's clear he's trying too hard to appear politely indifferent. His loose-limbed, stand-easy, shoulder-shruggy nonchalance doesn't fool me.

'Wes,' I say, 'do you remember me making notes on my clipboard when we were down among the cheap cars?'

'Course I do, Jimmy.' Rightly, he looks confused by my change of tack, and the wattage on his smile dials down a couple of notches.

'Well, here you are – you have them.' I take his clipboard, then attach my notes and hand it back to him. 'There's a car that needs cleaning and another without a price. Would you do me a favour, and sort them both out?'

'No problem, but why are you asking me now?'

'I'm trying to help you out by getting you gone from the showroom. Emma looks like she wants to kill you because of the way you're looking at that woman. And I want to kill you because the woman happens to be my missus.'

'Your missus? That's Charlotte?' His smile cranks back to maximum, and he actually pats me on the back. 'Jimmy,' he says, 'you're a lucky old so-and-so.'

'Less of the old, Wes, but I am lucky, that's true. You are as well. And a man can ride his luck too fucking hard. Trust me on that – I know all about it, and I don't want you to be doing the same.'

5.5) The Missus and the Ex

Everyone's watching as I walk up to Charlotte and kiss her softly on the lips. Then, taking a step back, I tell her, 'You look great.'

'Thanks.' She gives me the once over. 'So do you. Much better than earlier.'

'I've only perked up because you're here.'

'A likely story.' She laughs, and reaches out to wipe a smudge of her lipstick from my lips.

'Well alright, Charlie, I've had an energy drink as well.'

She laughs some more. That's a good thing. It means all is well, for the time being at least.

I take Charlotte's hand so that I can show her some cars. Everyone is still watching as we head for the door, and I'm suddenly aware of tears welling up in my eyes. I feel incredibly proud right now – proud of the gorgeous woman walking here by my side – but

I'm also deeply ashamed at how badly I've let her down. I walk Charlie quickly through the door, hoping none of these jokers have sussed out how emotionally overcome I am.

Once we're clear of the showroom and out on the pitch, I slow down again and take a couple of deep breaths. Outside of four walls, and away from prying eyes, that deep sense of shame feels manageable – manageable enough for me to carry on papering over the cracks in my fucked-up existence. I turn towards Charlie and say, 'I meant what I said in there. You really do look great.'

'Thank you, sweetheart. But you don't think I'm showing off?' It's then, when she holds it up, that I realise she's brought the Louis Vuitton handbag.

'I hadn't even noticed,' I reply. 'I had eyes only for you.'

She lets go of my hand and shoves me playfully. 'If you say so, Mr Cheese.'

'You show off your handbag. I'll show off my girlfriend. Now come on, there's a car I want to show you.'

I lead the way, but can feel her hanging back. When I stop and ask if everything's alright, she says, 'I need to know – has Ash been in to see you? And how did you get on if he has?'

'Oh, yeah,' I reply, glad to have a question I can answer honestly. 'Just as I thought, he wants to pull out. He's sticking with his current job, and so I'll need to change my plans.'

Charlotte seems to consider this news. Then she says, 'I'm sorry about that. I can see now how it must have been playing on your mind.'

'Well, it means I've got some thinking to do. I'll need to find a new mechanic.'

'You must know some, though.'

'I can think of a few who'd fit the bill. The challenge will be persuading someone to chuck in a secure job for the sake of joining me in a new start-up. I may have to offer a share in the business – but that's not an issue if I can get the right bloke. Ash was going to own half, after all.'

'Yes,' she says thoughtfully. 'I can understand why you might do that.'

I want to crack on and show Charlotte the cars – especially one car in particular – but before I can do that there's something she needs to say. She stands with her hands in her pockets and appears to think hard about where to begin. When she finally speaks, she does so slowly, making careful use of words. 'Regarding earlier, sweetheart, at home – I accused you of some crazy stuff. I'm sorry about that. I should have known you were worried about the business.'

'Don't apologise,' I tell her. 'I came home in a lousy mood. You weren't to know why, and you could have imagined pretty much anything.'

She sighs and says, 'Yes, but – '

'Yes, but nothing. Fault on both sides. We should leave it at that, Charlie. Let's not argue this.'

For a second, I think that arguing this is precisely what Charlotte wants to do. She stuffs her hands further into her pockets and stands with her chin thrust out. Looking over her shoulder, I can see that Kev has followed us out of the showroom and is tying promotional balloons to the wipers of the cars on the front row. Nobody is helping him, although I like to think I'd be doing so if I didn't have Charlotte with me. Then again, there are many things I like to think about myself that probably aren't true, at least not anymore.

Charlotte finally decides against a further argument. Her face softens and she shoves me playfully again. 'You're right,' she says. 'Fault on both sides, as you say. Come on – let's look at these cars, then.'

Once more, I take her hand. As we head down the pitch, she says, 'It's the title of a painting, you know.'

'What's the title of a painting?'

'"Fault on Both Sides". It's the name of an oil painting, by a Scotsman called Thomas Faed.'

'Yeah? What's it of, then – a car crash or something?'

She giggles at me. 'Hardly, sweetheart, given that it dates to the mid eighteen-hundreds. It depicts a married couple who've stopped talking to each other after a contretemps.'

'A contra-what?'

'Contretemps – an awkward situation that's arisen between them. Maybe an argument, for example.'

'Contretemps,' I murmur, filing the word away in my memory. I carry on leading Charlotte down the pitch, but we don't get to the Mercedes A Class I'd earmarked for her. That's because she slows down again and eyes up a different car altogether.

'I saw this one on the web,' she says. 'I quite like the look of it.'

The car she quite likes the look of is a six-month old Toyota Yaris.

I think: *fuck's sake.*

It's not that there's very much wrong with the car – I just don't think the Yaris in general is especially cool, smart or stylish, especially compared to the classy Mercedes I did have in mind. And it doesn't help that this particular Yaris is the same flat red as a Post Office van. It's the kind of motor I can imagine Charlotte climbing out of with two carriers from the supermarket, but not with a handbag by Louis Vuitton.

Charlie reads my expression and asks, 'Is there something wrong with this car?'

'Not really. It's just bland and ordinary, that's all. I mean, it's a Toyota Yaris in DKR.'

'DKR?'

'Dog Knob Red.'

Not laughing, she lets go of my hand to walk round the compact Toyota for a close-up look. 'Well, I like the colour,' she says. 'And I like the car overall.'

When I don't reply, she asks, 'Is it too much money?'

'Hardly. It's a bit less than I had in mind. I just reckon it's a schoolteacher's car, that's all.'

'And you've really forgotten what I do for a living?'

'I don't mean a hot and sexy schoolteacher like you. I mean a fifty-something bloke, with a scruffy beard and an old tweed jacket that reeks of pipe tobacco.'

'That's just a stereotype. There aren't any teachers like that – not really, not nowadays.'

I shrug. 'That's probably why this car's sat here unsold for three weeks.'

But it's obvious that she's keen on the bloody thing. She runs a hand approvingly down the roofline, and then stoops down to peer in through the driver's window. She smiles at me thinly when she straightens up again, and then says, 'I can tell you're not a fan, but Toyotas are actually good cars, aren't they?'

'Alright, yes they are. On a rational level, they're great cars. They're just not very exciting, that's all.'

'Exciting?' She looks at me like I'm just not getting it. 'I'm hardly a teenage boy, you know, with sports car posters on my bedroom wall. Nor am I a middle-aged man with a tiny willie. You know my interests, sweetheart – you know the things that excite me – and they've got very little to do with cars.'

Charlotte has a point. She's into cultural stuff, after all. Music, books and travel are the things that buzz her up, a list to which I can apparently add musty old oil paintings of marital contretemps. But never cars, not that I can remember.

'Okay, you're right,' I finally admit. 'I can't remember the last time you got goose-bumpy about nought-to-sixty times or peak torque curves.'

'I wouldn't know a peak torque curve if it poured me a glass of Pinot. Cup holders, though – they're important. Tell me the Yaris has got them.'

'I think there are two in the front.' Putting my prejudices aside, and deciding to finally make an effort, I step up to the driver's door and point in through the window. 'Yeah, the cup holders are low down in a Yaris. Near the base of the gear lever. Look, just there.'

'I see them,' she says. 'They look just fine.' Then she takes a couple of steps back and looks at the car in profile. 'So far, so good. But what else can you tell me about it?'

'Well this Yaris is the Icon version, which means it's got air conditioning, leather steering wheel, multimedia screen, plus Bluetooth connectivity for your phone. Safety wise, you've got antilock brakes, of course, plus stability control, and six airbags.'

'What about the warranty?' She sounds brisk and efficient, just like any other punter determined not to fall for my spiel. 'I read that it lasts for five years from date of registration.'

'It does last five years, Miss Hibbs – I see that you've done your homework. And because this car is only six months old, there are four-and-a-half years of warranty remaining. Parts and labour are both covered, so long as you keep the car serviced to manufacturer's recommendations.'

Charlotte walks another circuit around the Yaris. I tag alongside, pointing out how well the body panels are aligned, while waxing lyrical about Toyota's "bombproof" build standards and the proven reliability of their cars on the road.

When I finally run out of steam, she says, 'I thought you didn't do salesman's patter.'

'That's not patter. That's me apprising you of important information.'

She smirks and lets out a little snort. 'If you say so.'

'It's bloody true.'

'Alright, sweetheart,' she laughs. 'In which case, do you need to apprise me of anything else that's important?'

'Well since you ask, two things. Firstly, for a compact car, the Yaris has a damn' big boot, so carting your gym bag around shouldn't be a problem. Secondly, it's got a rear reversing camera, which should prevent your idiot boyfriend causing any damage when he parks up at the cinema.'

'Always assuming my idiot boyfriend's allowed to drive my new car.' She smiles, shaking her head at me in mock despair. 'Sweetheart, can you please show me the inside?'

'No problem. I'll get the keys. We can go for a spin if you like.'

Charlotte seems keen on a test drive, and so I leave her with the Yaris while I go back inside for the keys. Once I've got them, I let Graham know we're heading out and I ask him to value Charlotte's Clio while we're gone. He nods, grunts and mutters in agreement, but he's only half listening and is clearly distracted by whatever's showing on his computer screen. When I ask him what's wrong, he blows air through clenched teeth and explains that the marketing manager at head office – 'just some corporate fucking sprog, Jimmy, not much older than Emma or Wes' – has emailed his dissatisfaction with the number of appointments we've made for today. Quoting from the message in a posh-boy accent, Graham tells me that our tally is considered "disappointing for a weekend, even taking seasonal considerations into account".

I tell Graham to pay no attention, or to invite the bloke down here to have a go at making sales appointments this close to Christmas. 'I'd really like to see that, boss. What do those fuckers know about getting the job done?'

'My size ten up his fucking arsehole,' says Graham with a grim smile. 'That's a seasonal consideration he'd find disappointing.'

Then Emma comes into the office. Like me, she's going on a test drive. And like me, she wants Graham to value a car in part-exchange. But unlike me, she hasn't got time to stand around bitching. She's mad keen to get a deal done, and can seemingly scent blood in the water – Rudi's blood at that. Although her appointed punter has turned up on time, Rudi's so far hasn't, and she doesn't try to hide her pleasure that Rudi is currently pacing the showroom, still waiting for his man to show. I follow Emma back outside, from where she goes racing off with her customer in a sporty white Peugeot.

I wonder whether Emma's heading for a fall. I know, from experience, that it's easy to rush everything when you're pumped, causing you to lose a sale you'd have closed if you hadn't been in such a hurry. In comparison, I take my time showing Charlotte the interior of the Yaris. I demonstrate the reversing camera, and then I point out the stuff that's essential for a test drive, such as wipers, indicator and horn. After that, I make sure she's got her seat and mirrors correctly positioned before I tell her to start the engine. Charlotte seems to appreciate my taking the trouble, and soon she's driving us towards the exit, comfortable and in control. I'm a relaxed passenger, content to simply sit and chill.

Unfortunately I'm a relaxed passenger only for the few seconds it takes us to reach the junction with the main road. As we turn out of the car park, a purple Nissan Juke turns sharply in.

Fuck, I think to myself. *Fuckety-fuck-fuck-fuck.*

I glance behind as we pull away from the junction. One quick look is all it takes to confirm the worst. There are those oversized wheels, for one thing. And a glimpse of Isabel's face for another.

Then Charlotte and I are off down the road, making brisk progress in the Yaris. She's a good driver, and she susses the car straight away, moving smoothly through the gears and accelerating confidently. She's saying the right things for a punter, pointing out that the Yaris is smooth and quiet and speedy, but all I can think is

Shit.

And *fuck.*

And *bollocks.*

Shit, fuck, bollocks.

I'm asking myself what kind of scene Isabel will make in there – who she'll talk to, and what she'll say to them. Then there's the matter of what she'll say to me, or rather to us, once we're back. There'll be no chance her leaving before then. Charlotte and I could stay out in the Yaris until midnight, but Iz would be waiting for me afterwards.

I let Charlotte drive the car while I concentrate on what the fuck to do. So far as I know, the missus and the ex have never actually met. If I box clever, and get lucky, then maybe I can keep them apart at the showroom, and each of them can leave the premises without ever knowing the other were there. I'll need some help to pull it off. I'll be relying on favours from Graham, Kate and Rudi – I'm pretty sure they've all met both Isabel and Charlotte at least once – but with a bit of guile I reckon we can make it happen.

'He's really moving,' says Charlotte as a car whizzes past, heading the opposite way.

She's right – he was really moving. Also, "he" happened to be Carl, in the sporty Focus RS, motoring way too fast for these roads. And I don't reckon he'll be driving past the showroom – he'll be driving to it. Carl will be feeling pleased with himself now he's solvent again, and because we're the closest thing he has to proper mates he'll be wanting to inflict some of his happiness on us. But fuck me, I could have done without him turning up this morning. He's another one who's known me long enough to have met both Isabel and Charlotte, but he's more likely to be part of the problem than part of the solution – that's on account of his having all the discretion of a good, hard kick in the bollocks.

'Sweetheart, you don't seem to be listening,' says Charlotte.

We've stopped at traffic lights and the engine is idling smoothly. Everything is quiet and still in the Yaris's cabin. I have a big fucking sense of the calm before a storm.

'I'm sorry,' I reply. 'I just tuned out for a while.'

'You certainly did. I asked what route you want me to take.'

'Alright, let's see then.' I look ahead and try to plan a drive long enough to buy me some thinking time. 'Follow this road,' I tell her, 'all the way to London Avenue, and then turn left when we get there. After that, take the boulevard loop back to the showroom. That make sense to you?'

'Perfect sense,' she replies.

'Will that be a long enough test drive?'

'Certainly, it will.'

'We can go onto the dual carriageway if you like, and work up some speed.'

'No, this is fine.'

The lights go green, and Charlotte pulls smoothly away. 'What was it you were you thinking about?' she asks.

'When?'

'Just now. When you "tuned out for a while."'

'Oh, then? Nothing much. Just that I recognised the bloke driving so fast back there.'

But before I can explain to her that it was Carl, a young woman with a pram appears at the kerb, and Charlotte stops to let her cross. Unfortunately, someone behind us doesn't approve, and treats us to a long blast of their horn.

I'm not having that, especially when I'm as wound up as I am. I swivel round, ready to give someone the finger, but Charlotte says, 'Don't, Jimmy,' and places her hand over mine.

I mutter an opinion that whoever it is must be a dick, but to keep Charlotte happy I face front and don't do anything to escalate the aggro. Instead, once the woman and pram have safely crossed, I lower the sun visor as we get moving again, trying to angle the vanity mirror for a better view of the motor behind. I glimpse the front end of an old-shape BMW, but not for long, though, because the asshole at the wheel decides to overtake us, even though there are shops and parked cars on both sides of the road, and no shortage of pedestrians milling about. It's a moronic place to pass, but past us he comes, his custom exhaust making the banshee sound of a racing car. Charlotte slows to let him go, but once he's passed she flashes her lights and gestures to tell him he's a wanker. It's the first time I've ever seen her make a hand signal like that, and although I laugh out loud, I also worry for a short while. We'll have nowhere to go if the bloke decides to block the road for a fight – and it looks like there are two of them in there.

In the end, there's no problem. The BMW's driver, despite giving two fingers back, keeps his foot down and puts distance between us, his rear bumper bouncing loosely on worn mountings as his car skitters over a pockmarked section of road.

I take a deep breath and exhale slowly. What a week I'm having with all this fucking aggro – all these nearly fights. 'Charlotte Hibbs,' I say, 'that was miles out of character for you.'

'Maybe so,' she replies. 'But what an awful shithead he truly was.'

I sit quietly for a moment, and it dawns on me that the day may be coming when Charlie says something similar about me. Then I notice she's speeded up slightly – an adrenaline rush, I reckon – and I ask her, 'Are you alright?'

'I'm fine, thanks.' But maybe she senses my concern, because next second she lifts off the gas. 'Anyway, she says, 'you said you recognised the other boy racer. Were you about to tell me who it was?'

'Oh, yeah. It was Carl, from the showroom. You met him a few month's back, when we all went out for Rudi's birthday.'

'Oh, yeah,' she says. 'The overweight big-mouth. Wasn't he the guy whose wife had just left him?'

'That's the fellah,' I reply. 'His wife's back now, but if you thought he was fat then, well you should see him these days. He must barely fit that bloody car.'

'At least we know why he was driving so fast,' says Charlotte, here eyes searching out the Yaris's dashboard clock. 'It's gone eleven. He's really late for work.'

'Good logic, but he often drives like a prick. And he isn't supposed to be in work, anyway. Graham gave him time off to sort out some financial problems.'

'Doesn't sound like Graham,' she replies. 'How much time has he had?'

'He's been off since Wednesday morning.'

'Three days? To sort out financial problems?'

'I heard they were sizeable.'

'They flamin' well must have been.'

We drive on in silence, and when we stop at the next red lights Charlotte fiddles with some of the Yaris's controls. She switches on the radio, adjusts the heating, and gives the windscreen washers a blast. I'm getting anxious that I haven't come up with any kind of plan for dealing with Isabel, but it turns out that help is at hand. When the lights go green and we get moving again, Charlotte says, 'I've been thinking about finances, myself.'

'Okay. And what of it?'

She kills the radio and says, 'Sweetheart, I want you to listen to me. I know you said you can afford it, but this car costs a lot of money. And I think this is the wrong moment for you to be treating me, however much discount Graham will offer you. What with you having to find a mechanic for your business, I think you have other priorities right now. Who knows what you might need the money for?'

I don't reply straightaway. Charlotte glances quickly at me, and then returns her attention to the road. She fidgets in her seat, and adjusts both hands on the wheel. She'll be bracing herself for an argument, and who can blame her when we've already talked the subject to death and supposedly reached an agreement. But, actually, I'm not going to argue with her – very far from it. Charlotte isn't to know, but she's just offered up the answer to my Isabel-in-the-showroom problem. If Charlie doesn't want me to buy the Yaris, then there's no reason for her to come back to my desk. Instead, I can pack her off home from the car park, straight after our test drive. That way she avoids Isabel, and Isabel avoids her. Halle-fucking-lujah!

I take my time answering. I want to be seen to think things over. Finally I say, 'Alright Charlie, maybe you're right. Maybe this is the wrong time. Just so long as you don't think you've had a wasted journey coming here.'

'Not at all.' She slows as a Mini up ahead makes a right turn. 'Graham will still do me a good deal, won't he?'

'Whenever we're ready, I'm sure he will.'

'That's not what I meant,' she says. 'I didn't mean whenever we're ready. I meant now.'

'But hang on, you just said we shouldn't buy yet.'

'No, sweetheart,' she replies. 'I only said you shouldn't.' Charlotte glances at me impishly. 'I really like this car, and I'd like to buy it if that's okay with you. I'll need some finance, but from what you've said I'm sure Graham will offer me a low rate.'

'Charlie, no!'

'Jimmy, yes!'

'But wait a minute... bloody hell. You should think properly about all of this.'

'I have thought properly about it. I'd like to buy the car if it's affordable. Besides which, you need all the deals you can get. You'll win a thousand pounds if you finish top of your sales league this month.'

'And how the hell did you know about that?'

Another cheeky smile. 'Rudi told me while we were waiting for you.'

I think: *Fucking thanks, Rudi.* Then I see the junction for London Avenue coming up ahead. It's a busy, major road, and we may be delayed a couple of minutes while we wait to turn left. But once we've found a gap, we'll soon be back at the showroom. Back to face Isabel, unless I'm extremely cunning and even luckier.

Fuck. Shit. Bollocks.

Already, I can feel cold sweat dampening my collar. And matters get worse when there's hardly any delay at the junction. One car goes by, then two. But Charlotte has time to pull out and accelerate ahead of the third. She changes crisply through the gears, and sits smiling at the wheel as she hustles the Yaris back to base.

5.6) That's no Way to Sell Someone a Car

I've had some punters prang the car on test drive, and there have been an odd few – *very* fucking odd, I must admit – who've tried to seduce me while we've been putting a motor through its paces. I've also heard tales of carjacking, where the salesperson is ordered out of the car at gun or knifepoint, before the so-called punter drives off into the distance. But such goings-on are rare, and test drives are normally straightforward things. On average, they take twenty minutes or so, and as a matter of routine there are two questions I ask my punters once the drive is over. I ask the questions just as soon as we're back, while we're still outside after parking up.

My first question is simple. I ask the punter(s) whether they like the car. Assuming the answer is yes – and it usually is – I then wheel out my second question. It's a big question, the second one.

It's what Graham calls a "salesman's question". It's the one I ask to find out whether the punter is happy to buy the car there and then – and when I say "buy", I mean sign an order form and pay a deposit. There's more than one way of asking the second question, and I'll tailor my approach according to individual circumstances and my reading of the situation. For example, when someone answers the first question by telling me, plainly and simply, that they do like the car, I'll usually follow up with a straightforward, "So, would you like to buy it now?"

Alternatively, when I'm with cautious, more money-minded prospects, I might ask, "Will you be happy to go ahead now, assuming I can get you the right deal?"

And then there are people who've told me early on that they won't be making up their minds without going home and thinking things over, or that they need to compare the deal with others on offer elsewhere. To them, I'll put it this way: "Look, I know you said you weren't deciding immediately, but you've also said you do like the car, and I know you'll find our deals are the best around. Is there anything I can do to persuade you to go ahead while you're with me now?"

The word that crops up in all of these variations is: "now". I deliberately talk in the immediate, not leaving the timescale open-ended. I won't compromise on the use of "now"; I won't even say "today". It might only be ten a.m. at the time, and "today" gives someone eight more hours to go away and think things over.

No, I always say "now". However I phrase the second question, "now" is always part of it. That's because the job, in a nutshell, is about *now*. The job is about getting a punter's commitment to deal up there and then – there and then being the place and time that they're most likely to say yes. Quite simply, the few moments after completion of a test drive are the moments of peak interest on a punter's part, and so anyone answering yes to both the first and second questions will be brought straight back inside and immediately presented with an offer.

Unfortunately, though, we sometimes get punters who say they're undecided about the car but would like to see the numbers anyway, so that they've "got something to go away and think about". Well sorry, but bollocks to that. Time spent presenting an offer to someone who doesn't want to buy is time that could be spent talking to someone who does. That's why we ask the two questions immediately after a test drive – namely, to find out where the punter's head is at – and that's why we avoid talking numbers with anyone who doesn't answer yes to them both. If a punter says they're undecided on the car, I invite them to think about it alone for a few minutes. They can soon find me afterwards, once they've worked out whether they want the motor or not.

So that, in a nutshell, is what happens after test drives. Or at least that's what happens with normal punters.

And then there's Charlotte.

Charlotte isn't a normal punter. She's my beautifully awesome girlfriend, and I'm trying to manipulate her behaviour in a desperate, ragged attempt to keep her that way (keep her as my girlfriend, that is – beautifully awesome I'm sure she'll manage by herself, with or without my help).

My beautifully awesome girlfriend has, of course, answered yes to both questions without even being asked, and that's something which is rare but not unheard of. We call such people a "hands up" in the trade, and when one comes our way we normally we get down on our knees and offer thanks to the god of automotive retailing. But because this situation is far from normal, I don't offer thanks to anyone, and I don't hurry Charlotte indoors to look at an offer. Instead, I treat her like someone who's said they're not sure about the car. I tell her to spend a few minutes outside, alone with the Yaris, while I go back to the showroom.

'But I flamin' well want to buy it,' she insists, looking at me like I've flipped. 'What sort of salesman are you, that you want me to wait out here?'

'The sort who's seen too many people make the wrong choice,' I tell her. 'Please, Charlie, just five minutes, on your own, while I go back indoors. If you still want the car after that, I won't stand in your way. And I'll make sure Graham does you a storming deal.'

Finally she gives in, and I leave her standing bewildered and pissed-off in the car park while I head into the showroom, taking the workshop door rather than the main entrance. Five minutes, I said to her. Five minutes, she wearily agreed. That's the length of time I've got, if I'm lucky, to get a grip of whatever situation is occurring inside. Barely acknowledging the "Hiya, mate" and "Hello, Jimmy" from two of our mechanics – both happy because they finish at lunchtime on Saturdays – I hurry from the workshop down the corridor to the showroom, pushing open the connecting door just a fraction, so that I can peek in and figure out what's going on before making my entrance.

Things actually look more-or-less normal on the sales floor. It seems that Rudi's appointment still hasn't turned up, because Rudi is helping Wes manoeuvre a shiny silver Audi into the space created when Kate sold the Sirocco yesterday. Wes is at the wheel, and Rudi is directing him into position. But Rudi, as ever, is focused on the main chance – his eyes are constantly flitting from the Audi to the main showroom door, and he's ready to pounce if anyone walks in. Emma must still be on test drive, because the one and only punter currently in the place is a middle-aged bloke wearing a flat cap and wax jacket. He's armed with some motoring magazines and a notepad, the contents of which he's busily sharing with Marlon. Punters like this one always reckon we'll be interested in their research, but Marlon, of course, looks properly bored. I reckon Rudi probably spoke to this bloke first, before dismissing him as too much trouble or just a bloody time-waster.

Initially, I think that Isabel isn't even here, which make no sense when her Juke's still parked outside. But then I spot her in the far corner, sitting in reception and chatting to Kate. She's wearing the cashmere coat I noticed hanging in her hallway, and the good news is that she isn't causing any kind of scene, although that probably means she's saving one for whenever I put in an appearance. I'm unable to read the expression on her face because she's got her back to me, but I can see that Kate is nodding and smiling, and appearing politely interested in whatever it is that Iz has to say. I reckon this is no mean achievement on Kate's part, given that she'd sooner pass the time of day with an axe murderer or an undead zombie.

By now, I've managed to cobble together a plan – it's a bit half-assed, but the best I can do – and it needs me to get into Graham's office undetected by my ex. Remembering that time is short, I slip into the showroom, and begin skirting my way round the wall, trying all the while to stay out of Isabel's eye line. I glance across once or twice, but she doesn't turn around, and although Kate must have noticed me, she does nothing to give the game away. Rudi sees that I'm back, and briefly abandons Wes to come scurrying over. His eyes are wide with alarm, and he's gesturing frantically towards reception while quietly mouthing, 'Isabel's here.'

'I know,' I tell him, trying to keep my voice down and my profile low. I grip him by the arm and say, 'Look, I need to see Graham. Do me a favour, would you? Charlotte's outside. If she comes back indoors, come into the office and let me know.'

Rudi nods and says he will. I let go of his arm, and with another glance to make sure Isabel hasn't seen me, I hurry into Graham's office. That's when my luck starts turning to shit.

Carl's sitting at the big table, looking fat and ridiculous in ripped-look denims and a blingy gangster necklace. As ever, he's got his fucking phone out, and is cheerily showing whatever's on the screen to Kev – the same Kev who had his card marked by Graham this morning for not selling enough cars, and who, on that basis, you'd have to call an idiot for lounging around in here, even if he has put out the balloons since the meeting ended.

Neither of them notices my entrance, but at the desk Graham looks up from his keyboard, and when he sees it's me his face stretches in pained disbelief. 'So you're finally fucking back,' he says. 'You've got yourself some explaining to do.'

That's when Carl twigs that I'm here. He gets to his feet, happy to discard his new friend Kevin so that he can bend my ear instead. 'Jimmy!' he says, in the manner of someone greeting his latest guest at a dinner party, 'How are you?' If he remembers seeing me in his street when he was pissed, or has the slightest idea that I'm the reason why he got to pass Go and collect thirty grand, he doesn't want to discuss any of it now. Instead, he waves his phone in the air. 'You need to check this bad boy out. I was just showing it to Marlon.'

I can't help myself, even though the seconds are ticking down on my very own doomsday clock. 'Kevin,' I say to Carl. 'You mean you were showing it to Kevin.'

Carl glances behind. 'Yeah, Kevin – that's who I mean.' Then he pushes the phone at me, but I seriously don't have time for this. The fat prick can go fuck off.

I sidestep the oncoming handset. 'Give me a minute, Carl. I need to talk to the boss.' But then, not wanting to wind Carl up, or provoke a rant, I add, 'Good to see you back, by the way.'

'It's Monday before I'm back officially,' he says. 'I'm not working until then.' Then he edges closer, thrusting his phone pretty much in my face. The on-screen graphics depict a high-rolling casino scene. There's a hand of cards on a green-baized table top, and behind the table there's a smiling female croupier. She has high cheekbones, pearly-white teeth and breasts like intercontinental missiles.

'Carl,' says Graham wearily, 'get the fuck out of here, would you?'

'Say again?' Carl wheels round to face the boss. 'What have I done now?'

Graham looks to have run out of patience, but when he stands up at his desk he too tries to sound conciliatory. 'Look,' he says, 'I'm pleased you've got your shit sorted. And I'm pleased you've come in to see us. But the rest of us are working today, and I need to talk to Jimmy. So piss off home, will you? Piss off until Monday. And when come back, you need to be selling cars again.'

I actually put my hand in the middle of Carl's back and push him towards the door. 'Please, mate,' I say to him. 'I'll look at your app on Monday, or whatever it is you've got there.'

'Alright, alright,' he replies. Mercifully, he allows himself to be guided out, so maybe there is a god of automotive retailing, and maybe, for now at least, it's a god who has my back. 'I'll be on my way,' says Carl. 'I get what you're saying – I know you've got deals to do.'

Once Carl's gone, I turn my attentions to Kev, who's looking very shamefaced by this stage. He may be a rubbish salesman, but I don't reckon he's a bad lad, and I guess the only reason he was even in the office, looking at Carl's poxy phone and getting a talk through of online-gamblers-are-pricks-dotcom, was that nobody else could be arsed with it all. Now, in the wake of Carl's departure, Kev's already up from his chair. Although I'm sure he'd have left the office without being asked, Graham makes doubly sure anyway.

'You piss off as well, Kevin. And close the door behind you. But come and see me before you go home tonight.'

Mumbling an apology, his face flushed deep red, Kev slopes out and closes the door. I'd speak in his defence, but I haven't the time, and I don't even get chance. Straightaway, Graham gives me a scathing look and doesn't pull his punches. 'I don't know who's the bigger dickhead – you or fucking Carl.'

'I know, boss. I'm sorry.'

'Let me make sure I've got this straight,' he says. 'You get your missus to come in so she can buy a car. Well, alright, so far so good. But while you're on your test drive, your former missus also rocks up, disrupting business and demanding to see you. Well, how did that fucking happen – that they're both here at the same time?' Graham throws his hands in the air and shakes his head like a man trying to cast off the dizzying effects of a good right hander to the jaw. 'Seriously, Jimmy, what the fuck are you up to?'

I could reply to Graham belligerently. I could point to a near-deserted sales floor and argue that Isabel has hardly disrupted business when there's none out there to disrupt. But I really need the boss onside, and so I reply, 'Like I said, I'm really sorry. What is it she's been saying?'

Graham goes to the door and looks into the showroom through the thin strip of window. 'You'd need to ask Kate the fucking specifics. She's the one who's calmed the woman down, made her a coffee and got her sitting quietly in reception. Kate's not your biggest fan, be warned. And she was already spitting fucking feathers – something to do with Wes standing her up so he can go out on a date with Emma. I'll have to talk to him abut disrupting trade as well.' Graham turns from the door and stalks back behind his desk. 'I've had it all this morning. Wankers from head office. Carl coming in dressed like he's Bon Jovi or some sort of twat. And now I've got you and Wes stirring up woman trouble in my showroom. I need you to smooth this whole thing over, and to smooth it fucking quickly.'

I take a deep breath. 'I've no right to ask, but I'm going to need your help.'

The boss plonks down heavily in his chair. The leather creaks in protest and there's a wheezy swoosh of tired hydraulics. 'Why am I not surprised?' he asks.

I take a second deep breath, sidle closer to the desk, and start to go over my plan. 'Look, I'll explain everything later, and I'll do whatever it takes to make amends, but right now there isn't much time. Charlotte's outside, and she wants to come in and buy the car she's just driven. I need to keep her and Isabel apart; otherwise I'm dead fucking meat. Could you please talk to Charlotte, and get the deal done for me? I'll tell her you're taking over because one of my other customers has come back with a complaint, one which I need to sort it straight away. Then I'll go and talk to Isabel while you're concluding business with Charlotte. I'll get Iz calmed down and sent on her way.'

Graham just looks at me like he used to in the old days, back when I was new to the job and a pain in his arse. Back when I couldn't sell cars. Back when he wasn't sure I was worth all the bother. Back when he and everyone else, and not just Carl, would call me Cooter most of the time.

'Of course,' I add, 'the whole thing is my fuck up, and I wouldn't expect you to pay me for Charlotte's deal. Nor would it count towards the thousand pounds bonus, or my position in the league table.'

He looks at me some more, and then appears to think for a second. But I'll never know what he was going to say because the door swings open and Kate walks in. She stands there, hands on hips, and she too looks at me like I'm a useless streak of piss. 'I've made your next appointment comfortable,' she says sarcastically, 'and I've even fixed her a coffee. Think you can take it from here?'

'Kate, I'm really sorry. And thanks for doing this. I didn't plan it you know– I didn't ask Isabel to come in.'

'You didn't ask her?' she hisses. 'James, you fucking shithead. You might not have asked her, but whose fault is it that she's here?'

'Come on, I didn't mean it's not my fault. Look, we don't have time for this right now. I was just about – '

'Oh, so we don't have time? I go out of my way to cover your back, and then you stand there telling me we don't have time to talk about it?'

'Kate,' says Graham, waving at her to take a seat, 'I know what you're saying, but just give him a break. Jimmy knows he's fucked up, and when this is over we're all having a big drink on him.'

Kate doesn't sit down, and hers is another reply I'll never get to hear, because it's then that Emma arrives in the office. And it's not just the way she smiles that tells us what's going on in her world. It's the look in her eye and the spring in her step; it's the confident way she stands at Graham's desk and tosses her hair back. Every little foible announces that Emma has a deal on the go.

'Got my offer, boss?' Emma asks.

'I don't want to be rude, Emma,' says Kate, 'but we're having a private conversation.'

Emma smiles sweetly at her. 'You are being rude,' she says, as if putting a badly-behaved child in its place. 'I need some numbers for my punter.'

'And we are here to do deals,' says Graham, hurriedly, before Kate can answer back. He quickly resumes typing, saying to Emma, 'I'll soon have it done. Is your man having the car, do you reckon?'

Emma's reply reminds me of how Rudi answers when Graham asks him that question. Rudi will say: "What do you think?" And he says it in such an easy, self-assured way that what he's really saying is: *Need you bloody ask, Graham. It's me you're talking to – Rudi, the king of car sales. Of course my punter's bloody-well having it.* So when Emma tosses her hair again, and says to Graham, 'What do you think?' she's sending a clear message. The rest of us in here – Kate, Graham, and even me with my brains all scrambled – pause for a second and let that one sink in. It was Emma announcing her claim to the number one spot. She reckons she's top dog now.

Graham squares his shoulders. 'Alright,' he says, 'so your man's dealing up. Now, I know you said earlier that he wants to pay cash, but I'll put some low-rate finance into his offer – it makes us a couple of quid more. Go through it with him, and tell me what he says.'

'That's fine,' she replies. 'No problem at all.'

I look at my watch, and then I look at Graham. 'Boss,' I say, 'that help I just asked you for? There isn't much time.'

He glances up from his typing. 'I have to do this for Emma. It wouldn't be fair otherwise. Look, I'm sure Kate or Rudi will help you.'

I turn to Kate. She looks ready to kill somebody – either me or Emma, probably the both of us. And before I can actually ask a favour, she grabs my arm and leads me into a corner, away from the desk. 'What's going on?' she asks, lowering her voice to prevent Emma overhearing. 'Why has Isabel picked today to come in, demanding to see you? And why did you have a face like a smacked backside first thing this morning?'

'Kate,' I plead, 'it's complicated.'

'Bullshit is it complicated. You've shagged her, haven't you? After everything that happened last time, and everything you told me yesterday, you've gone and shagged the dreadful cow.'

I don't answer her.

Kate says, 'Tell me you haven't'

And then another voice, barely audible, says, 'But you have, haven't you?'

I whirl round. I should have noticed that Emma had left the door open, and having noticed I should have closed it again. But I didn't notice and I didn't do anything, and now Charlotte's standing in the doorway with so much hurt on her face that I want to die right here and now. There's an awful moment of icy silence, during which I wonder what happened to Rudi and the warning I asked him for. But I know the answer before I've even framed the question. A punter must have come in. And Rudi must be talking to him. Rudi always has an eye on the main fucking chance.

'Oh, God,' says Kate, her hand going to her mouth. Then another frozen pause, before she adds, 'I'm so sorry, Charlotte... how much did you hear? I didn't mean for you to hear any of that.'

Charlotte takes a wary, tentative little step into the office. She looks at Kate. Briefly, bravely she tries to smile. 'Not your fault,' she says in the same quiet tone as before.

I say, 'Charlie... I... '

Graham has stopped typing, Emma has gone all quiet, and Kate looks to be holding her breath. I hear a burst of chatter from somewhere in the showroom, alongside the clunk of a car door slamming closed. They sound like noises heard underwater, what with my pulse yammering in my ears, threatening to burst out of my head.

'Alright,' murmurs Charlotte, apparently to herself, 'so now I know the truth.' She looks at me and draws a breath, but in the end finds nothing to say. Instead, she turns to Emma and Graham at the desk. 'Sorry to have interrupted,' she says to them, again barely loud enough to be heard. And with that, she turns and walks quickly from the office.

A few seconds pass. Nobody moves and nobody speaks.

Then Graham says, 'I guess she won't want the car anymore.'

Emma says, 'Oh, God. Like, I'm sorry, Jimmy. I wouldn't have come in... '

Kate shakes me by the shoulder. 'What the hell are you waiting for?' she says. 'Get after the woman.'

I take one faltering step towards the door. I tell Kate, 'I don't know what to say to her.'

'Jesus, James.' She throws her arms out wide. 'Tell her something. Anything. Talk to her about your money in the bank. That might bloody help.'

But I just feel rooted to the spot. Another couple of seconds pass. Then Graham asks, 'What money in the bank?'

Kate shakes her head at him. 'Never you mind,' she says, sinking into a chair at the head of the table. 'Fuck, what a mess!'

Graham tells me, 'You can't just stand there all fucking day. Go and talk to the other one if you won't chase after Charlotte. You've still got things to sort out.'

Emma looks at me and asks, 'The other one?'

Kate looks at her and says, 'Never you mind, either.'

Graham does have a point, though: I can't stand here all day. And so I take another heavy step towards the door, but I'm unsure who I'm going to talk to, or whether I can catch up with Charlotte anyway.

And then Carl has to bloody well walk in. He's got his phone in one hand, a coffee in the other, and an insolent grin on his fat fucking face. 'Jimmy,' he begins, that moronic grin growing ever wider, 'isn't that your old missus out there? Fit thing, you know, what's-'er-name.'

At the table, Kate holds her head in hands and groans. 'Not now, Carl.'

'Carl,' says Graham, 'what the fuck did I tell you about going home?'

'I'm just saying, that's all,' replies Carl. 'What's the problem with everyone today?'

I size Carl up. He's just inside the office, standing where Charlie stood a minute ago. I ask him, 'That thing you wanted to show me earlier, on your phone? Was it something to do with gambling?'

'Yeah,' he says. 'Online poker.' But maybe he's picked up a vibe from me, because his tone is suddenly wary and he takes a half step backwards. 'Why do you ask?'

'You'll never learn,' I tell him. 'Put down your coffee, Carl.'

'What for?' he asks.

'James,' says Kate, 'don't do this.'

'Not in here,' says Graham.

'Put down your coffee,' I order Carl. 'Because you'll need to defend yourself in a fucking second.'

He shuffles back some more. He's standing in the doorway, half in the office, half in the showroom. 'Bollocks to you, Cooter,' he says. 'Fuck off with you.'

I lunge forward. I'm vaguely aware of Kate and Emma yelling at me, and of the grin falling from Carl's pudgy big face. Then I smash him hard, right on the fucking nose. There's a crunching noise, and also the sort of squelch normally produced by someone walking ankle deep in mud. A thin spray of blood arcs through the air, and I feel some it spatter my face. Carl falls backwards from the doorway, down onto the sales floor, hitting it hard. I stride out towards him, my fists still balled. This is what you'd call a fucking contretemps.

Carl groans and rolls on the floor, his hands to his face and blood spilling onto the lino. His phone has gone skidding away, and his fucking coffee with it. Rudi's standing close by with a punter, and they're both looking on with their jaws hanging open in shock. Somehow, seemingly in slow motion, I notice all these things, and I think to myself that this is one downside to sitting outside Graham's office that not even Rudi can make light of. I can see something else as well: I can see that Isabel has risen to her feet on the other side of the showroom, and even from here I know that she's gaping in horror.

Given the chance, I'm not sure whether I'd have hit Carl again or not. I might have put the boot in, or I might have jumped on him and pummelled his face. Then again, I might just have stood by and watched him squirm. But I don't actually get chance to find out, because Wes moves like lightning, and from nowhere he has his arms around me and is pulling me away. 'Whoa, Jimmy,' he chuckles, actually laughing at all this mayhem. 'What are you playing at, big man?'

What am I playing at? Wes's question was probably rhetorical, meaning I don't need to answer, at least not right here and not right now. Which is just as well, because I haven't got the least idea what I'm fucking playing at. None at all. But this I do know: a lot of things have changed in the last couple of minutes. Changed massively, probably for all time.

And I reckon not for the better, not by a long bloody way.

THE END

But while you're still here, I'd firstly like to thank you for reading. And I do have three points to wrap things up with, if you don't mind...

1) In the opening paragraphs of the book, Jimmy takes the wrapper from his sandwich to the waste bin in the kitchen. There he finds from Cheryl from Accounts, and he tells her a joke which he says Graham told the sales team at that morning's meeting.

Now of course, as the reader, you're perfectly entitled to imagine for yourself what Graham's joke was about. But in case you're wondering, the one I had in mind was this:

> *The barman says, 'Sorry, we don't serve time travellers.'*
>
> *A time traveller walks into a bar.*

Please don't ask me why that's the joke which was in my head. I know it has no sexual content, nor any bad language, and so it may not be the kind of joke you'd necessarily expect from an old bruiser like Graham. Nevertheless, when I was writing about Jimmy repeating a joke previously told by his boss, that's simply the one which occurred to me. Maybe Graham has a subtler side to him than the story ever revealed, or maybe he told it as an example of how not to be funny – at least to his way of thinking. Either way, I thought I'd share the joke with you, and so I hope you don't hate it.

2) I'd be very, very grateful if you'd please take a few minutes to post a review of *All These Nearly Fights* on Amazon. The reason I'm asking – and, yes, this is naked self interest on my part – is that the more reviews my work gets, the better the chances of people (punters?) finding it when they're browsing for something to read, especially if the reviews happen to be good ones!

If you still have the email from Amazon confirming your purchase of this book, click on the link inviting you to "Review This Item" – you'll find it next to the image of the book's front cover. Otherwise, you can simply find the story again on the amazon.com site, and go from there. (Sorry if it sounds patronising when I tell you how to post a review – please keep in mind that I need to cater for readers who might not know how it's done.)

3) I am working on a sequel to *All These Nearly Fights*. If you'd like to be kept informed of its progress and release date, just drop me a line at **r.cunliffe@yahoo.com** (again, this may sound patronising, but please remember the dot between "r" and "c", rather than forgetting, as people sometimes do), putting "ATNF Sequel" in the subject line. Also, do feel free to use the same address if you'd like to correspond more generally – I will respond to email which is written civilly and is NOT spam). Finally, if you'd like to connect via Twitter, I'm **@CunliffeRich** and I look forward to hooking up with you there.

Thanks very much once again (and if you'll forgive me, here's another reminder: do <u>please</u> post that review).

Richard Cunliffe

August, 2017

Printed in Great Britain
by Amazon